EXODUS

GARDEN OF EVIL SERIES

EDEN – BOOK 1
EXODUS – BOOK 2
GENESIS – BOOK 3
ELYSIUM – BOOK 4

Shade Owens & Ash S-J
www.shadeowens.com

Edited by Nikki Busch
www.nikkibuschediting.com

RED RAVEN PUBLISHING

ISBN: 978-1-990271-07-6

This is a work of fiction. Names, characters, businesses, places, events and incidents are either the products of the author's imagination or used in a fictitious manner. Any resemblance to actual persons, living or dead, or actual events is purely coincidental.

PROLOGUE

The weight of the pistol empowers me. With my index finger, I rub the cold metal trigger and shivers run down my arm. I want to close my eyes, if only for a minute, to take it all in—the silence, the fear, the confusion among the women before me.

I press the gun's muzzle into the back of his curly black hair. He attempts to pull his head away, and I fight the urge to smile.

His life is in my hands.

The women remain still, their eyes enlarged and fixated on this man, Gabriel. They resemble frightened children during a school lockdown. Their lips are parted, but not a sound escapes their lungs. The air around me is so still I can hear my heart pulsating in my throat.

What did he expect? Did he think that it would be so easy? That I would simply integrate him into Eden, among my women? He's promised me safety—promised my women a haven that could sustain us indefinitely.

It's hard to imagine what Gabriel is thinking. I'm certain he's terrified—wondering why I would allow him inside of Eden only to turn around and kill him now.

He says he wants to be a part of the new world, but the truth is, he is still a man.

He doesn't belong in the new world.

CHAPTER 1 – EVE

"How can I trust you?" I ask, and he looks up at me like a beaten dog.

His dark curly hair dangles over his crystal blue eyes and he leans the weight of his body on one elbow, his shoulders large and round and his abdomen muscles bulging. I want to believe that there's goodness inside him, but all I see is an animal—a beast made of muscle capable of destroying all that I've worked for.

And what will the women think of me when I announce to them that a man will be guiding us to new territory? Will they view me as weak? As a hypocrite? As a leader incapable of leading her people?

It's my job to protect these women. The last thing I want is to accept help from a man.

"I guess you can't trust anyone," he says. His bright eyes look even brighter above the candlelight's glow, and they never leave mine. He's staring into me as if trying to analyze my very core—trying to decipher what made me who I am and what led me to be so mistrustful.

I glower at him. Who does he think he is?

"I'm not trying to hurt anyone," he adds. "I promise you this place exists. Why would I have risked my life bringing back one of your injured women? For all I knew, you could have had guards waiting inside the gates"—he suddenly grabs the skin over his ribs and grimaces in pain—"trained to k-kill any man they see."

I raise my chin, my gaze fixed on this hairy beast. "Go on."

"I'm not on *their* side if that's what you think."

I'm assuming he's referring to the male species in general, but I can't be certain.

"Men," he continues. "They're tearing each other apart out there. But believe it or not"—he bares his teeth again—"we're not all like that."

I don't believe it. How can I? I've seen what men are capable of. I watched them slaughter thousands of women during the gender war. They have no remorse for anything they do.

He must sense my hatred, because he lets out a soft sigh and lies back down, his bare back touching the cold concrete floor.

"You don't have to trust me," he says. "But believe me when I say this: you aren't safe here. Adam and his men"—his eyes dart my way when he realizes I have no idea who he's talking about—"men like the ones who attacked your women are everywhere. You have no idea what I've seen. You can live your peaceful little life in here all you want. You can pretend you're living in some paradise garden, but the truth is, you're surrounded by so much danger. It's only a matter of time before rebels come barging in—"

"And how would they know of Eden?" I spew. I'm prepared to crush my heel into his broken ribs. "What did you tell them?"

His eyes enlarge, and he pulls his head back. He's staring at me as if I've lost my mind. "How should I know? Word spreads. How do surviving women find their way here? Because they do, don't they? Haven't they been told to look for Alpa?"

I clench my fist at the sound of that word slipping off his tongue.

Mount Alpa.

Only women should know of this mountain—of this beacon—that leads them to safety.

"All it takes is for one woman to let it slip," he continues. He rests his arm on his forehead and his bicep muscle bulges. "And you've been hiding here for what? Five years? I'm honestly shocked you haven't been attacked by now."

"We have," I growl through clenched teeth.

"You know what I mean," he continues. "Attacked as in completely infiltrated. I guess survivors are too busy fighting each other. But the bad ones... They're looking for you. They're trying to find women. You and I both know why—"

"Enough," I hiss.

"Look," he says. "I know you hate me. I know you hate men. I don't blame you. After everything I've seen, I understand why you do."

My heartbeat slows down a bit. I can't believe what I'm hearing. I've never heard a man speak like this before.

"They're egotistical, prideful"—he sits up again and winces—"they're the reason this country fell apart. I mean, think back to history. Men have always been fighters."

"I'm listening," I say.

"You don't have to like me. But I swear to God I'm not like those pig-headed pieces of shit. Men aren't *all* like that. There are good ones, same as there're bad ones. There's another man out there. A dead man. He fought by my side trying to stop Adam and his dogs from raping your women."

I clench my fists again and my knuckles crack.

"Are they all dead?" I ask.

"Adam and his boys?" he asks, and then he nods.

I loosen my fists and my fingers dangle at my sides.

I turn around and pace across the room, my heels ticking on the hard floor. What do I do? I don't trust him—I never will. But at the same time, he *does* seem different. What if this is a setup? Perhaps he's luring us straight onto male territory, straight into a painful world of slavery. If men are in control, that's precisely what will happen. We will revert to an archaic age where men ruled women as if they were mere objects—where men decided when they wanted to fornicate and did so without the consent of the other party involved.

You can't do this, Eve.

Think about how far you've come.

These women trust you to be their savior.

You're putting them all at risk.

"Shut up!" I hiss.

"I didn't say anything," Gabriel says from behind me.

I grab my hair at the sides of my temple and pull gently until a slight pain sets in. A wave of relief washes over me and I take a deep breath.

You can do this.

The man is right—you can't stay here.

"Where is this place?" I ask, swinging around.

He sits upright even farther, using his hand against the concrete to inch his way up. "About three hundred miles south."

"Three hund—" I say, but I can't even finish my sentence. I turn back around and start pacing again.

Is he insane? How on Earth am I going to relocate 382 women 300 miles from here? It isn't like we have adequate transportation. I can't risk the lives of all these women simply to reach some unknown destination. And what is this place, exactly? What if other survivors have already claimed it?

I pinch the bridge of my nose and walk back toward him. "Say we go to this place... What is it? What are we walking into?"

"Area 82," he says as if this should mean something.

"What is *that*?" I sneer. I don't mean to come across as snarky, but my patience is wearing thin. "Some sort of underground facility?"

"There is a massive underground bunker, yeah," he says. "But it's a top-secret military base. It's surrounded by twenty-foot fencing... There are vehicles, aircraft—"

"What good is any of that with damaged wires?" I ask. "You know as well as I do that the EMP fried everything."

"Not everything," he says. "Adam and his crew were able to start an old pickup truck. People think that everything got fried, but the truth is, EMP attacks don't necessarily damage everything—especially when the electronic device is turned off. What did us in was the limited supply of gas. The gas in tanks started evaporating, and with gas stations not up and running, there was no way to replace the fuel." His eyes widen as if he's telling some exciting tale. "If we could get ahold of a military plane, though… If we could find a way to fix whatever's been damaged, if there's damage—"

"Then what?" I say. "We magically fly a plane over here and scoop up the remaining women? Is that your brilliant idea?"

I clench my teeth just looking at him. I'm not an idiot—I know this man is military. And although I want to slit his throat for it, I can't. I need him.

He tries to shrug, but his shoulders barely move. "What other option do we have?"

"What makes you think there will even be a plane for us?" I throw my hands in the air. "Listen to me—I sound ridiculous even saying it aloud. A plane…" I let out a laugh. "And if some vehicles are still up and running, why aren't people traveling across the country? Why haven't I seen one vehicle approach Eden over the last five years?"

He's lying—he has to be. Everything stopped working after the attack.

"Who's gonna drive? 'Case you haven't noticed," he says, "most people are dead. You haven't seen what I've seen… Cities full of dead bodies. The smell alone is enough—" He turns away and places two fingers underneath his nostrils as if he's still able to smell the decay. "I don't think you—" For a moment he pauses, seemingly pondering how best to word his next statement. "I don't think the women fighting for their freedom realized the devastating effects of an EMP attack."

"We knew what it meant," I say coldly. "We would rather live in a world of chaos and destruction than be ruled by men."

"All I'm saying," he says, "is that millions of lives were lost. I know all about this. I took part in military equipment testing in Area 82. The biggest danger of all isn't not having electricity… It's not having access to food, a heated shelter for those living up north, and most of all, clean water. Without electricity, sewage pumps don't work. Filtration systems shut down. Water becomes a luxury, so most people resort to drinking from ponds, lakes, or rivers, and a lot of those are contaminated. I'd be willing to bet that the few people who survived were country folk… People who live off well water, grow their own food, have livestock, and heat their homes with fire. And these people aren't gonna go looking for military bases."

I don't say anything, so he clears his throat and keeps talking. "I doubt anyone will be in Area 82. The only people who know about it are those who've entered it. And these people… these soldiers… Most of them died after the attack. It was the most gruesome thing I've ever seen."

He turns away and brushes his fingers through his curly locks.

"What?" I say. "Were women slaughtering what remained of your military?"

His puppy eyes shift my way, and he looks like I've shattered his heart. Did I strike a nerve?

"I don't agree with what those men did," he says, "but they were all brainwashed. You don't know about any of that. You weren't there. You didn't see the way they were made to hate their spouses, their daughters, their mothers. These men were still human beings, same as we are."

"We?" My voice rises.

There is no *we*. There is myself, my women, and then there are men.

"You know what I mean," he says.

I wave dismissively. I don't care to hear his humanitarian speech.

"Say we make it to Area 82," I start. "Hypothetically speaking, I send a group of women along with you to this place. Then what? I take it you're going to tell me you're a pilot, too?" I almost burst out laughing. I'm beginning to think that this man is insane. "And that you're an electrician? That you'll be able to repair the damage?"

"Actually," he says, "I was hoping you had those specialties here in Eden."

Is he trying to aggravate me? He offers me help, then expects me to provide the resources? I'm about to slap him across the face when I realize something—Jaqueline, one of my women here in Eden, is an ex-military combat pilot.

CHAPTER 2 – LUCY

Emily sits at the edge of my bed, playing with the tip of her honey-brown hair. It's braided to the side like it usually is. She hasn't been feeling well and didn't go to class today or yesterday or the day before that. If there's one thing I love about Eden, it's how nice the teachers are about kids missing class. They're always telling us that our health is the most important thing in the world.

Some days, I miss going to class. I miss being brought outdoors and taught things like how to read time based on the sun's position, how to start a fire, how to build a shelter, or how to get drinkable water. Sometimes I wonder: if we ever go back to how things were before all of this, are we going to be stupid kids in the eyes of society? In regular school, we're supposed to learn all about science, history, math, and English.

They do teach that here, too, but not in the same way as schools did back in the real world. I say the real world, but I guess this is the real world now.

"Aren't you a Healer now that you've graduated?" Emily asks, her porcelain-like skin looking almost gray. "Can't you *heal* me?"

I smirk at her and she smiles back, but then her lips droop down like she's about to throw up. I wish it were that simple, but choosing to become a Healer didn't give me powers overnight. I'm not some magical fairy who's able to wave a wand and make everyone better.

Besides, Mavis and Perula aren't teaching me as much as they should. I guess they don't want a sixteen-year-old knowing all their tricks. And that's what they are, I think—tricks. I still don't know what to think of them. They're being sneaky about certain things.

Like giving Devil's tea to the women of Eden.

That still doesn't sit right with me. Mavis blew up at me and said that Eve does everything she does to keep her women happy. The way I see it is if women need drugs to be happy, they're obviously not that happy.

"Abracadabra, you are healed," I say, twirling my finger in her face.

She slaps it away and lets out a chuckle but then covers her mouth with the inside of her elbow. Her cheeks balloon.

"Please don't get sick on my bed," I say. "The laundry ladies are busy enough as it is. I'd feel pretty bad about bringing them more work."

The worst part is only three of them work outdoors doing laundry for everyone in Eden. They use well water and the sun, mostly, and it does the trick. But last I heard, there are three hundred and some people living in Eden.

I remember when we first got here. We were a

group of about two hundred. We should have been more, but a lot of women didn't want to leave their homes. They said they'd rather stay in the cities because soon enough, help would be coming.

I don't think help ever came.

I suspect they all died, though I don't like to think about that. Even little kids stayed behind. Their moms didn't want to risk traveling far outside the city. I don't think that was fair for them to have to stay behind when Eve promised them safety.

She promised us all safety, and that's exactly what she gave us.

A knot forms in my stomach and I feel guilty about everything that's happened... the doubts I've had about Eve... Aunty Eve. But she's brought us this far. Why would she be trying to hurt the people she saved?

"Maybe I should go lie down," Emily says, holding her belly. "Try to get some rest." She then lets out a loud cough into the elbow of her arm.

"Good idea," I say.

I have to go see Mavis and Perula anyways. I've been avoiding them for a few days, ever since Mavis blew up at me. Maybe I should apologize. Besides, I don't know what kind of consequences there are if I don't show up for my lessons. Now that I've graduated, I'm supposed to be working. This is supposed to be a job—a way for me to contribute to the little society Eve's built.

Can they fire me? I'm not technically being paid for this, other than the shelter, the food, and the clean water I'm given here in Eden. Shoot. Maybe I'm being immature. I should probably apologize.

"I'll see you later," Emily says, but it comes out all muffled and she scurries away.

I'm shaken from my train of thought when I hear her throw up down the hallway. Then, little kids screech and squeaky footsteps run down the corridor.

Poor Emily.

I'll ask Mavis and Perula if they have anything I can give her for nausea. They'll probably say ginger, though.

Ginger!

The thought makes me smile. It means I've retained some of the information they've shared with me. Maybe my lessons are helping after all.

I hop off my bed and slide my favorite book—*Magical Herbs* by Fiona Lynch—under my mattress. There's never been any theft in Eden per se, but some of the kids, especially when they run loose during class, tend to take things that don't belong to them. They're not doing it to *steal*; they're looking for new shiny toys to play with.

And who can blame them? There isn't much around here in the way of games or toys. I think of my H-Cap and let out a long breath. Frig, I miss that thing. I had so many games at the tips of my fingers—literally. I smile at the thought of my mom playing it. She used to jab her fingers through the hologram instead of on the hologram. The screen would scramble every time, and she'd slap her knee all frustrated.

I take a peek behind my little dresser to make

sure it's still there, and it is. I haven't been able to use it since the EMP attack, or whatever it's called. The battery got fried. I can't think about that too much, though. Every time I think of my H-Cap, I think of my mom... Though I think of my mom all the time anyways.

Eve still never told me exactly what happened to her. Every time I've brought it up, she got all weird and started rambling about how tragic it was. So, I stopped asking.

I miss her so much.

"Heading for your lessons, missy?" comes Nola's voice.

I swing around in a panic like I've been caught doing something wrong. "W-what? Oh. Yeah."

She scratches her long fingernails through her poufy sandy-brown hair. I don't know why she bothers trying to look so good all the time with those perfectly manicured nails and clear, shiny skin that's obviously being washed every day.

"I don't think I've seen you leave your room in a while," she says.

She walks right into my cell, brushing her fingertips against the iron bars as she comes in, and plops herself down on my bed. Why is everyone always sitting on my bed? Maybe sometimes, I want my space. Is it too much to ask?

"Are you okay?" she asks.

Her thin eyebrows move up, and her forehead forms little rolls that look like tire tracks left in the sand.

"I'm okay," I say. I don't know why Nola's always

asking me if I'm okay. Even if I weren't, and most of the time lately, I'm not, I wouldn't tell her. I don't want to worry her. Besides, she'd think I was crazy if I told her I'd been having doubts about Eve's rulership.

She claps two hands together. "Well, chop chop—go on, then."

I force a smile and hurry out of my cell. When I glance back briefly, she's smiling back, a motherly tenderness in her eyes.

"Hi, Lucy!"

"Hey, Lucy!"

They run past me like they have springs for legs, and I barely have time to see them. Their little ponytailed heads bop up and down in the distance and they run around the corner, entering the main hall. But I know who it was—Alexa and Sabrina. Two six-year-old twin sisters who say hi to me every chance they get, even if that means multiple times in one day.

I wonder if they've escaped class again. That'll be three times this week that Mrs. Pottery chases after them, and she's getting too old to chase the younger kids around Eden. The last time I saw her chasing them, she got Ruby, Eden's golden retriever, all excited. The playful dog started chasing Mrs. Pottery, and then other kids joined in until they formed a long train that snaked around every Division.

I enter the main hall, the sound of my footsteps bouncing off every piece of furniture in sight. It's pretty quiet here today, which means it's sunny outside. The main hall is only full when it's yucky out there or when Eve calls everyone in to give some big announcement.

I also hate winter for that. When we get cooped up in here for a few months, people start to become irritable. We've been lucky over the last few years. In total, we had snow maybe three or four times. It doesn't snow here often, but it gets chilly. It's never stopped the kids from going out to play, but in general, the moms and the women stay inside.

I cross the hall then turn down Division Three's corridor and make my way to the back exit. This is where most of the garden work is done and where Mavis and Perula's garden shed, or Herb Shack, is. I only recently found out they call it that. I blast the door open and the sun's afternoon glow lands on my face. It's hot against my skin, which is nice since the air around me is mild.

I have a homemade calendar in my cell. Well, it isn't a real calendar. It's an old sketchbook that I've been using to keep track. I write in it every day as small as possible to keep track of the date and the day of the week. Unless I miscounted a month somewhere, we're now October 24 of 2069. Soon, Mavis and Perula will start bringing in a few plants. They say that some of them can't survive the cool weather.

I cross Division Three's courtyard, past a small group of little girls sitting in the grass. Their tiny pigtailed heads are tilted back, and they're listening to Mrs. Greensmith like she's the smartest person in the world. Mrs. Greensmith's holding signs that have alphabet letters on them, and she looks up at me from behind the small circular-rimmed glasses on her nose.

I can't help but smile. I love Mrs. Greensmith and the kids love her, too.

When I reach Mavis and Perula's Herb Shack, I squeeze the wooden handle and twist it open. It always seems like I'm intruding when I enter their space—like I'm about to walk in on them brewing something up—something bad I shouldn't know about.

"Oh, there she is!" Perula exclaims.

She gets up but starts limping as soon as she does. She rolls her shoulder to move her long salt-and-pepper hair out of the way and extends an arm in my direction, her pointed nails tickling the air.

Is she trying to grab me?

"There she is," Mavis repeats, and she couldn't sound more unexcited to see me.

I wish I knew what her problem was. Perula is the one with chronic pain—the one who got shot during the revolution and now has to deal with permanent nerve damage. On top of it, she has hip problems, too. What's Mavis got to be so damn cranky about?

"Where in heaven's name have you been, child?" Perula asks me. Her eyes look like apple-flavored candies—bright and shiny underneath the shack's glass ceiling. Most days, especially when she's hurting, they look brownish yellow.

"I was sick," I lie.

I can't tell them I've been avoiding them. It'll only

worsen Mavis's thoughts of me. She already thinks I'm "just a kid." If she finds out I've basically been sulking in my cell, she'll never stop calling me that.

"Silly girl," Perula says, flicking her wrist. "We're Healers. You're a Healer now. Why didn't you come to us?"

I shrug. "Just need rest, that's all."

Mavis lets out a scoff but doesn't say anything.

"Well, come on then." Perula keeps wiggling her fingers in the air.

I wipe my feet on the doormat, not that it makes any difference. The whole shack is made of wood and it's rarely ever cleaned.

When I step inside, Perula wraps her delicate fingers around my wrist and guides me toward Mavis's cauldron—well, her soup pot, but I like to think she's a witch. Why's Perula so excited, anyway? She's pulling at me like she's trying to show me the world's next best invention, or better yet, the return of electricity.

"What is it?" I ask.

But she doesn't answer me. Instead, her sunken cheeks rise and a goofy smile forms under her crooked nose. She looks at me and then down at the table by Mavis's cauldron. I step closer and follow her gaze.

Beside the cauldron is a small pot with soil, and at the very surface of the soil, a small bud is coming through.

"What's that?" I ask.

"The offspring of this poor little thing here," Perula says, throwing her thumb toward the back of the cabin. I know what she's pointing at—their dying nightshade plant. It's what they use to create something called scopolamine... what they've been using to create their Devil's tea—the brew they give to the women of Eden without their consent. Apparently, it makes them happier and more willing to listen to what Eve has to say.

"And 'ere we thought it was gone-a-gone-dong for good," Mavis says.

I raise an eyebrow. Why does she always have to talk so funny?

She smacks the wooden table and I flinch. "Look at that beauty! If two leprechauns fornicated and birthed a plant, it wouldn't even be as fine lookin' as this little guy."

She wiggles her long-nailed finger over the bud like she's trying to tickle it.

What's wrong with her?

Her eyes shoot up at me. What does she want? A compliment?

"Looks great," I say through clenched teeth, but what I want to say is, *You guys are horrible people.*

CHAPTER 3 – GABRIEL

Everything feels like a dream.

I keep going through this never-ending cycle of waking up and falling back asleep. I can't tell if I'm actually waking up anymore or only dreaming about it.

"Come on, get up," a voice says.

It's tender but authoritative at the same time. I crack my eyes open to find her standing a few feet away from me, arms crossed over her chest. She has a stiff posture, straight as a piece of plywood, and I wonder if she's ex-military or ex-police.

Her long dark brown hair is pulled up into a high ponytail, showing off her high cheekbones and piercing eyes—one green, one blue. It's mesmerizing. I've never seen anything like it. Her jaw is squared off and small bulges pop out on either side of her face as though she's biting down repeatedly.

My vision's a bit fuzzy, but from what I can see, this woman's beautiful. She's slender but still has an hourglass shape, and she's wearing military cargo pants, a gun belt, and a padded vest over a long-sleeved shirt. Without uncrossing her arms, she makes her eyes go big like she's trying to say,

What're you looking at?

I rub my face and sit up, but then the pain kicks in. It's a sharp, hot pain that spreads from my ribs to my chest and even into my stomach. Even my fists hurt, but that could be from punching Adam and his dogs in the face more times than necessary.

"Drink up," she says. "It'll help."

Her face barely moves when she talks. It's like she has no emotion. I follow her stare and find a cup of steaming liquid on the concrete floor. It's a small ceramic cup, probably over twenty years old, with a chip on its brim.

What's in it? More drugs? Because that's what they've been giving me.

"Mavis made it for you," she says.

"Who's Mavis?" I ask, and my voice comes out sounding like I have a toad stuck in it. I'm exhausted and dehydrated. How long have I been down here, anyway? That's where I am, isn't it? In a prison's basement?

"Someone who's trying to help," she says.

Again, she doesn't move. Her legs are shoulder-width apart, and she reminds me of a drill sergeant with that cocky look on her face. The only difference is her face doesn't piss me off.

I reach down and scoop up the tea. It looks like a kid's teacup in my fist. It's so small that if I closed my fist, I'd probably hide it completely. "This for pain?"

She nods.

I sniff it. It smells like earth, kind of, with a hint of perfume. Like a bunch of plants were thrown into a blender and then a flower was dipped in it to add a scent. Can't be any worse than some of the stuff I ate when I was traveling with Adam and the gang.

I take a sip.

Jesus Christ.

It takes like shit, but that probably means it's strong.

"Let's go, buddy, I don't have all day."

I look up at her with the cup pressed against my lips. What's the big hurry? She makes her eyes go big again, so I hold my breath and dump the rest of the fluid into my mouth. I almost cough it out trying to swallow, but I manage to bring it down.

"There you go," she says.

She moves toward me, her heavy combat boots clapping against the solid floor, and scoops the cup right out of my hand. I wipe my mouth with the back of my forearm and lick the air a few times. Maybe a bit of oxygen will get the taste of shit out of my mouth.

"Who are you?" I ask. "How long am I staying down here? Eve said—"

"Until Eve says otherwise," she cuts me off.

"What about Eve's plan?" I ask. "We can't waste any—"

"Look," she cuts me off again. This time she drops the weight of her body on one leg like an annoyed mom who has to keep repeating herself. "All I know is that you're supposed to help us, and you can't do that until you're all healed up. So shut up, tough it out, and keep taking your medicine when someone brings it to you."

Why's she being so cold? I haven't done anything

to her. She's acting like I'm some ex-boyfriend who broke her heart long before the revolution started.

"What's your name?" I ask.

She lets out a laugh and shakes her head.

It wasn't genuine, but it was pleasant to hear. There's something different about her. She's not like Eve. I don't know what it is, but I can see it in her eyes.

"What's so funny?" I ask.

She looks me in the eye for the first time and I feel like I'm staring at an Egyptian goddess. Her skin is fair but tanned, and her eyes look like emeralds. Her lips look bright red, but not red like lipstick red. It's her natural lip color.

I have to keep my mouth closed although it keeps wanting to open on its own.

"You are," she says, and her lips curve into a crooked smile. I can't tell if she's amused or annoyed. "I'm not here for conversation."

"No, you're here to babysit me."

Her glare narrows and a knot forms in my stomach.

"Do you work for Eve?" I ask.

She raises her chin and her perfectly arched brows draw together. "What's it to you?"

"I'm curious. I don't know anything about this place. All I know is I'm basically being held a prisoner in the basement of some prison. That's more insulting than being an actual prisoner if you ask me." I know I'm ranting, but I can't stop talking. "But I know you don't like me because I'm a man. I honestly don't want any trouble. I was only trying to help those women. I know you hate me. Everyone here's gonna hate me—"

"You're not hated," she says, and I shut my mouth. "But keep in mind that the women here haven't seen a man in over five years, and the last time they did, they were being shot at by them."

A big, nasty ball of guilt sits in my throat and I look away. If this woman knew I used to be in the Black Marines, she'd probably chop my head off right here. I still don't understand why Eve didn't question me about Area 82. It's like she knew I was military but wanted to ignore it to get what she wants. This woman though… She seems more levelheaded. I can't tell her… Even if I didn't kill any women during the gender war, I still can't tell her. That's like telling someone you belong to the KKK, but you don't attend the meetings. I was still a part of what these women were fighting against.

"I'm sorry," I say. "This whole war—"

"Stop talking," she says.

I look away and give her a brief nod. I don't know what's wrong with me. I think of myself as a pretty confident guy—the kind who's able to hold up a conversation with either gender without choking up or stuttering. But this woman…

"Hello?" she says.

My eyes meet hers again.

She points at the floor beside my knees. A small loaf of bread, a single serving size, sits on a sky-blue ceramic plate. "You have to eat."

"You're making sure I eat?" I ask. "What am I gonna do? Use the bread as a pillow instead?"

She doesn't seem to find this funny. "Just eat it," she orders.

I pick up the baguette and the smell of fresh bread fills my nostrils before I even sink my teeth into it.

Oh God.

If this isn't heaven, I don't know what is. I haven't smelled fresh bread in forever. The last time I ate bread, it was in the White House during the war. They'd passed slices around to tide us over, and I remember it tasting like cardboard.

This is different. I squeeze my fingers into the cooked dough and it bounces back like a sponge. I close my eyes and slide my nose along it, inhaling the smell as if that alone will satisfy me.

"What the hell are you doing?" she asks.

I open my eyes and reality sets back in.

"Sorry, I—" But I can't even finish my sentence. I sink my teeth into it and let out a moan. I don't mean to, but it tastes so goddamn good. The outside's a bit crispy, and the inside is as soft as air. It's like biting into a cloud from heaven.

"Never had bread before?" she asks.

I roll my eyes, but not because of her. It's too good.

"Not in years," I say with a full mouth.

"Well, get used to it," she says. "We make a lot of it around here. A lot of soy, too."

"For protein?" I ask. I'm probably drooling, but I don't care.

She nods.

My throat sticks together on the last bite and I

swallow hard. She walks toward the back of the room, reaches for something inside a metallic cabinet, and pulls out a big stainless steel jug.

"Here," she says.

I twist its cap off and pour the cold water straight into my mouth, almost choking on it. If there's one thing I miss more than food, it's fresh water. Finding clean well water or leftover grocery store stock hasn't been easy these last few years. Everything has a shelf life.

"When you're done," she says, "put the empty bottle by the door. Someone'll keep an eye out for you."

I'm still chugging it back.

"And once that goes through you... There are two buckets behind you."

She's right. There's a white one that looks like it's spent its life rolling around in the dirt and a red one that looks like it used to be shiny.

"I'll let you pick which one you want for... you know." This time, her smile looks genuine.

Is she taunting me?

"What am I?" I ask. "A caged animal?" I pick up the bucket and the plastic base scrapes against the cement floor. "You want me to shit in a bucket?"

She rolls her eyes, but the corners of her lips are still pointing up. "Our pipes aren't exactly functional right now."

I let out a sigh. It's not like I haven't shat in worse places before. Not like I haven't taken a dump in front of a dozen guys with my pants down to my ankles.

"There's toilet paper there"—she points beside the buckets—"if you want to use it."

"If I want—" I shut my mouth. Now she's being a smart-ass. "How do you have toilet paper?" I ask, but then I realize it isn't *actually* toilet paper. They're small sheets of thin material piled overtop one another. It's hard to tell what it's made out of, but it's obviously plant-based.

"Well, don't I feel special," I say. "Is it organic?" I try to be funny. "'Cause I only use organic—"

"Shut up, Gabriel." My name sounds so good coming out of her mouth. I can't help but smile, even though she told me to shut up.

She makes her way toward the main door but turns around when I say, "So you know my name."

She rests a hand on her gun belt. "I think every woman in Eden will know your name soon enough."

"My friends... Well, when I had friends, called me Gabe," I say.

She doesn't even blink. "We're not friends."

I shrug. "Still think it's only fair I know yours."

I'm not trying to be smug, but I can't help myself. There's something so alluring about her. She might be some crazy feminist extremist who thinks all men deserve to have their dicks cut off, including me, but I still need to know her name.

"It's Freyda," she says impatiently. She then turns around, pulls the door all the way open, and casually waves a hand over her shoulder. "God knows why I'm telling you..."

And the door slams shut behind her.

CHAPTER 4 – EVE

I pace back and forth, the sound of my breath aggravating me.

What have I done?

Why on Earth would I accept help from the male species? Or worse, from a military man? This man, Gabriel... He promises my women safety, but how can I trust him? Who's to say this isn't all some clever plan to infiltrate the paradise I've built for these women?

Perhaps he wants me to trust him—trust him enough to guide my women outside of Eden's barrier and onto male territory.

I slip off my red heels and fall into bed. Why does everything have to be so difficult? If only I had my little sister with me...

Oh, Mila.

She was always so much fiercer than I. As I gaze at the yellowing ceiling, I wonder if maybe I'm out of my depth.

A knock on the door shakes me from my trance. I swiftly sit upright and run my fingers through my short hair.

I clear my throat. "Come in."

I know it's Freyda before she even enters my room. She always slips her fingers around the doorframe, peeks an eye through the crack, and steps foot inside. She's well-mannered in every way, and as I watch her enter, those broad shoulders drawn back and chin level with the floor displaying confidence, I remember that I'm not alone in all of this.

I have Freyda, and if there's one person I want by my side, it's her.

"Freyda," I breathe, relieved by her very presence.

"Eve." She nods with her hands fastened behind her back and remains silent. She does this every time she approaches me. It's her way of showing me that she is prepared to obey any command I give her; she is always ready to do anything I ask even if it means putting her life at risk.

But she hasn't always been like this.

* * * * * *

Jesus Christ. Has this woman always been so obnoxious?

"Do you even know where we're going?" she asks me.

Everyone else is following me to Eden, yet this woman chooses to question everything I do. I have no idea who she is, or who she thinks she is, but she's walking in front of the others like she owns them. Her eyes are the strangest thing I've ever seen. One is green, and the other, a bright blue full of starlike specks—a galaxy. Her dark hair is pulled into a high ponytail, giving off the appearance of slick wet hair atop her head. She wears a gun belt with numerous pistols attached. I've seen her fire them—it doesn't take a genius to know she's trained in combat. On her back are two long blades that cross over one another. They're both covered in rusty blood and their handles are showing obvious signs of wear and tear. I'm happy to have her here by my side, whoever she is, but she needs to understand that these women are following me, not her.

And there are thousands of them—mothers, children, and many elderly women who are finding it difficult to keep up. But they followed me for one reason: I promised them survival. I spent weeks alongside Vrin's most highly trained military women, learning all of the necessary steps to take following an EMP attack.

I was prepared for this. I didn't realize how difficult it would truly be—but I was prepared.

Deep down, I'm scared. I'm not certain where we're going, but all I know is that we need to keep moving. We must remain as far away from Washington, DC as possible. If we don't, these women's lives will be at risk in a matter of hours or days. There are still men out there, and there are still women who believe that their men are worthy of saving.

But the truth is, they're all going to kill each other.

They're all going to turn on one another when they run out of food, clean water, or shelter. Their survival instincts are going to kick in, and they're going to become animals. I, for one, don't want to stick around to see that happen.

I think back to Vrin after I killed the president of the United States and the way she looked at me before we left the White House. She'd readjusted her military vest, tilted her head, slid a hand over her greasy blond hair, and said, "Whatever you do, get out of the city. Don't waste time, and don't stop unless it's to gather supplies. As soon as people realize that help isn't coming, they're going to turn on each other. Find a safe location outside of the city, at least fifty miles away, and start building a civilization. Find doctors, electricians, plumbers, any profession you can think of—make sure you have these specialties in your group of women. You'll need them. We've been in communication with our resistance groups across the states, and they're going to do the same. The more women you can bring, the better. Leave the men behind. We're going to rebuild America, but the filth needs to be exterminated first, and the best way to do that is to leave them to kill each other."

Then, we parted ways.

I turn toward this woman who's asking me so many questions. How am I supposed to answer her? Tell her I have no idea where I'm going? These women are relying on me. I grab Lucy's cold little hand and hold her close to me. She latches on like a koala bear and looks up at me with green, bloodshot eyes. She hasn't stopped crying since I came for her—since I took her out of that basement shelter.

Poor Lucy.

If only she knew what happened in the White

House. If only she knew I was responsible for her mother's death... She'd never forgive me. I haven't even begun to forgive myself. I swallow hard and instead of wallowing in my guilt, I focus my attention on my aching legs and burning muscles. The pain is the only thing keeping me going. We've been walking for hours, collecting stray women as we move forward through Washington, DC's surrounding cities.

Everything is eerily quiet—not a single car engine is running, traffic lights aren't humming, and electrical wires aren't buzzing. Every few miles, we come across a small band of men, but they look at us like wild dogs in hiding. Their heads pop out from behind abandoned cars, eyes wide, and they disappear as we move closer.

This is precisely what they deserve and I grin with satisfaction. They deserve to fear women—to fear for their lives the way we've feared for ours for centuries upon centuries; they deserve to feel like they belong at the bottom of the food chain. There are thousands of us and only a few of them.

Sometimes, we find one or two men dressed in military attire. Some have tried to fire at us—some have succeeded. But now, every time we spot a military man, my armed women at the front draw their weapons and fire.

And every time this happens, I flatten my hand over Lucy's eyes and hold her tight. She doesn't need to see violence even though all that remains of this reality is precisely that. But not for long. Where we're going—where I intend to take these women—

violence won't exist.

There won't be mass shootings or sharp weapons being thrown. Women will live in harmony, free of fear, hatred, and pain. Life will be spent living in prosperity and seeking only happiness. This place that I'm searching for, although I don't yet know where it is, will become a paradise like no other, its doors open only to women.

Although I'm not entirely sure where we're heading, I can already picture it. Beautiful trees will fill most of the space and the grass will be as vividly green as freshly plucked grapes. We will have an abundance of fruits and vegetables that will feed us all, and livestock for animal products such as eggs, milk, fur, and meat.

Over time, these women won't understand the concept of violence.

Every child will be raised to believe in a world of everlasting peace.

It's the least I can do... for Mila. So much violence and devastation have filled the hearts of these women. I glance back over my shoulder, seeing sweaty faces scrunched in pain and desperation. Many of the women have skin as gray as a stormy sky due to the ashes and cinder that followed the war.

I know our journey will be long, but at some point, we will find this sanctuary that is so clear and vivid in my mind. It's out there, waiting for us.

I turn toward this woman—the one with all the weapons attached to her—and offer a smile.

"We're going to Eden," I breathe.

* * * * * *

"What is it?" I ask Freyda.

She never enters my room for no reason.

"The man is fed, hydrated, and medicated," she says.

She's drawn her shoulders back and barely makes eye contact.

"Relax," I tell her.

I often need to remind her that she isn't a police officer anymore. Conversations don't always have to be about business or combat.

This time, she makes eye contact, and I smile at her.

"What happened to you, Freyda?"

She seems taken by surprise—her shoulders slump slightly and she lets out a soft breath. "I'm sorry?"

I laugh, which seems to amuse her. "You used to be such a bigmouth," I say. "Remember when we first met?"

She shakes her head and offers a crooked grin—a beautiful smile that has me staring longer than intended.

"I remember," she admits. "I thought you were—" But she stops herself as if she's only now realized who she's talking to.

I flick a wrist in the air. "You can say it, Freyda."

But she doesn't. I'm not sure if she's fearful of me or if she's placed me on a pedestal over the last few years.

"A stubborn bitch who wasn't fit to lead thousands of women after the revolution?" I ask.

She smirks, but her lips remain sealed as if to say, *You said it, not me.*

I stand up, and without my stilettos, my forehead reaches the height of her chin. "I'm starting to miss the old you. The *bold* you."

"You miss having someone to argue with?" she asks.

I brush my chin with my thumb and index finger, my eyes playfully narrowing on her. "Sometimes."

"Well," she says, "things have changed. And besides, I learned pretty fast that arguing with you was pointless."

I nod slowly. "It's hard to argue with someone who's always right."

She lets out a laugh and I feel at home.

"I consider you a friend, Freyda," I say. "Please don't forget that."

She smiles, her perfectly aligned teeth resembling chalk, and I can tell this means a lot to her. Freyda has a big heart, though she hides it from everyone. She's been through a lot, and I only found out about it several years after we migrated to Eden. She has a habit of bottling everything inside and swallowing it down as if hiding it from the world will somehow make it all better.

But it never does.

Her eyes reflect pain even when she's smiling.

All she has is Eden, and all she wants is a purpose, so that for a few hours out of her day, she can focus on something other than the family she lost violently to the war—her two little girls who were slaughtered at the hands of the military and her husband who died trying to save them. When the truth came out—when I first learned of her tragic past—she explained to me that her husband was unlike any man she'd ever met, that he was sweet, nurturing, and protective of his family.

I didn't believe her then, and I still don't. I think poor Freyda is heartbroken over her little girls and she's created a delusion in her mind. With time, she will come to realize she is better off without him. Deep down, men are all the same. There is no difference between them, and the truth is, we are all better off without the male species.

I think of Gabriel, and my stomach sinks.

I don't trust him, but what he promises is exactly what we need.

"Freyda," I say, and she stiffens like a police dog on the verge of being given a command. "Gather the women for me."

"Would you like Mavis and Perula?" she asks.

I give her a brief nod and wave a finger in the air. "Yes, please. And ask them to bring extra tea. I have a feeling this isn't going to go well."

CHAPTER 5 – LUCY

I'm surprised to see Freyda standing at Mavis and Perula's doorstep.

She has both hands on her gun belt and looks pretty serious. I can't help but stare at her guns. Do they even work? I mean, she hasn't used them in years. I remember seeing her shoot them when we were leaving Washington. It was the sound that scared me more than anything. It sounded like an explosion right beside me, but thankfully, Eve kept covering my eyes and ears.

I wonder what they're talking about.

Mavis and Perula are nodding and making hand gestures. I was told to wait at the back of the Herb Shack, so I don't know what's going on. Then, Perula looks back at me over her shoulder, guides Mavis out the front door, and closes it behind her.

Why do they always do this? Everything is some big secret around here. I already know about the tea. What else could this be about? What's the point of graduating and starting a *profession* if they're still treating me like a kid in school? And when will this stop?

Come on. I'm sixteen now. In two years, I'll be

eighteen, which is basically adulthood. Especially with the new drinking age that took effect in the states a few years ago. Well, before the war. I remember watching it on TV and how my mom was pretty upset about the age restriction dropping from twenty-one to eighteen. I guess she didn't like the idea of me ever touching alcohol.

What was the big deal, anyway? In parts of Canada, the legal drinking age has been eighteen for a long time. Or maybe it's nineteen. I don't remember. But I do recall hearing people complain about it.

Point being—if I can drink at eighteen, I'm technically an adult, and I'm only two years away from that.

I grind my teeth and glare at the Herb Shack's dirty wooden floorboards. A purple-shelled beetle runs across one of them and disappears into a hole in the wood.

"Dagnabbit!" comes Mavis's voice.

The twins come in with hunched postures, throwing their arms around animatedly as they bicker.

"Oh, this is bad," Perula says.

She rushes by me, her long green dress brushing against my cotton T-shirt. She hovers over the plant they showed me—the nightshade plant that's only starting to sprout. Then, in one swift motion, she turns around and scoops up the other nightshade plant, the one that's either dead or dying, from the shelf on the wall.

It looks like it's been set on fire. Not a single

flower is growing from it, and the tiny dark balls it once had aren't there, either.

"I thought Eve wasn't 'avin' another meeting for least another month!" Mavis rants. "That's what it's supposed to be! Once a month. Oh, frog-on-a-stick!"

"Calm down," Perula says, her gentle eyes fixated on her sister. She's always the calm one, but I can tell by the way she keeps biting her bottom lip and playing with her thumb that she's nervous about something. "We have other ingredients."

"Other—" Mavis shouts, and she swings a closed fist at the rotten plant Perula placed on the table.

My shoulders jerk forward and I take a step back.

"We need the Devil's tea," Mavis says. "You 'eard Freyda! This meeting's about the *man*."

"Man?" I ask. "What man?"

Mavis's eyes shift my way, and after a moment of silence, she flicks her wrist in the air. "There's a man in Eden. He's being held in the basement. Eve is calling a meeting to announce—"

"Mavis!" Perula exclaims.

Mavis cocks a curly-haired eyebrow. "What?" Her eyes dart from her sister to me. "She's gonna hear about it sooner or later."

Perula lets out a soft sigh. "I suppose you're right."

"So, what?" I ask. "Eve wants Devil's tea to keep the women calm? Because she knows this is all gonna blow up in her face?"

I'm about to keep ranting when Mavis points a stiff finger in my face. "Bite your tongue, girl."

I hold my breath and count to three. It's

ridiculous that Eve has to drug up the women of Eden to have meetings with them, but Mavis is a huge believer in Eve's methods. Questioning Eve's ways in front of Mavis again is going to get me nowhere fast.

"What's the problem, then?" I ask, my tone a bit calmer now. "You don't have enough of the ingredient for it?"

Mavis lets out a growl, and I'm assuming that's her way of saying, No.

"There are other ways," Perula says. She turns around and plucks a few plants from their shelf. As soon as she places them on the table, Mavis lets out a loud scoff.

"Do you have a better idea?" Perula says. She's getting impatient.

Mavis rolls her eyes. "Eve isn't going to like this. Not one bit. Not one wrinkle-toed bit."

* * * * * *

"She isn't gonna like this," I hear someone whisper.

Aunty Eve's holding onto my hand like it's going to disappear forever if she lets go. I don't know how long we've been walking. A few days, at least. We've stopped to sleep a few times, but when we do, we don't sleep long. We even walk at night, when the air gets a bit cool against our cheeks.

"We don't have a choice," says another voice.

"Excuse me!"

Who are they yelling at? I turn around and see two older women waving their arms over their heads like people do when they're trying to call a taxi.

They're looking at me. Well, maybe not directly

at me. But they're looking over here. Eve's talking with the woman who's been by her side this whole time. The one who keeps shooting her guns and protecting us. She's the reason Aunty Eve has to keep covering my eyes and ears. I think her name's Vrayda or Horayda.

Not sure what kind of name that is, but that's what I hear coming out of Aunty Eve's mouth when she talks to this lady. They seem to be getting along well.

"Excuse me!" the voice yells again.

This time, Aunty Eve turns around with her hand still wrapped around mine, and everyone stops walking.

"Eve," this woman says, "we need to stop. We can't keep walking."

She looks twice as old as Aunty Eve. She has gray hair that's short and sticks out from behind her ears. She looks so tired. She must be tired. Even I'm tired. Looking at her makes me sad. All I can think about is Grandma.

Aunty Eve said it would be too dangerous to go back for Grandma, so what am I supposed to do? It's not like I can go find her on my own. I wouldn't even know how to get to her house. Mom always drove us there. I just sat in the car playing my H-Cap.

"We can't stop," Aunty Eve says.

She doesn't sound like she used to. She used to be kind to strangers, but now, she talks to everyone like she hates them. I wonder if this is because of my mom and whatever happened to her. Maybe Aunty Eve is hurting inside like me. The only reason I'm not crying all the time is that my legs hurt so bad and my feet feel like they're bleeding inside my shoes. If I cry, I'll look weak, and Eve will think I can't continue walking. Mom wouldn't want that. She'd want me to be strong. She'd want me to get to this safe place, wherever it is.

"We have to," another woman says.

This one looks a bit younger, but it's hard to tell with all the dirt on her face. She has beige lines that run from her eyes to her jaw. A lot of women have them. They've been crying a lot. They're probably hurting in so many ways, not only their bodies.

Aunty Eve tries to protect me from all the awful things out there, but I've seen some of it. I know how violent everything got. I've seen tons of dead bodies, and I've smelled them, too. I wonder if these women saw their friends' bodies or dead family members.

I don't know what I would have done if I saw my mom...

I swallow hard. I can't think about that right now. I need to be strong.

Be strong, Lucy, be strong.

"Some of us can barely walk anymore, Eve," the woman with the tear lines says. "We're starving... dehydrated... exhausted beyond belief."

A few women around her start cheering at what she's saying. They're probably tired too.

Eve looks at her friend, that Vrayda lady, then back at the huge crowd following her.

"If we stop, we could die," she says. "We don't know who's hiding here." She points toward the damaged buildings and abandoned cars.

We're walking through a small town right now. It looks like something you'd see in an ancient photo. In one of those black-and-white pictures from way before Grandma's time. Everything is dark gray or black, including the sky. Even colored cars look black, but that's only because of all the dust and ash.

I can understand why Eve doesn't want to stop here. I don't want to stop here, either.

"If we continue," the older woman says, "we could die."

Aunty Eve bows her head and lets out a soft breath. She places a hand behind my neck and tickles my hair. Mom used to do this to make me feel better when I was scared.

"I'm sorry," Aunty Eve says, and she *actually* does sound sorry. Maybe she's still in there somewhere. "But we can't stop. If you can't follow, be sure to stay in numbers. Hide as often as possible. We need to keep moving. I can't risk the lives of so many by staying here."

A lot of women are upset. They start arguing over each other, but Aunty Eve doesn't stand around to listen. She tugs on my arm and we keep walking toward the sunset.

"You go, sweetheart," someone says.

I follow the voice. It's a woman with long blond hair who looks like she's about to collapse any second. Her face is all twisted, and she keeps grabbing at her leg.

"Mom, I can't—"

"Go, Elizabeth. Once you've made it, you can come back for us. You can take us all there."

The younger lady, this woman's daughter, nods fast and wipes tears from her face. She grabs her mom by the back of the neck and presses her forehead against hers.

"I love you," she breathes, and her mom says the same thing.

I look up at Aunty Eve, but she's staring straight ahead. The setting sun makes her blue eyes look orange right now. Everyone behind her is heartbroken, but she keeps walking. They're all saying their goodbyes because the crowd is splitting up in two. Those who are strong enough to keep going are coming with us, and those who can't do it anymore are staying here in this destroyed town.

Are they all going to die?

Aunty Eve looks down at me from the corner of her eye. I think she knows I'm staring at her. Her jaw muscles pop in and out, like whatever she's going to tell me is some big secret only she knows.

"Sometimes, Lucy, sacrifices have to be made for the greater good."

* * * * * *

"You deaf, you little brat?"

Mavis is looking at me like she wants to kill me.

"Been callin' your name for the last five minutes!" She slaps her forehead. "Kids these days... Couldn't use regular electronics. Had to use holographic ba-heegies and all that fancy shi-zaz. See? See what it did?" She flicks her wrist at me. "Fried 'er brain up like cauliflower mashed potatoes."

"Cauli—what?" I ask. "Cauliflowers are vegetables, not potat—"

Mavis lets out a bark-like laugh and reaches for my cheek. I pull back. She could probably slice me open with those long nails of hers.

"Oh, sweet soul," she says. "Bet ya woulda turned out as a Holo-Model in the real world."

I glare at her. Aside from having indirectly called me beautiful, this isn't a compliment. Holo-Model is a job given to people with good looks and nothing else. You sit there, in a room, reading off a script like a robot while they record you. Then, they use you in holograms around shopping malls or on city billboards for advertising purposes.

It pays well, but everyone makes fun of the hologram people. My mom told me that in her day, when it first came out, it was a huge thing and it was something to be proud of. But now, since holographic ads are so common, it's an insult.

She probably thinks I'm too stupid to know that, too.

I almost say, "Better a Holo-Model than someone's old broom closet," you know, because of that crazy hair of hers, but I keep my mouth shut. It would have probably made me sound immature.

"Mavis is only teasing," Perula says, smiling at me. The look she gives Mavis is like something out of a horror movie.

When Mavis finally stops laughing, she leans forward and sniffs the air like she has a cold.

"Get yourself on over to see Georgia," Mavis says.

"Who's Georgia?" I ask.

"The one who runs the gardens," she says, slapping the table again. "For cryin' out loud... What d' they teach you in school? You should at least know who runs what round here!"

"She's often wearing overalls," Perula says. She reaches two fingers a few inches over her head. "About this tall. Gray hair tied into a bun at the back of her neck."

I nod. I know who they're talking about. She's always outside, even when it's raining. If it weren't for her, the women of Eden would starve. I've seen this woman maintain dozens of gardens at a time. She has people who help her, but for the most part, she does all the work.

"I need forty-five strawberries, seventy-three blueberries, and three handfuls of blackberries," Mavis says, counting on her fingers.

"Was that seventy-four, or seventy-five blueberries?" I ask, and although I'm laughing inside, Mavis doesn't find this funny at all.

"Seventy-three!" she spits.

I don't bother questioning her. She probably needs these fruits for the tea they're putting together. My only guess is that whatever drugs they're putting in it are strong enough to taste, so they're going to try masking it with a fruity flavor.

I pluck an empty wooden box from the end of the table and make my way to the door. I look back at Mavis. I should keep my mouth shut, but I can't help myself.

"If I don't make it back," I say, "I probably got caught up practicing my Holo-Modeling."

Mavis's upper lip curls up over her front teeth, revealing dark red gums and browning teeth, but I don't stick around long enough to hear her lash out. I hop out of the Herb Shack and let the heavy door slam shut behind me.

CHAPTER 6 – GABRIEL

The orange glow reflected on the ceiling grows smaller and smaller, like a flashlight's zoom being turned all the way to the right. The candle's wax has melted on its little ceramic saucer, and the flame's dancing around, fighting to stay alive even if only for a few more seconds.

Any minute now…

It flickers one last time before everything around me goes black.

I let out a sigh.

How long do they plan on keeping me down here?

Alone in the dark?

I suppose it could be worse.

I could have entered some crazy society where any man found is strung up by his penis and left to die. I've been given shelter—even though it's freezing down here—food, and water.

That's all I need. I shouldn't be complaining. I shiver with my back against the hard floor, and goose bumps travel along my skin. What'd they do with my clothes, anyway? I'm wearing a pair of old briefs and nothing else. I'd say I was a bit embarrassed when I met Freyda, wearing nothing more than underwear, but in this world, nothing embarrasses me anymore. When you live every day knowing it could be your last, you stop caring about the small stuff.

Like nudity.

Like smelling like a rotten asshole.

Like shitting yourself in public.

The last one on that list was a one-time thing when I got jumped and beaten badly by a group of women. I didn't do it on purpose. It just happened. But I'm over it now. Besides, that's probably what saved my life. What better way to get your attackers to back off than to fill the air with the smell of fresh shit? To soften their blows with a warm, mushy texture in your pants?

Either way, after that, I'm lucky to be alive.

I stare into the darkness above me and think of that woman's beautiful face. Will I see her again soon? Will she come back to check on me?

Flashes of women screaming and blood splattering in the air suddenly fill the dark space around me. Back on the day the war ended, I remember thinking, is it truly over? How could it be over?

But it was over. And where was I? Hiding in the Oval Office, too scared to step out. If I did... if I stepped out, I'd see President Price's body. I'd see his lifeless face, looking like pale playdough on the floor, and everything would become too real.

* * * * * *

This can't be real.

My shoulders jerk forward when another explosion goes off outside.

“Let’s get outta here,” someone says.

I’ve pressed my back against the inside of the cabinet’s cool metal, my heart thumping against my ribs. I don’t want to look through the keyhole. I can’t. I won’t. I already saw her… that blond woman. She stabbed that bayonet right through President Price’s heart.

Maybe if I stay here and close my eyes, everything will go back to the way it was.

I won’t be hiding in the Oval Office, scared for my life. It’s pathetic, really. I’m a goddamn marine. I shouldn’t be hiding, and I shouldn’t be scared, but if I step out, I’m a dead man. I’d rather be hiding than dead. Maybe this is all just a dream and I’ll wake up at Mama’s house to the smell of baking cookies. I’ll have listened to her when she told me not to join the forces, and I won’t even be a Black Marine.

Why didn’t I listen to her?

“I-I-I.” The blond woman gasps. The last thing I saw was her swinging that rifle around and accidentally slitting her friend’s throat with a bayonet. She’s probably still hunched over her friend’s body, sobbing. I know she didn’t mean it, but it happened. And it wouldn’t have happened if she hadn’t killed the president. “Oh… Oh…”

I rub my palms against my eyebrows and slide my fingers through my hair.

“Ophelia,” the blonde moans. “Oh God…”

“We have to go, now!”

“I can’t leave—” the blonde says, and now it

sounds like someone's pulling at her. "Get off me! Get your fucking hands off me!"

She's lost her mind. Her voice breaks and she screams at the top of her lungs.

"Eve," someone says. "Please. There's no time."

This woman, Eve, doesn't say anything. She sniffles, then movement fills the room. Another bang shakes the White House and I cup my hands over my ears. What the fuck is going on?

Heavy footsteps shuffle until finally, I can't hear anything. No more voices, no more footsteps. Did they leave? I'm afraid to check. All I want to do is sit here and pretend none of this is happening. But I can't sit here forever. I'm about to piss myself and my legs are cramping up.

I stick my face against the cabinet's door and press my eye up to the keyhole.

Everyone's gone.

With my elbow, I give a little nudge to the door and it creaks open. I poke my head out.

Nothing. Not a single sound. They must have left the White House as fast as possible. I slowly stand, my knees popping and my legs almost completely numb, and limp my way over to President Price. He's lying flat on his back with his chair still under him. His legs dangle in an odd way and his shiny shoes point up toward the ceiling.

His eyes are wide open, and it looks like he's staring at me. I don't bother checking his pulse. His skin is dull and his lips are pale. Blood stains his collar, his shirt, and his wrist cuffs, probably from trying to fight off this woman.

A few other bodies fill the room. Two of them wear fancy suits and wired earpieces, but the other guy has full tactical gear on. How the fuck did these women pull this off? I think back. I remember running in here, into the Oval Office. I didn't do it on purpose. I was being fired at, and the doors burst open.

It's all coming back to me now.

Those blasts. They were like nothing I'd ever heard before. Homemade explosive devices or grenades. The women must have set a bunch of them off. And they weren't alone, either. Every hallway, every room, every space in the White House was filling with smoke and gunfire.

President Price didn't anticipate them bringing the fight inside.

That's how they pulled this off.

It was a surprise to everyone. All military personnel were too busy fighting them off on the outside.

I straighten my back and walk toward the Oval Office's window. Everything outside looks gray. The grass, the trees, the people...

The people.

I duck behind the president's desk and peer over through the window.

Hundreds of women are running wild, waving weapons over their heads. Some have broomsticks, others knives, others pieces of wood. Five of them beat down on a man wearing military gear and he isn't moving. He probably died a while ago, but they keep bashing him and the sound of bones crunching fills the air.

The shouting sounds like something out of a horror film, and even though the Oval Office's windows are still in one piece, it's as though I'm standing right out there with them.

A combination of anger and hatred almost seeps through the walls.

My heart beats hard, a pounding drumbeat that lets me know I'm alive… and terrified. I don't know what to do. I can't go out there. They'll kill me. They'll beat me until my bones turn to soup. They're killing off any man they find. I crawl my way back over to the cabinet and slip inside.

Call me a coward, but I'd rather rot in here with piss and shit all over myself than be beaten with sticks and stones out there.

******

I wake up to the smell of sulfur near my face.

"Freyda?" I moan.

She's crouched beside me, waving a flameless match over a freshly lit candle.

"You'd better get cleaned up," she says. "The women of Eden are going to want to meet you after they find out about you."

CHAPTER 7 – EVE

"What do you mean, you don't have it?" I hiss.

I pace back and forth in the theater's Preparation Room and run my fingers through my hair.

"We have something else," Perula says. Her voice is soft, as it always is, but this isn't enough to calm me.

I need my Devil's tea. How am I supposed to tell these women that we're hiding a man within Eden's walls? I'll lose their trust, their loyalty. For years, I've advocated against the male species, and today, I stand to risk my rulership by contradicting what I've fought so hard to prove to these women—men are the reason our world fell apart.

Why associate with a man? I think of Zack, Madelaine's son, and my world begins to crumble around me. First, a boy, and now, a man. And what will happen when this boy reaches adulthood?

I clench my teeth. I won't let it happen. He will be gone before his sixteenth birthday—I will make sure of it. Sooner or later, his instincts will kick in, and he will show the women of Eden his true colors.

But that isn't the problem. Right now, Gabriel is the problem. Not having my Devil's tea is the problem. I grab the back of my neck and tug on the skin. My skin is moist and warm, and sweat drips from my hairline.

“Eve?”

“What?” I snap, but the frightened look in Perula’s eyes reminds me to compose myself.

“This’ll work,” Mavis cuts in, pointing at her big glass jug.

The liquid is reddish brown with little fruit pieces floating in it. Blackberries, strawberries, and blueberries.

“What is this?” I ask. “Alcohol?”

“It’s a brew,” Mavis says.

Is this supposed to make me feel better? I slow my breathing when I realize my chest is heaving and wipe my clammy palms against my pantsuit.

“Sorta like Devil’s tea,” Mavis continues.

She’s a lot bolder than her sister, which is what I need right now. I need someone to take charge—someone to explain to me that this is our only option and that it’s *going* to work. Someone who can put up with my anxiety by calming me, not cowering from me.

I tilt my head back and close my eyes, the fluorescent lights making me see yellow through my eyelids. I inhale a deep breath, eyes still closed. “What’s in it?”

“Does it matter?” Mavis asks, and I’m about to lose it on her when she says, “Don’t you worry yer pretty lil’ head, Your Majesty. We wouldn’t let you down, Eve. No, ma’am.”

Your Majesty?

I let out a long breath, almost instantly relieved. I've fought long and hard to regain the respect of these women after we separated—after families were torn apart so that the strong-bodied survivors could make it to Eden.

To be addressed with such respect is all I've ever wanted.

I'm the reason these women are alive.

I killed the fucking president of the United States. I killed my best fr—

I turn my head away. They should worship me for what I've done.

You aren't this person, Eve.

Some days, I wish that little voice inside me would disappear forever. I'm not little Eve anymore—I'm not Mila's big sister or my mother's daughter. I'm Eve Malum—ruler of Eden. If I allow myself to remember who I once was, I'm afraid Eden will collapse.

"You're sure this will work?" I ask, hovering over the jug of dark tea. I lower my head over the liquid and breathe in. It smells like a combination of herbs, nuts, flowers, and fruit. "And what's it taste like? Because the women are used to their Devil's tea."

"Oh, it's fine-dandelion-fine, my queen," Mavis says.

My queen? I'm a little taken aback by all of her royalty references, but I can't say that I mind them. She smiles at me, and her eyes narrow and cheeks lift.

"Mavis, are you high?" I ask.

"No, ma'am." But she lets out a chuckle, followed

by a tiny burp.

My eyes shoot toward Perula, who cowers further into herself and raises two open palms. “We had to test it somehow.”

“Oh, for God’s sake!” I say, and the pacing starts up again. “You two are like children!”

“Calm your knick-knockers,” Mavis says, and I glare at her. “You should be ’appy!”

“Happy?” I say. “Why the hell would I be happy about one of my Healers being as high as a kite?”

“It’s only temporary,” Mavis says. She chuckles again and makes her way to toward the jug. “Let me get ’em all ready for these fine ladies.”

She reaches for the jug’s handle, but Perula rushes to her sister’s side with a noticeable limp. “I’ll do it.”

“Oh, huff and puff, you big ole stick,” Mavis says.

“Is this how the women are going to behave?” I ask, giving her a full up and down. “Like petty children?”

“No.” Perula sticks a thumb out at Mavis who’s now grinning from ear to ear for no apparent reason. “She tried each ingredient as we mixed it in, you know, to make sure everything was in”—she makes air quotes—“‘working order.’ She *may or may not* have also eaten some of my new edibles thinking they were snacks. Clarisse made me a new batch yesterday—”

“Edibles?” I say. “What on Earth are you talking about?”

And why is Clarisse, Eden’s Chef, involved in this mess?

"Edeebables?" Mavis blurts out. Then, as if the memory of it has flickered on in her brain, she points a stiff finger in the air. "Oh, right. Well ya shoulda told me—hey, would ya look at this?" and she moves toward the big wood-framed mirror standing at the back of the room as if seeing it for the first time—as if she hasn't spent hours in this room.

"They're for my pain," Perula says. "Clarisse agreed to make me some marijuana biscuits."

I pinch the bridge of my nose, shake my head, then wave a few fingers in the air. I don't know how much longer I can handle these two. "Just make the drinks, Perula."

* * * * * *

"I don't know how much longer we can keep going," Freyda says.

If this were coming from anyone else, I'd probably snap. But Freyda means well, and she's only vocalizing what everyone is thinking. I'm even beginning to wonder if this place—this paradise that I envision so clearly—exists.

When will I know when I've found out? How will I decide what's a safe space for us to build a society? What am I even looking for? A cavern? A bay? A forest? I look down at Lucy. She's so exhausted she can barely keep her eyes open.

Poor kid.

I have blisters on my feet that scrape against my socks and shoes that are now damp inside. I don't understand how I'm still walking, but I can't stop—I can't give up. We've been walking for over three days with limited supplies—a few water bottles taken off the shelves of a grocery store, snacks that have to be eaten sparingly, and suitcases full of supplies such as clothing and tools that the women take turns dragging.

Surely, we're close.

Soon, we'll find land that's safe and habitable.

"Eve," Freyda presses. "We've already lost another dozen women. If we keep going like this, you'll be the only one who makes it to wherever it is you're taking us."

I look back. Only several hundred women remain out of the thousands who initially followed me. Their eyes are sunken in, their bodies are shaking, and their steps are slow and staggered.

"All right," I say. "Let's take a break."

Freyda waves an arm over her head and shouts out, "Let's rest!" and everyone drops to the ground in a dramatic motion. Sighs and bellows are released as women land on the grass. Children burst out crying and grab on to their mothers or caretakers, and Lucy lets go of my hand to lie flat on her back. She stares up at the sky, her bright eyes darkening underneath the thickening clouds.

I can't even begin to imagine her pain.

I don't want to think of it. When I look at her, she reminds me of Ophelia and of what I've done.

"Oh God... Oh God!"

I scan the crowd of women until I see heads moving about sporadically. What's happening? I push my way through, nudging bodies out of my way.

"What's going on?" I ask.

But no one answers me—no one has to answer

me. Lying in the tall grass is a little girl, no older than six years old, with clammy skin and a shiny forehead. She looks pale beside her mother, a frantic woman who rocks back and forth beside her daughter's body.

Is she dead?

The mother focuses her hateful eyes on me. "This... This is your fault!"

She tries to stand but trips and lands on her hands and knees. "P-p-please, help her!" Her face is wet, covered in tears. "If you'd have let us stay longer in Acitok, we could have found medication!"

Acitok is the last town we walked through. Many women raided the stores for supplies—clothing, food, batteries, electrical wires, light bulbs, anything that might be useful to us in the future was collected. But after several hours, I decided it was time to go. Some women argued, stating that we could build a new home in Acitok, but it was too risky. It wasn't a safe space.

"I didn't stop anyone," I say. "You could have stayed."

Her eyes narrow into hateful slits and she bares her big, gummy teeth at me. "You know damn well we would have died if we stayed behind!"

She shifts her body weight upward, and this time makes it up onto her knees. She's about to lunge at me when Freyda's pistol appears in front of me, its muzzle aimed straight at the woman's head.

"Back off," Freyda says, and the woman's eyes go wide.

She takes a few steps back, as do several women

behind her, and raises her arms in submission.

"What're you gonna do?" she asks. "Kill me? You promise to take us to safety, but we're all dying! You aren't protecting us! Where are we even going?" Her voice cracks.

A few women start arguing back and forth.

Freyda's the only one who knows that I'm walking into this blind. If I admit to these women that I don't have a destination in mind, I can't protect them. All I sense in my gut is that if I keep walking a bit longer, I'll bring them to safety.

"No one's killing anyone," I say.

"So where are we going?" she cries, and others join in.

"We want answers, Eve."

"Where're you taking us?"

"How long do we have to keep walking like this?"

I turn around, my gaze fixated on the horizon. What do I tell them? How am I supposed to—

But then, I see it, and memories flash in my mind like photographs. That mountain—I've seen it before. It has a dip in the middle, almost as if forming the letter "M."

Where have I seen it?

I bite down on my teeth.

Think, Eve, think.

And then it hits me. There's a prison located near this mountain—a massive penitentiary that used to house prisoners. A news article I found lying on Ophelia's coffee table said as much. The picture, which was black and white, was of the prison with flames and smoke coming out of it. The damage was so severe they relocated the prisoners.

They were in the process of renovating and landscaping before the revolution began.

This is it.

This is where we'll establish Eden.

I point toward the mountain that was referenced as Alpa in the news clipping. "That's where we're going."

* * * * * *

"The women are ready," Freyda says, poking her head into the Preparation Room.

I give Perula a brief nod as a way of telling her to distribute the tea, and she scoops up the first tray of drinks. I sit down on the velvety red couch and scrape my nail against one of its big yellow buttons.

Everything will be fine.

Everything will be fine.

I know why I'm nervous—I'm afraid of retaliation. I'm afraid to lose all that I've worked for. What if these women turn against me? What if they no longer view me as a strong, capable leader?

But then something crosses my mind.

Why didn't I think of this sooner?

Just as I did with Zack, the young boy, I will give the women of Eden the illusion of a choice. If something goes wrong—if Gabriel turns out to be like every other man on the face of this planet—the women will blame themselves.

I swing my body forward and land on my feet.

"Where ya goin'?" Mavis asks.

She's seated on the floor's filthy gray carpet that smells a thousand years old, her legs crossed in front of her. I wish this room had caught fire. Maybe then this carpet would have been replaced with tile.

I stare at Mavis. With that old body of hers, she'll regret her position the moment she tries to stand.

Perula comes in for the second tray and gives me a big thumbs-up as if to say, "They're loving it."

I cross the Preparation Room, my heels barely making a sound against the carpet.

"Let's get this over with."

CHAPTER 8 – LUCY

"Lucy? It's Lucy, right?"

I turn around, though I'd have recognized that voice anywhere. It's the only male voice in Eden. Zack scratches the back of his neck and his bushy eyebrows move up on his face. He looks uncomfortable. Probably as uncomfortable as I am right now.

I wipe my blueberry-stained hands against my pants.

What does he want?

A dozen little girls poke their heads out from behind a garden bed as if playing hide-and-seek. Every time Zack turns his head to the side, even in the slightest, they all duck and start giggling.

"Yeah, that's me," I say.

"S-sorry to bother you," he says, "but have you seen Emily?"

What, are they best friends all of a sudden?

"She said she'd meet up with me today for school, but I haven't seen her," he rambles on.

I'm not sure how to feel about Zack. For the most part, he strikes me as a good person. He has soft brown eyes and a skin tone that reminds me of wet sand at the beach. I know I shouldn't be judgmental because he's a guy, but it's hard not to be. With everything that Eve's taught us, it feels like he's the enemy.

"She's sick," I say, and it comes out meaner than I'd hoped.

"Oh," he says. He looks around Division Three, still scratching the back of his head.

"Nice clothes," is all I can think of saying.

He smiles at me, then rubs his palms against the fabric of his shirt. It's beige, like most dresses here in Eden, but it's a guy's tunic with short sleeves and a small V-cut at the neckline with thick thread giving it a unique design. His matching pants look soft to the touch—almost like pajama pants.

"That Indian woman," he says, "Sahana—"

"I know who she is," I say.

He's still smiling at me, but his expression is forced and uncomfortable. It's hard not to feel bad for him. He seems likable.

"Do you know where to go?" I ask.

He shrugs his broad, bony shoulders and his shirt slides up at the same time. "No… I was waiting here for Emily. We were supposed to go to class together."

I smirk at him. "Let me take you before you end up being found by someone like Mavis or Perula."

"Ma—who?" he says.

I shake my head and let out a laugh. "Don't worry about it. Come on."

He follows me like a lost puppy with his head bowed forward and his feet too big for his body. He's wearing blue-and-white sneakers that don't match his new clothes at all, but they look comfortable.

"Appreciate those while you have them," I say, eyeing his shoes.

He glances up at me, a crooked smile on his face. His teeth look like they've been polished. They're so white and shiny. "Yeah, these are my favorites."

The rest of the walk is quiet, so I try to focus my attention on anyone walking by until we finally reach Division Six.

"This is your spot," I say, reaching a crowd of older kids in Division Six's courtyard. "Big kids meet in Division Six."

"Big kids?" he looks like he's about to laugh.

"You know what I mean," I say. "Fourteen-to-sixteen-year-olds start their day off—" But I pause, realizing I'm not even sure how old he is.

"I'm fifteen," he says.

It's like he read my mind. "Turning sixteen soon, though. I'm a Capricorn."

I cock an eyebrow. "A capi—what now?"

"Capricorn," he repeats, and the only thing I can picture is some kind of unicorn. "Don't you know zodiac?"

He probably thinks I'm an idiot because I have no idea what he's talking about. But he's not looking at me like I'm an idiot. He's looking at me like I'm a little kid, like I'm younger than him, and I'm not sure how to feel about it.

He waves his hand in the air like he's trying to erase something. "Sorry. I've spent a lot of time around adults. Sometimes I forget I'm only fifteen.

My mom pulled me out of school when I was eight. She said it was too dangerous. You know… Because of little boys disappearing."

"What?" I say.

"Well, she didn't want to—"

"No," I cut him off. "What're you talking about? What boys? I didn't hear anything about boys disappearing."

"Yeah," he says. "Well, I guess it wasn't on the news. But my best friend went missing"—he kicks at the grass with the tip of his sneaker—"and then my mom said that some of our neighbors lost their sons and were hysterical. I heard them once… the parents, I mean. They were fighting so bad I could hear them through my bedroom window. Mr. and Mrs. Garner, I think it was. They were such good people. And they always looked so happy together. But after Alex and Skyler went missing, it's like they turned into different people."

"What happened?" I ask.

"To the boys?" He shakes his head and kicks at the grass again. "Mom thinks the government had something to do with it. I don't know. I mean, I thought the government was supposed to protect us."

"The government isn't—" I start, but I can hear myself on the verge of getting upset. I close my eyes and take a deep breath. "The government isn't on our side. If they were, they wouldn't have killed all those people. They wouldn't have forced women to kill their girl babies."

"I know, it's awful," he says.

For a second, I think maybe we can be friends. He's levelheaded and easy to talk to. I don't think of him as a boy when I'm talking to him. I think of him as a person.

"Mom thinks they were trying to make clones," he adds.

I burst out laughing, but I slap a hand over my mouth when I realize he isn't smiling. He's serious.

"Clones?" What for?"

He smirks and shakes his head again. "Not 'clone clones'"—he makes air quotes with his fingers—"I mean like, they were probably trying to figure out a way to use the boys to create male babies."

"Like, without a mom?" I ask. "That was all over the news a few years ago. I saw my mom watching it. Parents could create a baby without the mom being pregnant. Like, they grew in tubes. So, what? The government stepped in and wanted to start making a bunch of male babies?" I almost start laughing again. This is ridiculous.

"I don't know why you think it's so funny," he says. "It's not like it's impossible. They were already doing it."

How many adults *has* he been talking to, exactly? But then I remember seeing Grandma on her laptop and the videos she used to watch. I always call it a laptop. That's what Grandma says it was, but Mom used to shake her head every time Grandma said that, and she'd tell her, "Mom, laptops are a thing of the past, now. They're Projexers." And then Grandma would shake her head, grab her old plastic keyboard, and slam it on the counter, refusing to give into the whole holographic stuff. She wanted nothing to do with the colorful projected keyboard, using the excuse that pressing plastic buttons was how it should be, not tapping your fingers on the counter. My mom would even try to get her to use the slim virtual reality headpiece, but she'd refuse. I was happy about that—I got to see everything she saw floating up in front of her face.

And there was so much outrageous stuff on there that I thought was fake—like the time I saw a policewoman talking to the camera and telling everyone how she'd been fired for being a woman. And then she said that the police were trying to design guns that only worked with fingerprint technology. That way, their weapons couldn't be used against them and they couldn't be used by women. It sounded like a bunch of garbage, like she was upset for having been fired and wanted to get back at the police force. But I found out a few weeks later that it was true. A bunch of policewomen came out and said the same thing. And then, another time, I heard that some high-security buildings were designing access control that didn't allow women to enter at all. Something to do with fancy cameras and hormone-detection machines. It sounded so farfetched, but everyone started talking about it.

What am I supposed to believe? Anything could be true.

"Think about it," Zack says. "If they have thousands of little boys, they could do all kinds of tests on them to figure out why they were born a boy and not a girl. Or, they could keep making boys and stop women from having kids, you know, naturally."

"That's disgusting," I say. "They can't force women to not have babies. That's horrible. Some women want to be mothers. And boys aren't lab rats. They can't make people by putting them in an incubator and sticking tubes down their throats. It's revolting."

I'm taken aback by my own words. For the first time in I don't know how long, I'm actually defending boys.

"Or," Zack says, and his eyes are wide open like he's about to tell me all about a cool book he read, "maybe they're making little soldiers."

"Soldiers?" I ask. "For what? And you're talking in the present tense. Everything's gone now."

He rubs his fingers through the few little hairs on his chin. "Maybe some secret underground government lab survived all of it. Maybe they're keeping the babies hidden too, you know, train them how to fight as they get older. And years from now, when there's literally nothing left in America... When most survivors are dead, they'll come out from hiding and take over."

I smirk. "Well, that's stupid. If there's no one left, why even bother to take over—"

"Yeah, yeah," he says. "It sounds crazy, I know."

He seems a bit embarrassed, like he took it too far and assumes I think he's an idiot.

"It's not *that* crazy," I say, and he looks at me, his big eyes fixed on me for a moment. "I mean, you never know anymore, right?"

His smile comes back and he nods. “Exactly.”

“Listen,” I say, “I’d better get going. I need to get a few ingredients for Mavis and Perula. And I think you’d better hurry.” I point at Mrs. Lewenburg, the Life Lessons teacher, and at the students who are all getting up from the grass. “It looks like they’re going somewhere.”

“Oh!” he says, walking backward. “Okay, I’ll catch you later. And, um—thanks for the chat!” and he runs toward the group of kids, his long, lanky legs kicking behind him.

Poor guy. Mrs. Lewenburg stops talking as she watches him approach, and everyone in the group turns to him. Awkwardly, he places his hands behind his back, and although I can’t see his face, he probably has that cheesy grin on it—the one that says, “Please like me.”

Some of the girls look disgusted by him, and a few others at the back start giggling and whispering.

I hope I’ll run into him again later.

Even if his stories sound insane, they’re fun to talk about.

CHAPTER 9 – GABRIEL

I hear her footsteps against the iron staircase before the heavy door swings open. I sit upright, stretch my neck, and blink away the fuzziness from my sight until I see Freyda standing there, hands on her hips.

"Miss me already?" I say, my voice sounding like a toad. She doesn't even smile.

"Get up," she orders.

"I'm not even dressed–"

"Now," she says like I'm a disobedient dog.

I slowly roll onto my hands and knees and get up on my feet. It feels like my ribs are being pulled out of place.

Something soft, but surprisingly warm, smacks me square in the face. "Put these on."

I grab the clothes and stare at her. She looks much smaller now that I'm standing, and I don't think she likes that. Her chest is puffed out like she's trying to make herself look bigger than she is. She probably feels threatened by me, which makes me a bit sad.

I don't know why, though. I'd never hurt her.

She clicks her fingers together and widens her eyes at me. "Let's go."

I slip the cotton, or hemp, tunic over my head. It hurts to put it on, but if I don't hurry, she'll let me know. It's soft against my skin, like fleece, but it's a bit tight for me. It contours my shoulders and my chest, which makes my biceps bulge out. It's probably making me look bigger than I actually am, and I'm a pretty big guy. If they're presenting me to a bunch of women who hate men, wouldn't it have been better to make me wear something a little less… showy? Maybe a sweater or something. Better yet, how about a bunny outfit? Something cute and innocent that screams, "I'm not here to hurt you."

All right, all right. I'm being an idiot. But I don't want their first impression of me to be a bad one. I slip into the pants. They're beige, and they match my new shirt, and thankfully these aren't snug. They're comfortably loose, so they don't sit tight around my junk.

I scratch my chin, feeling the rough hairs of my beard. There's another problem. My beard. I don't think women are ready to see some six-foot-two man with muscles, a beard, and dark curly hair that's starting to hang by his ears. I'll probably look like a goddamn caveman to them.

Shit.

"Here," Freyda says, and she passes me a silver blade, its sharp tip flat in her palm.

I let out a soft laugh, and even that hurts my ribs. "Must have read my mind."

"No," she says. "I looked at your face."

Is this supposed to be an insult? Even if it is, I can't be upset with her. Just looking at her makes everything about this hellish basement seem a little less awful. She narrows her eyes at me, but I don't mind. Let her hate me all she wants as long as she keeps coming to see me.

"What're you, anyway?" I ask. "Ex-military?"

She crosses her arms over her chest and purses her lips like I'm an idiot for even trying to make conversation.

"Special Ops?"

Nothing.

"Black Marines?" I try, even though I know it's highly unlikely. It was a fairly new division in the military, and most women were booted out by the time the war started.

"You gonna shave, or what?" she asks.

I'm surprised she's standing so close to me. First off, I'm a man. But secondly, I'm holding a weapon in my hand. What if I were some crazy bastard? Some piece of shit pig with only one thing on his mind? I'd have her pinned against the wall in a second. I shake away these thoughts. I shouldn't even be having them, but with everything I've witnessed over the last few years, my mind automatically finds the worst-case scenario in every situation.

My eyes shift to her gun belt. Maybe that's why she's so confident. She has two pistols tucked away in holsters. And if she is ex-military, she knows how to use them.

"I don't have a mirror," I say.

"Oh, for fuck's sake," she says. "Give me that." She snatches the blade right out of my hand. "Hold still."

Hold still? A woman who hates me and all men of the world is holding a razor blade by my face.

"You're too tall," she says. "Bend down a bit."

"You're too short," I want to say, but I don't think she'd find it funny.

I stare at her. Is she serious? Am I supposed to trust her to shave my beard? She rolls those beautiful eyes and lets out an annoyed breath, probably sensing my hesitation. "I know what I'm doing. I've shaved my husband's beard many times before."

I blink, but I don't move my face.

"You have a husband?" I ask.

I realize it's none of my business, but it's too late to take it back. The words already came out. She grabs my face with one hand and gently scrapes at the side of my jaw with the other.

"Had," she says, and she doesn't look at me.

"I'm sorry—"

She's so focused that her forehead has wrinkles and her lips are sealed tight. Her nose is medium-sized and neither round nor pointy. It's this perfect combination. And those eyebrows. It's obvious she doesn't pluck them. I mean, who would in a postapocalyptic world, anyway? But she doesn't have to. They're perfectly shaped into half-moons. Not too thick, not too thin. She has this cute little beauty mark over her lips, too. It sits right at the top corner of her mouth. She even has one on her thick bottom lip. A little brown freckle. I've never seen that before.

"Stop staring at me," she says.

"I wasn't—"

Her grip tightens around my jaw. "I can feel your eyes. Look somewhere else."

"Sorry," I mumble, and I roll my eyes up toward the ceiling, awkwardly trying to find something to focus on. All I see are old pipes full of cobwebs and wires that probably haven't worked in years.

"Those pipes up there," I say, and I flinch when she cuts me.

"You shouldn't be talking," she says.

I don't say anything and stand with my back hunched forward and my hands behind my back. I feel like I'm in a scene from *Beauty and the Beast*. Like I'm being cleaned for some big celebration by someone who thinks I'm a monster.

I close my eyes, and her touch, even though she's brushing a blade against my skin, is the nicest thing I've felt in years. I can't remember the last time I felt a woman's touch.

Her hands are so soft, but incredibly strong at the same time. She's breathing out through her nostrils, and it smells like perfume, or like flowers. Like she's eaten a whole bouquet of lilies or roses. How does she do that? Manage to keep up with her hygiene? Then again, this place is full of women. Hygiene is probably an important part of their everyday activities.

"There." She pulls back from me. With my jaw still held firmly in her hand, she moves my face from side to side to make sure she didn't miss anything. My skin feels completely irritated, but I don't mind. She licks her thumb and wipes the side of my cheek, probably where she cut me earlier. "Good as new."

She shifts her eyes to meet mine, but only briefly. The second she realizes we're looking at each other, she turns away and I straighten.

"Thank you," I say, but she doesn't say anything back.

"Come on, let's go."

"Hey, Freyda—"

She tilts her head and looks at me, obviously feeling empowered again now that she's at a safe distance.

"Is there anything I need to know? About this place, I mean. Should I be worried? I get that you guys—you women, I mean. Women. You're not a fan of men. I know that. But am I walking out there to be stoned to death? I know Eve said that she'd accept my help, but I don't know if she was serious. All I'm saying is if I'm gonna die, could you please tell—"

"You're not dying, you idiot," she says. She lets out a long breath, and it sounds like she's trying hard not to be mean to me. "You seem like a decent guy. I hope you are. Eve will be telling everyone that you're going to help us in some way. I don't have all the details yet. So, if you are this good guy you say you are, be yourself. Don't be an asshole, and most of all, don't be misogynistic."

"I'm not—"

"And don't interrupt someone when they're talking to you."

"Sorry."

"You're a huge minority here in Eden," she says. "I honestly have no idea how it's going to go. I'm sure some women will be pretty excited about having a man around"—she gives me a quick up and down—"but most are probably going to hate you right off the bat."

I let out a soft laugh even though I don't think any of this is funny. "I guess this is karma. Women have been fighting to be treated as equals for centuries, and now, in this place, men are a lesser being."

"You're not a lesser being—" she tries, but I shake my head, my curly hairs tickling my forehead.

"It's okay," I say. "Honestly, you all have every right to be hateful. I won't take that from you. I hope I can make a difference, though."

She bows her head and rests her thumb on her gun belt. "If you're genuine, Gabriel, you're one hell of a guy. I'm trying to be positive, here. I'm trying to believe you." She then raises her chin and flares her nostrils. "But if I find out you're dishonest in any way." Now she's pointing a finger at me. "If I find out you're doing all of this for some sick fucking reason—that you're a piece of shit like the rest of them—so help me God, you'll be looking at me upside down, the weight of your body held only by your fucking dick wrapped in barbed wire."

CHAPTER 10 – EVE

I watch the women before me. With their pupils dilated, they lean in various directions, whispering into each other's ears. Have they heard of what happened outside of Eden's walls? Do they already know about Gabriel? About the attack on my women?

How could they? Gretchin has been placed in an isolation unit in the medical center along with the three women who were attacked that morning. I haven't done this to punish them. Rather, it's to allow them time to heal their physical and psychological wounds before being reintegrated into Eden's society. The women of Eden must continue to be surrounded by love and positivity—not by victims of abuse who will frighten them into believing that danger lurks nearby.

I want my women to enjoy their lives unburdened by anxiety. And unfortunately, several bad seeds risk ruining an entire garden. I have ensured that Gretchin and the others receive the utmost care during such a delicate time. Penelope, a former psychiatrist who worked in one of Washington's leading anxiety and trauma clinics, will be visiting them every day for the next two weeks. This woman is a godsend, having helped hundreds of women deal with their traumatic memories following the war. I cannot imagine Eden without her.

And then I spot her. She's seated at the far back corner of the Theater Room. She's always at the back—always in a position where she can observe without interaction. I suppose this has to do with psychology. Today, her dark hair is tied up in a bun at the top of her head—a typical librarian look that suits her well. When she ties it like this, I can see her thick gray stripe of hair that runs from her temple all the way to the bun. It's the oddest thing I've ever seen.

We have a clear understanding, Penelope and me. She is to help the women of Eden move past grief, anxiety, trauma, and abuse, but she is not to attempt to counsel me in any way. I do not want her pity, nor do I want any insight as to why I do the things I do.

I watch as Perula limps her way through the crowd, careful not to trip over anyone's feet or knees. Penelope sits quietly, her eyes shifting from left to right, scrutinizing every word shared among the women. I notice that Perula does not pick up an empty teacup from Penelope, which is no surprise, as Penelope despises any sort of mind-altering substance.

A knock at the back door captures my attention. It's Freyda.

She's leaning sideways, her head poking into the

Theater Room. She offers a brief nod, which I know translates to *He's here*.

I clear my throat and prepare myself. Everything is about to change.

* * * * * *

They aren't ready for change.

"A prison?"

"Is this a joke?"

"We're supposed to live in... *there*?"

I clear my throat and turn around, Lucy's little hand still tucked in mine.

"These walls will protect us," I say, extending an open palm toward the penitentiary behind me. It looks old like an ancient Irish castle, with stone walls that are at least thirty feet high and massive wooden gates that are currently hanging open.

Not a single sound escapes the abandoned prison, which leads me to believe it is perfectly safe. Freyda has already gone inside with her guns drawn to scope the place. Going in there alone seems a bit foolish, but this woman is more stubborn than Mila was when it comes to protecting others. She is always on the front line, refusing to back down against anyone. I'm lucky to have met her.

"Protect us from what?" someone shouts. She holds a tight fist in the air as if prepared to start a riot. "Look around. There's no one here."

The others join in on the debate, accusing this woman of being too "picky" regarding our location. And then, there are some who don't comment at all—they simply stand there, waiting for the argument to blow over. It's apparent they're exhausted. All they want is to rest, regardless of where they might be.

I do understand where this woman is coming from. I look around, seeing nothing but open field and a nearby forest with an abundance of trees. Behind the prison lies Alpa, the quaint mountain that looks like nothing more than a small "M" in the distance. Nearby, birds chirp, water flows, and insects hum in the tall grass.

Why hide in a prison in the midst of all of this? It will guarantee our safety. These women fail to understand that the surviving males will venture out of large cities in search of women—they will tear through pretty much anything to get their hands on a woman.

We're not safe out in the open or in nature. We need a barrier between us and them.

"It isn't over," I say, and everyone goes quiet. "This war—this intolerance we face from the male species. They're not extinct. They're out there, somewhere, and although they may never come this way, there is always a risk. And I will not put your lives in danger because some of you don't like the idea of being within prison walls."

I expect anger, but to my surprise, the women slowly nod, their lips sealed.

"Eve's right," someone shouts. "Who cares what it looks like in there? At least we'll be safe."

Freyda suddenly appears by my side. She nods, her firm, square jaw barely moving an inch, and slips her pistols back into her holsters.

"All right," I say, my voice carrying over the women and children. "Let's hurry inside. You"—I point to the mother whose sick little girl still sits in her arms—"bring her in first." I crane my neck and scan the crowd. "Who here has a medical background? This girl needs immediate care."

A curvy, middle-aged woman with poufy sandy-brown hair and a pair of crooked glasses takes quick, deliberate steps toward the front of the crowd. "I'm a nurse," she says, shoving her way through. "Well, used to be."

She looks like the kind of woman who, at whatever hospital she used to work at, would have gone above and beyond to make sick children laugh. There's a certain goofiness to her even though it's deeply hidden right now.

She leans in over the little girl and her lips stretch into a huge smile. "Hi, sweetheart. I'm Nola." Swallowing hard, she turns away. She's obviously quite sensitive, too. I wonder who she's lost. Who does this little girl remind her of? A daughter? A granddaughter? She clears her throat and wipes a tear from her eye. "We're gonna make you all better, okay? Here." She angles her shoulder to one side, and a massive backpack falls to the ground with a *thump*. She digs into it, her back round and her hat-like hair moving from side to side.

"Aha!" She pulls out an apple juice box and pierces the straw. "Here, drink this." She then stands up by pushing down on her knees and turns toward Freyda and me, the smile on her face vanishing as if it were a mask. "Was there a medical facility in there? Did you notice if they had any supplies?"

Freyda gazes toward the sky as if analyzing the

image she's saved in her mind. "Yeah, there was."

"They might have something," Nola says, but she hesitates, and her eyes shift between the young girl and me. She's probably thinking the same thing I am—what exactly is she looking for? We don't even know what's wrong with the girl. But she's doing everything she can to reassure the little girl. She looks down at her and offers an exaggerated grin. "All right, sweetie, let's go make you all better."

Everyone starts moving forward, their footsteps heavy and pained. A few women, however, cross their arms and stare at me.

"Is there a problem?" I ask. I'm getting upset now. After everything I've done...

"Is this a long-term thing?" one of them asks. "Are we going to spend the rest of our lives in a prison? Because—"

I point my finger straight at the ground. "You have two choices here." They take a step back and keep their mouths shut. My words must have come out as more of a hiss. "You can either come inside and be a part of our society—a part of someplace safe where we will all be happy together. Or, you can turn around and leave. The choice is up to you."

"Let's just go in, Vee," one of them says. I'm assuming they're sisters. They look alike, with long blond hair that reaches their hips.

The other one, assumedly the more dominant sister, doesn't break eye contact with me. It's like she wants to challenge me, and right now, I'm not in the mood.

"No one said this life would be easy," I say, trying

my best to remain soft-spoken even though I'm about ready to tell her to go fuck herself. If it weren't for me, she'd still be in Washington, DC, probably hanging onto her sister's dead body. "But I'm trying, here. So again, you can follow me, or you can turn around. If you follow me, I promise I will do everything in my power to give you the life you deserve."

She lets out a long breath, picks up her bag, and throws it over her shoulder. "All right, let's go." And she brushes past me.

I take a deep breath and stare into the open field, focusing on the crisp air entering my nostrils.

"You okay?" Freyda asks.

I turn toward her, my scowl quickly transforming into a pretentious smile. "What? Yeah. I'm fine. Let's go in and get some rest."

* * * * * *

"Thank you all for coming, my beautiful women of Eden," I say.

I smile as sweetly as possible and my lips twitch. The women return the smile and watch me as if awaiting my blessing. They all sit on their gray-padded chairs, their knees close together beneath their hemp dresses and their hands over their laps.

"As you already know, a few women were granted the freedom to venture beyond Eden's walls."

A mixture of curiosity and anxiety fill the room. One chair scrapes against the floor, and a gasp comes from the back.

"What you do not know, however, is that male

rebels attacked these women."

And voices erupt like an active volcano. Scowls appear throughout the room and women begin yelling over one another—some out of fear and others out of anger.

"Where are they?"

"Oh, dear God, what happened?"

"Are they all right?"

"What happened?"

I raise a hand, level with my face, and silence returns.

"The women have survived," I say, and a unanimous sigh escapes everyone's lungs. I walk across the stage, my head bowed and my gaze fixated on the floor in front of me. "But they wouldn't have." Without raising my head, I look up at the women—at their wide eyes and parted lips. "They wouldn't have survived if it wasn't for one person."

I need to portray Gabriel as some angelic savior, even though it makes me sick to my stomach. Although I'm grateful that he saved my women, I can't help but feel as though he has ulterior motives. Saving four women does not make him a hero—it makes him likable, which is perhaps precisely what he wants.

But, I need my women to *want* him in Eden if my plan is to work.

"Who?" someone calls out.

"Who saved them?"

"A man," I say.

Some women gasp while others clutch at their hearts with bulging eyes and open mouths.

"His name is Gabriel," I say, but no one moves or speaks.

Have the drugs even kicked in? I glare toward the Preparation Room and spot Perula's worn face poking out of the doorway. She grins and gives me a tight, fisted thumbs-up.

I clear my throat. "Freyda."

Within seconds, she appears inside of the Theater Room with Gabriel following behind. He looks like a giant compared to everyone else in the room. He has rope fastened around his wrists, both of which hang loosely in front of his abdomen, and he's wearing basic hemp clothing made by Sahana—a special request of mine. He's also cleanly shaven.

The mixture of voices that explodes around me is enough to give me a migraine. Then, one woman stands, fists partially raised, her face beet red.

"That mother fuckin' piece o' shit! What the fuck is a man doing in Eden?"

"Sit down, Tye!"

"Don't you dare tell me to sit down! After everything they've done—"

"Shush, Tye!" someone else cuts in. She looks much younger, and she stands, her back muscles tightened and her head sticking too far out from her body. "I don't see anything wrong with having a man around." She then turns to Gabriel, gives him a full up and down, and winks at him. "Think of him as a new toy."

A few whistles form a melody in the room, and Gabriel shifts uncomfortably.

"Men have torn America to bits, and you're

thinkin' about sex?" Tye says.

"Nobody said—"

"Enough!" I shout, and the bickering immediately stops.

I clench my teeth, wanting nothing more than to walk into the Preparation Room and grab both Mavis and Perula by their throats. The cocktail was supposed to mellow them out, not make them fight with each other. Then again, I suppose that this topic cannot be numbed by substances.

"He isn't being integrated into Eden," I say.

"We sure hope not!"

I raise my chin and stare at this woman—Tye. What I would do to wrap an old cable around that thick neck of hers. Who does she think she is?

Freyda clears her throat, and I'm propelled back to reality—back into the very moment that could change Eden forever.

CHAPTER 11 – LUCY

"Is it true?" I whisper, and Emily flops over in her bed. Her eyes are bloodshot, and her braid looks like haywire tied with an elastic.

With the back of her hand, she rubs her eyes and then the white muck from the corner of her pale lips.

"What?" she says, but it comes out sounding more like "Ahh."

She's holding a stuffed bunny, something that I assume used to be white. It looks more yellow than anything now, and its ears look like they were soaked in liquid sugar. The fur appears sticky and hardened. She tries to sit up but instead starts coughing, her lungs sounding like little bubbles of water. I take a step back involuntarily. The last thing I want is to catch whatever the heck she has. And with all the kids around here, viruses spread pretty fast.

"Sorry," I say. "I didn't know you were sleeping."

She shakes her head as if to say, "It's okay," then pushes herself up with her elbow. Poor Emily. She looks awful. Her usual porcelain-like complexion is more gray than white, and her brown eyes look almost black. I'm glad her room's all the way at the back end of Division Five. I hate to be selfish, but I wouldn't want her near my room. Not with a cough like that.

"We should get you to see Dr. Lewis," I say.

Dr. Lewis (she always tells me to call her Ezri, but I feel weird doing that because she's the same age my mom would be) takes care of sick people in the Medical Unit. In a way, it's funny. Mavis and Perula are supposed to be Healers, when in reality they're just potion mixers. They work with natural ingredients to create remedies for stuff. Dr. Lewis, though, is a real doctor. I've gone to see her a few times, mostly for small cuts and scrapes from playing outside. She's nice, and she's especially good with kids. She has beautiful shiny brown skin that always looks so clean, and the coolest hair I've ever seen. It's an Afro, fluffy and round on her head, but sometimes she braids it tight against her skin. I like it in an Afro, though. It suits her.

The first time I went to see her, I had a cold that was going around Eden. She was so welcoming that I didn't want to leave. She let me lay in a padded bed with fresh white sheets for hours. She gave me lemon honey drops for my throat, which I now know were probably made by Mavis and Perula. I wonder if I'll be working closely with her as I get older. Maybe I'll be making all kinds of recipes for her to give to the women of Eden, like Mavis and Perula do.

Emily furrows her brows. "No, no, I'm fine. Wh-what're you talking about? Is what true?"

Her voice sounds like music from a radio with too much bass.

"There's a meeting," I say, "about some guy."

She tries to smile, but she starts another coughing fit. This time, I hear the phlegm come loose in her lungs. She swallows hard, and I'm not sure if her throat is bothering her, or if she swallowed whatever came up. Either way, it makes me want to be as far away from her as possible.

"Seriously," I say. "Go see Dr. Lewis. If you don't go, you're being selfish. Little Angelica sleeps right there—" I point at the empty cell across from Emily's room. She's probably in class right now, but a six-year-old doesn't need to catch something like this. "You should be isolated."

She coughs up again, this time, into the elbow of her arm.

"Y-yeah. You're right." Her glassy eyes meet mine, and drool drips from the corner of her mouth. "God, this is horrible."

I make a come-hither hand gesture. "Come on. I'll take you. Don't touch me, or anything, for that matter. And try not to cough on me."

She makes a face that says, "Shut up." At least she still has her sense of humor.

I extend my arms, prepared to catch her if she falls, but I hope she doesn't. What scares me most about kids getting sick in Eden is that they don't all make it. As much as Dr. Lewis is a great doctor, and as much as Mavis and Perula make some pretty strong stuff, it isn't always enough. When we first came to Eden, a bunch of kids got sick and then almost everyone caught it. It was horrible. Kids were throwing up in their rooms at night, and adults came in as often as possible to comfort them even though they were just as sick. That's why Eve decided that in every Division, there should be adults every few cells to watch the children. And there's a lot of us, too. Kids, I mean. Many of the adults weren't strong enough to make it all the way out here, so they sent their kids, pleading with Eve to take care of them.

Eve said we were supposed to go back to get the rest of the survivors, but then she told everyone that the small town—the one where the grandmas and weaker women stayed behind—had been attacked by male rebels.

I don't know where she got that information, but it's what she told us. All of that to say... the first year here in Eden was pretty dark. A lot of kids cried, and a lot of adults, too. And to make things worse, a lot of kids died. It's hard to forget the first girl who ever died in Eden. She looked so sick. I remember her skin most of all: clammy and cold-looking. She kept shaking in her mom's arms, and everyone kept rushing around them trying to figure out what to do.

Dr. Lewis wasn't in Eden yet. Maybe she's the one who told Eve about the town being attacked because she found Eden a few months after we did. I don't know.

But at the time, Nola was the one trying to help. She said she used to be a registered nurse. She did everything she could, but all I remember her saying was, "There was nothing we could do."

That poor little girl died that night, the first night in Eden, and it was one of the worst nights for everyone. Eve and a few of the adults took her body outside of Eden's walls. I don't know what they did with it, but I guess they didn't want to start burying bodies inside of Eden.

I watch Emily as she takes little steps down Division Five's corridor. She's having such a hard time. I loosen my hand when I realize I'm making a fist. Why am I so stressed? Am I afraid of getting sick, or am I scared something will happen to the one person I've started thinking of as a friend?

Oh God, I hope she's okay. It's only a cough, right? Just a bug.

She trips over her own feet and lands face-first against the iron bars of someone's empty cell.

"Emily!" I say.

"It's okay," she croaks. "I'm okay."

She straightens up and walks toward the main hall, all the while brushing her fingers along the walls. I hope she isn't spreading her germs, but at the same time, she needs something to support herself. Sweat drips from her hairline and she shivers. She's probably running a fever.

"What the hell's wrong with you?" I ask.

"I-I don't know," she says. "I don't feel good."

"That's not what I mean," I hiss. I don't mean to come across as angry, but deep down, I am angry. I'm pissed off that she wouldn't be smarter than this. She knows that we're not living in a big city with tons of doctors, antibiotics, and hospitals. You don't mess around with sickness here in Eden. "What were you thinking? Why didn't you go straight to the Medical Unit when you started feeling sick?"

She tries to shrug, but it looks like she's shivering

even harder. "I don't know."

I let out a sigh. At least she's going now, so there's no point getting upset with her. It's not like she has a mother or a guardian to force her to do anything. And I can't go back in time. I'm scared. I don't want anything bad happening to her.

I guide her through the main hall and toward the main entrance of Eden. It's so quiet in the main hall that our shoes squeak on the tiles. The kids are all outside, enjoying what's left of the mild weather, and the adults are probably all in the Theater Room right now, having a meeting about that *man*.

I'm so curious.

Down the main entrance's corridor, there are several rooms along both sides. At the far back is where the main door is, the one where only Eve is allowed to go through. There's a solar-paneled security system that requires a keycode to open the front door. We're not allowed anywhere near there, so I don't step too close. Instead, I turn left down a small hallway with about a dozen individual rooms. They're like doctor rooms—you know, when you go to see your family doctor and they make you wait for about an hour. I miss that. I wouldn't complain about the long wait times if I could go back.

Some of the doors have curtains over the windows, and some don't. Curious to see how many people are sick right now, I try to peek inside. I see a few kids in some of the rooms, but halfway down the hall, something odd catches my eye. It looks like there are four women in the same room. They don't look sick, exactly. They're talking to each other. One of them has frizzy orange hair. I think I know her. I think that's the adult that Eve said could go outside.

If they're okay and they weren't hurt out there, why are they here in the Medical Unit?

It even looks like there's a lock on the door.

But then, the one with the orange hair catches me looking, and she jumps up and runs toward the door. My heart races. She's going to open the door and yell at me, isn't she? Maybe tell me to mind my business? Instead, she reaches for the window's curtain and slides it over until all I see is a blue material with yellow polka dots.

Emily's head is hanging in front of her and her shoulders are so rounded she looks like an old person. I don't think she saw any of that. I walk a bit faster, all the way to the back of the hallway. Dr. Lewis is usually in the last room.

The glass on her door is thick and translucent. It looks like frosted glass. That's where she does all her exams (probably because it's the biggest room, and it's private) and where she keeps all the medicine. The door's closed, and beside the door, there's a plaque that reads, M-12. I'm assuming that's for medical room number 12, but I could be wrong.

On the door itself, there's a metallic slab that looks like it used to hold a name plaque. It probably did, but it obviously wasn't Dr. Lewis's name, so she must have taken it off.

I knock on the door and wait.

Emily's swaying from side to side, her arms wrapped around her body like she's standing outside in the middle of winter.

Within seconds, a shaded figure moves toward the door and the handle turns. Dr. Lewis's shiny brown face appears in the crack of the door. When she realizes it's us, she pulls the door wide open and smiles so big her beautiful white teeth, which are as bright as the long coat she's wearing, take up half her face.

"Come on in, come on in," she says.

I love Dr. Lewis. She's not like any other doctor I've ever met. She doesn't look annoyed or act like she hates her job. She's always happy to help others. Today, she has her usual Afro, and it's even bigger than it was when I saw her a few weeks ago. Sometimes she lets it grow out and it looks awesome.

"Oh, goodness," she says, eyeballing Emily. "What happened to you?" She reaches a slender arm out and presses her wrist against Emily's clammy forehead.

Emily shrugs and starts hacking again. It's like every time she tries to talk, the air she breathes in irritates her lungs.

"She hasn't been feeling well," I say, "and today, I found her like this in her room."

Dr. Lewis's eyebrows pull close together and she nods. "You did the right thing bringing her here," she says to me. "Don't you worry about your friend, love, I'll take it from here."

Emily's dark eyes meet mine. I don't want to leave. I need to know she's okay.

"Don't worry," Dr. Lewis says as if reading my mind. "Come back in a few hours and I'll give you an update. You shouldn't be here, though. You don't want to catch this."

I know she's right, but it still sucks having to leave my only friend behind.

Emily's pale, cracked lips form a smile and her bloodshot eyes meet mine. "Do me a favor," she says. I stare at her. I'm happy to give her whatever she needs. "Go to our spot"—she makes her eyebrows dance up and down on her forehead, but then coughs up again—"and find out whatever you can. Then, tell me all about it."

Our spot? What's she talking about? But then it sinks in—the closet behind the Preparation Room. She wants me to sneak in on Eve's meeting? Alone? Dr. Lewis is looking at the two of us like we're speaking another language.

I swallow hard and give her a quick nod.

I'll do it.

CHAPTER 12 – GABRIEL

I feel like an animal at an exotic pet exposition.

They're all staring at me as though they've never seen a man before. How long's it been since the revolution, anyway? About five years?

The woman who stood up earlier, Tye, I think they called her, looks like she's about to climb over the crowd and strangle me. I pick at the rope around my wrists. It's making my skin itchy. It looks like hemp, but I can't be sure. Their clothes, including what I'm wearing, look like they're made out of hemp, so I suspect the rope is, too. A few wear beige dresses with mixed color splattered on the shoulders. It kind of looks like they used berry juice to stain the material. Maybe they were hoping to bring a bit of life to this place. It is pretty dull-looking, at least from what I've seen.

Most walls in here are gray. With the huge windows on the ceilings, there's a lot of natural light. They're pretty lucky to have that. This place doesn't compare to Area 82, though. They'd be way more comfortable there.

The only problem is, I'm not so sure they'll want to go. They hate me. I can see it in their eyes. Aside from a few who obviously yearn for a man's touch, they all look mortified. Eye contact seems to piss them off even more, so I avoid it. It's like I'm filth. Like I'm unworthy of breathing the same air as them.

Is this Eve's doing? I think back to the first time I saw her in the Oval Office. Something about her has changed. Five years ago, when I watched her through the cabinet's keyhole, she was driven by her emotions, pacing around the room like she was completely out of her element. She was scared and angry all at the same time. Now, she looks composed no matter what. Even when she gets upset. It's like she's holding everything in. She's scarier now than she was with a bayonet in her shaky grip.

The women in the room start going at it again, but the second Eve lifts a hand, they all stop talking. They evidently respect her. I can't figure out if that's a good thing or a bad thing. Maybe deep down, Eve means well. But there's something in her clear blue eyes that warns me she'd do anything to anyone who got in her way when it comes to this utopian place she's trying to create.

I think she's delusional, but that's just me. The atmosphere she wants to create is an impossible one. You can't have a society of only women, same as you can't have a society of only men. There's a reason there are two genders. We need each other. We each have strengths and weaknesses that complement one another.

Mama always taught me that intelligence isn't all about facts and knowledge. Human intelligence is far more than that. It's about emotional intelligence, and women have a lot of it. On the other hand, Mama always told me that men have an easier time coping with stressful situations. We tend to focus on facts and don't dwell on how the situation makes us feel.

That's what balance is all about. It's about making up for our weaknesses and sharing our strengths.

"Let me remind you," Eve says, pulling at her white overcoat and stiffening her back, "that very recently, you all agreed to accept a young boy into Eden."

This seems to have thrown them off guard. They turn their heads from side to side, looking at each other as if they'll find an answer on someone else's face.

"I'm not suggesting this man will be integrated into Eden," she continues, and their faces turn toward us at the front. Freyda still holds my rope in her hands, and it hangs between us with barely any slack. It's like she's ready to take me down if I take one step too far. And she'd probably succeed. She looks like she can handle herself.

She yanks on the rope when she catches me looking at her, and I shift my eyes to my feet.

"Then what are you suggesting?" someone asks.

I can't tell where the voice came from. There are so many women in here that half of them are stuck standing at the back without chairs.

Eve takes a deep breath and lets it out nice and slow as if her breath alone has some important meaning tied to it. "We can't stay here."

And we're at it again. Everyone starts shouting over each other:

"This is our home!"

"This is all we know."

"What're you talking about, Eve?"

I feel bad for them. They look terrified... as though they've learned they only have a few months to live. They weren't expecting this at all. I wonder how long Eve's wanted to leave this place. Her mind seems pretty made up. It's do or die. If they stay here, according to her, they won't make it.

"We're running out of resources," she shouts over them.

It's the first time I hear her raise her voice, and it doesn't suit her. Her voice sounds strained like she's holding back an even bigger explosion. She probably is. She's probably fighting as hard as she can to not go all neurotic. I know that look. Her jaw muscles keep popping in and out. She reminds me of some Black Marines who didn't make it, who were taken away and never seen again because they couldn't control their anger.

But the women don't stop bickering.

This time, she shouts, "Enough!" and her voice cracks and a few strands of her perfectly combed hair fall in her face.

It worked, though. The room goes so quiet I can hear everyone breathing out through their nostrils. I look up to catch Eve's eyes locked on me. She throws her chin out at me but doesn't say anything. I know what this means. She wants me to talk. To tell these women what I told her: that male rebels know about Alpa, and that they're not safe here.

I clear my throat and take a step forward, but

Freyda's quick to give me a warning tug. A snap of the rope tells me if I try to go any farther, there'll be serious consequences. So instead, I shift my weight, feeling like a dinosaur standing beside Eve and Freyda with my heavy combat boots.

"My name's Gabriel," I say, but I pause, expecting to have something thrown at me.

Surprisingly, nothing happens. Their eyes are glued to me as they lean forward.

This is it, I tell myself. You have a chance to show these women that you aren't their enemy. Don't mess it up.

I clear my throat again, my deep voice sounding like a monster's growl.

"I was raised by my mother." Half the room scowls at me, confused by how I'm approaching this. "Believe me when I say I have the utmost respect for women."

They're about to blow up again, but I see Eve wave a hand in my peripheral. I turn to Freyda. I know we're not friends, but something about her comforts me. Even just a look. She doesn't say anything, but her eyes tell me to keep going.

I let out a sigh. The only thing I can do is try to be as honest as possible. "This place isn't safe anymore." I pause, but not long enough for them to start yelling over me. "I got caught up with a band of male rebels out there. Trust me when I say these men are extremely dangerous. I don't know how, but they knew about *Alpa*"—I make air quotes in front of me, though it looks like I'm clawing the air with my wrists tied together—"and they were constantly on the hunt for women. I didn't know what Alpa was until they told me. But if they knew..." I look up, and for the first time, make eye contact with some of the women in the front row. "Who else knows?"

"Why're you telling us this?" someone asks.

"I'm a human being like you. I don't want to see you get hurt."

Someone scoffs, but I do my best to ignore them. "I'm sure some of you had husbands, sons, fathers, brothers..." This time, my eyes move toward the back of the room, and I catch a few women nodding. "I'd be willing to bet my life that most of these men weren't okay with what President Price was doing. With the abortions. With the unfair treatment."

They're still nodding. I'm doing something right.

"I get it, trust me, I do. But somehow, everything got out of control. The government became corrupt. People were brainwashed." I shake my head. "It doesn't matter. It's over. But now"—I point into nothingness—"out there, people are dying. People are suffering. Both men, and women. And in those men, some of them are bad people. A lot of them are bad people. The guys I ended up with were horrible. Most of them, anyway. You have no idea the things I've seen... The amount of violence I've witnessed. Or, maybe you do." My eyebrows slant as I stare at them, the desperation and pain evident in their eyes. I know they've suffered. "For those of you who remember your husbands"—my eyes shoot toward Freyda, but only briefly—"your brothers, your fathers... your sons. You know these men were good people."

"My husband beat me and took off with my son!" someone shouts, spitting saliva into the air. "You call that a *good person*?" Her face is so contorted she looks like a wax toy that's been left in the sun too long.

"My only son told me he hoped I'd rot in hell!"

I bow my head again. I'm fucking this up.

"Some men are pieces of shit, okay?" I say, my voice a bit louder than before. "Some of them are led by their dicks and think that women are lesser beings."

The two women who were red in the face slowly sit back in their chairs.

"I don't know what it is. I don't know where this misogynistic bullshit came from. It's been around for centuries. A lot of men, especially men in power, believe they're better than women."

Rapid nods fill the room, and some women lean back, arms crossed over their chests. They don't like me, but they're willing to keep listening.

"All I ask is that you have an open mind," I say. "I genuinely want to help. There's barely anything left... You may be living in some beautiful garden, protected by concrete walls, but out there"—I point into the air again—"it's a disaster. People are killing each other over territory. Women and children are being abducted and abused. Men who don't belong to crews or gangs are being violently beaten to death."

Looks of disgust and horror spread throughout the room. I glance over at Eve who shifts uncomfortably with her arms crossed loosely over her stomach. I don't think she was expecting me to be so descriptive. I don't think she wants her women fearing the world. Or, maybe she does. Maybe this is her way of controlling them. Of having them want to stay inside of Eden's walls.

Is she playing me? Is this a setup? I can't try to understand her. All it does is create a ball of anxiety in the pit of my stomach. Something about this woman is terrifying, and I don't trust her one bit.

I focus my attention on the frightened women.

"I'm not telling you this to scare you. The point in all of this is that while you're safe in here, people out there are suffering. Not only that, but it's only a matter of time before some of those *bad men* find this place."

"Then what're you tryin' to do?" Tye asks. "What's the whole point of this? Why're you here?" She's not as aggressive as before, which means I'm doing good. She wants answers, and I don't blame her.

"I know a place," I say. "It has over sixty acres of land, protective walls, and advanced technological defense systems."

"And you want us to go there?" Tye asks.

I peer over at Eve again. She isn't saying anything. I'm assuming this means it's up to me to keep talking.

"Yeah," I say. "I think that's what's best for everyone."

I flinch when someone yells, "He's a fucking man!" Everyone starts getting rowdy again, and I take a step back on the stage. Women swear left and right; others try to calm them down. It's like there are two types of women in this room: some who are open to the idea of receiving help from a man, and others who are opposed to it no matter how many facts I present to them. They won't budge. I could tell them an army is coming, but because I'm a man, they wouldn't listen. How am I supposed to work with this?

Eve brushes past me, her heels ticking against the stage tiles, though I can barely hear it over all the shouting. I turn my head to follow her. Where's she going? Is she leaving?

Jesus Christ, please don't leave me here.

But she doesn't leave. She stops in front of Freyda, looking incredibly tall in comparison in her bright red heels. She extends her palm faceup and wiggles her fingers like she's asking for something. Her lips move, but I can't tell what she's saying to Freyda. It's too loud in here.

Freyda leans forward, and with her right hand, pulls her pistol out of her holster. It all happens so fast, I don't have time to process anything.

The next thing I know, cold metal touches me in the back of the head and I can't hear anyone bickering anymore.

All I hear is the sound of the gun being cocked.

CHAPTER 13 – EVE

The pistol's grip feels all too familiar in the palm of my hand. I wrap and rewrap my fingers around it, feeling the rough texture on my fingertips. There's something so empowering about holding a gun.

Gabriel's head is pulled away from his body as if he's trying to create space between the pistol's muzzle and his skull—as if this space is going to save him. What he doesn't know, however, is that I don't intend to kill him.

I fight the urge to smile. Truthfully, I feel whole.

I am in complete power. Everyone's eyes are on me as they wait for my next move. No one dares to raise their voice—they're afraid I might pull the trigger. I suppose they're wondering what's going on. I can only imagine what Gabriel is thinking.

He's probably terrified—confused as to why I would make a deal with him only to turn around and point a gun at his head.

"I can't watch you suffer like this," I say, shifting my eyes to the crowd of frightened women. "You women have been through so much. I can't—" With my other hand, I pinch the bridge of my nose as if on the verge of crying, even though I'm doing everything in my power not to smile. I need to get my point across. I need these women to believe that I would do anything. Otherwise, why would they follow me? "I can't watch you suffer. If this man makes you fear for your life"—I eye each one of them individually, my stare lingering for a few meaningful seconds—"I will do what's necessary."

I expect someone to stand up at any point and argue that taking a life is never the answer, but they all remain tight-lipped, so I continue. "He is a man, after all. If you believe him to be dangerous, let me kill him. Let me protect you—that's all I want. I want you to feel safe. I do not want any of you going to sleep at night afraid for your lives. Afraid that this *man*"—I look at him with utter disdain—"is going to break out of his containment cell and harm one of you."

Gabriel tries to raise his tied hands, probably in an attempt to plea for his life. If he had an ounce of intelligence in that thick skull of his, he would know that this is all a ruse. Why would I kill the one person who knows the whereabouts of this safe space he speaks of? Area 82.

My plan will work because my people are women.

Women do not want violence, nor do they want to see others harmed—especially not someone who appears to be innocent. The women who fought against male soldiers during the revolution were led by anger and instinct, but right now, at this very moment, these women aren't in immediate danger. Their lives aren't at risk. Should these women decide to kill Gabriel, they will all have blood on their hands. Women are nurturing, not primitive. They won't choose his death.

"What's killing him gonna do?" someone asks.

Then, someone else shifts on the cushion of her chair before standing up. She's young and introverted—her eyes never leaving the floor. "We came to Eden to live a life without violence."

Her words are barely audible—a muffled mumble—but everyone heard them.

"She's right," someone else says.

"We can't take a life just because he's a man. He didn't do anything to us. Right, Eve?"

"What if he does?" I ask. "What if he turns against us?"

I need to push them—I need them to be certain that they want Gabriel to live. Weeks, months, or years from now, when his true colors surface, they will all be reminded of their decision. They will all realize that they cannot think for themselves—that I am better suited to make decisions here in Eden.

"It isn't right," says the shy woman. "This isn't what you've taught us, Eve." This time, her dark eyes shift in my direction. She bites her bottom lip and wraps her arms around her belly, her shoulders drooping. She reminds me of a helpless turtle trying to return inside its shell.

"I-I'm only trying to help," Gabriel cuts in. "This place... This place I'm talking about. It could save hundreds of more women. You don't have space here. And like Eve said, you're running out of res—"

I press the gun's metallic muzzle harder into the

back of his head, through his curly hair, and he stops talking. I hate hearing someone rant. It's unbecoming and quite honestly, irritating. His voice sounds like the deep rumble of a rusted car's engine in comparison to the beautiful feminine voices of Eden.

"We don't all trust him," someone else says, "but that's not a reason to kill him. You said it yourself, Eve—he saved some of our people. Maybe this place he's talking about can save more lives. You've guided us this far through peace, Eve."

I raise my chin, my eyes fixated on the middle-aged woman. She extends her sun-damaged hands and makes a gentle up-and-down motion, like she's trying to convince me to put the gun down.

I have them right where I want them. The corner of my lip twitches upward, but I consciously correct this. Two minutes ago, these women were fighting over his presence, and now, they're defending him to save his life.

The amount of empathy and compassion women have for living beings astonishes me. If this were a room full of men and Gabriel were a woman, they'd have beaten her, gang-raped her, and left her for dead. I realize I'm pressing the gun even harder into the base of his skull as I think about this, so I shake these thoughts from my mind and unclench my jaw.

Stay calm, Eve.

* * * * * *

How am I supposed to stay calm?

"She's barely breathing!"

I don't know what to do with myself. I clasp my

fingers together, then let them go.

"Someone do something!"

The little girl's mother holds her tight against her chest. She kisses her daughter's sticky forehead and brushes her thin blond hair out of her face.

"Oh, baby, hang on, baby," she says through broken sobs.

Then, at the end of the long corridor, Nola comes running through the crowd with her arms flailing over her head. They're empty. Why are they empty? She was supposed to find something—anything. Antibiotics, maybe.

As I stare at the little girl's face—at those light eyes that keep rolling in the back of her skull—I'm reminded of Mila, and a wave of emotions washes over me; I am hopeless, terrified, and enraged all at once. In a flash, I see Mila's bloody face, and then I see her black-rimmed glasses on the pavement, broken.

Every time I think of her, that's all I see. And every time I think of Mila, I'm reminded of my mother. Is she even alive? Does it matter? I clench my fists and my knuckles pop. If my mother hadn't been so involved in the revolution, maybe Mila wouldn't have turned out the way she did—maybe she wouldn't have wanted to fight, and she wouldn't have gotten herself killed.

"I-I couldn't find anything," Nola says, little wrinkles forming at the corners of her lips. She straightens her back and wipes a line of sweat from her cheek. "I don't know what to do. We've already given her a bottle of juice. I assumed maybe her sugar was low. So why isn't it working? When's the last time she ate?"

The mother barely responds. She's too preoccupied trying to comfort her daughter. Nola kneels on one knee and rests a gentle hand on the woman's shoulder. "When was her last bite of food?"

The mother shakes her head, her mouth open and droopy. "I-I don't know. I've been trying to keep her steady with the few s-s-snacks we found."

"When?" Nola repeats. She's so calm—more than me, and I'm not even helping. I feel like these women rely on me to save this little girl's life, but how can I? I'm not a doctor. I never promised to provide medical help. I was supposed to find a doctor for Eden, and I did, just as Vrin instructed me to do, but she was shot during our migration—killed for no reason by a band of male rebels.

What have I done? If I hadn't forced these women to keep moving, maybe this wouldn't be happening. Maybe this little girl would be alert and lively, playing with her friends—not on the verge of death in her mother's arms.

"M-maybe last night," the woman says. "I-I think. She had... She had a granola bar. We picked it up from—"

Nola inches her way closer to the little girl and presses the back of her hand on her forehead. "Does she have any other medical problems?"

The woman bursts out crying this time and she squeezes her little girl closer to her. "Oh, baby," she says. "We haven't been to a doctor in years. I-I don't know." Her words are barely comprehensible, but

Nola seems to be catching everything she's saying. "Because... Because of all the men. I couldn't work... They fired me... I-I couldn't afford medical bills." She's crying so hard now that her face is beet red and squiggly blue veins bulge out from her temples.

Nola glances up at me, a somber look in her eyes. Why is she looking at me? Why is everyone looking at me like that? My heart races and I wipe my palms against my jeans. I did what I promised—I followed through. I brought these women to safety. What more do they want from me?

But everyone's attention returns to the little girl when a long breath escapes her parted blue lips.

"Baby? Baby? Lina?" the woman gently taps her daughter's face over and over again. "Oh, baby, no, no, no." She clutches her daughter's little body and squeezes her so tight I fear the little girl's bones might break, then lets out a pained bellow that immediately pulls me back to the day I watched my little sister die.

The pain on this woman's face is enough to bring me to my knees. I want to rip my own skin from my face, pull my fingers until they snap, and bend backward until I break. I want to hurt—I need to feel excruciating physical torment to forget the pain inside.

I can't handle this.

One second, I see Mila's crippled body and I watch as blood spews from the gunshot in her neck. It isn't real.

It can't be real.

That never happened.

Mila's alive.

She's alive.

Then, the crying woman comes back into view. Her mouth is open so wide that I can see her tonsils. She keeps repeating her daughter's name and pulling her limp body into her arms. The little girl's head hangs loosely over her mother's elbow and her pale lips are parted underneath glazed blue eyes.

She's gone.

She's dead.

Mila's dead.

Mila's dead and she's never coming back.

No, it's not true.

You killed the president.

Why won't my mind shut up? Why am I having these thoughts?

You're a murderer... a fucking killer. You're the reason Mila's dead. You should've never brought her with you to help Ophelia from that bastard stalker. That's why you killed Ophelia. You wanted to kill her, you little bitch. You blame her for Mila's death. You avenged your sister.

What? This isn't true. I never wanted to hurt Ophelia—

Oh God, what have I done? Who am I? I stare at my hands, and although completely dry and dirt-stained, all I see is thick blood filling the cracks around my fingernails.

It's everywhere.

Why is there so much blood?

Vivid flashes of women being shot at with machine guns cloud my mind. Gunsmoke pollutes the air, and women dance backward with flailing arms as bullets come blasting through their chests and out of their backs.

A grenade goes off and pieces of muscle, bone, and tendons fly in every direction.

This didn't happen.

Why am I seeing this? Why is there a constant war playing in my head? A sharp pain shoots through my chest, and I clutch at my heart. I want to fall to my knees, but then I'm reminded of who I am—of who I became that awful day.

I was the first woman who made the decision to attack. After the EMP, I was the first woman to come walking out of the White House—to march through the front doors with the president's rifle in hand and blood splattered all over my shirt, neck, and arms. I was the first person to utter the words "It's over" to thousands of broken women before me.

That day, I became their leader—their savior.

There's no going back for me. These women need me. I clear my throat and the tightness I felt in my chest only minutes ago disappears instantly. I inhale a slow breath through flared nostrils, and relax a little as the oxygen makes its way into my lungs and through my entire body.

The tips of my fingers tingle and my heartbeat slows.

These women need me—they need a savior.

I cannot be weak.

As I gaze at the wreckage in front of me—at the woman whose heart is shattering into a million pieces as she holds her little girl's dead body—a strange sensation comes over me; it's a feeling I've never felt before.

I feel nothing.

* * * * * *

I loosen my grip, bend my elbow, and point the gun at the ceiling. Gabriel lets out a relieved breath and turns to look at me.

"Very well," I say. "Gabriel will stay here with us." I squint at the crowd as a way of expressing love and tenderness, though I feel nothing inside—nothing but hatred toward this man and toward any woman who feels his presence is welcome here. I'm content that my plan has worked. I do need Gabriel if we're to build a better society—if I'm to gather more women into my paradise. But that's all he is—a pawn. After that, I'll figure out what to do with him. "If anyone has missed a meeting tonight, please share with them our plan. Tell them that soon, we will be moving to a better Eden." I pause and extend my hand toward the women who are reaching for me. Our fingertips touch and their eyes soften with satisfaction. "Oh, and one last thing, my beautiful ladies. Please don't share this with the children, at least not yet. They need to focus on their education, not worry about having to relocate what they've come to know as their home."

Everyone smiles and nods like perfectly programmed robots.

CHAPTER 14 – LUCY

I hate it when my heart beats this loud. I always think someone's going to hear it. It doesn't help that I'm hiding someplace I shouldn't be, but I want to know what's going on.

I'm not brave enough to open the door—the one at the back of the storage space with half its white paint peeled off. Emily likes to open it a crack to see inside the theater's Preparation Room, but I'm not that brave. Instead, I press my ear against the door. I've always been good at that. Sometimes, I'm sorry I never told my mom how much I used to listen to her and Eve talk in the living room. She thought she was protecting me, but I heard it all.

Thinking about that makes me feel guilty. Now, I'll never be able to tell her how much I used to pretend I was sleeping. I won't be able to grow up with her at my side; I won't be able to make jokes with her about when I was young and how much of a rascal I could be. We won't laugh about those times because she isn't here anymore.

I seal my eyes and a warm tear glides over my cheek and drips from my chin. I take a deep breath, but I don't let it make any sound as it comes out. I can't think about my mom right now. I need to focus.

"You're the one who let me try it all, you wart-faced donkey!"

I don't even have to listen to her voice to know that's Mavis.

"It's called portion control," Perula says.

"Portion, farortion!"

I don't know why Perula bothers trying to argue with her sister. She's always coming out with the funkiest things, and half the time, it doesn't make sense. Although I can't see Perula right now, she's probably shaking her salt-and-pepper-haired head with a palm flat on her forehead, a gesture that says, "Why is my sister such an idiot?"

"Mavis," Perula says. Her voice is calm. I don't think she wants to argue. "Do you think it's a good idea?"

Mavis grunts.

"For us to move, I mean," Perula says. "We have so many plants in the Herb Shack. How're we supposed to transport that to some new Eden? Do you honestly think this Gabriel man wants to help?"

I pull back from the door and glare at the wall beside me. New Eden? What's she talking about? And who's Gabriel? Is that him? The man Mavis and Perula were discussing? If so, why is she talking about us receiving help from him? My eyes dart from side to side across the white-paneled wall and my mind races.

What's going on?

Why would we move?

Everything is going so well here. If we move,

history will repeat itself. Who knows how long we'll be traveling? What if more people die? Why would Eve do this? Is this about resources? I heard someone say that's why those women were sent outside of Eden. Apparently, Eve wants to start letting women go out to get things more often.

Why isn't that happening, then?

Why does she suddenly want to leave? Is it the space? I close my eyes and picture every Division. All of the corridors, all of the long narrow stretches filled with dozens upon dozens of cells. In these cells, I see girls and women of all different ages. Aside from most of Division Seven, I can't remember the last time I saw an empty cell.

Are we running out of space?

I'm about to press my ear against the door again when the sound of a box being kicked echoes behind me. My heart nearly jumps in my throat and I swing around with my fists up by my face the way a rat curls its little paws it's grooming.

I probably look like a complete moron.

At first, all I see is a pair of legs on the floor, and I can't tell who entered the storage space.

"Lucy!" comes Nola's voice.

She crawls onto her hands and knees, gives me the stink-eye, then stands up. She must have tripped over a box. I'm about to laugh but realize I'm probably in trouble. I hold my breath, ready for her to rip my head off when she walks toward me with horrible posture and awkward footing.

Is she trying to be sneaky?

"What're you doing here?" she asks, her voice a

sharp whisper.

"Why're you whispering?" I whisper.

"You tell me!" she whispers, and her eyes narrow on me.

"Did you follow me?" I ask.

She shifts her weight on one leg only and tilts her head to the side.

"Yeah, I followed you," she says as if this were obvious.

"Why?" I mouth.

She twirls a finger in front of her face as if drawing circles on mine from a distance. "I've been watching you," she says. "You've been acting kinda funny... Lying to me about where you are. Skipping your lessons with Mavis and Perula. Just like my daughter... Adventurous. Then, I see you sneaking your way down toward the main entrance." She crosses both arms over her chest. "I left the meeting to go to the bathroom when I saw you heading toward the main entrance! No one goes to the main entrance. And you looking over your shoulder every few seconds didn't help your case."

She caught me. I feel like an idiot. What am I supposed to tell her? That I've been having doubts about Eve? I can't do that. I don't know where Nola stands. I don't know which side she's on. Heck, I don't even know which side I'm on anymore. What am I even doing?

"What's on the other side?" she asks, wiggling that finger toward me again.

"Preparation Room," I say and avert my eyes to the floor's carpet.

Game over.

"Prepa—" she steps quickly toward me and plops herself down like an excited toddler. Her thick legs almost squish mine, and she pushes me to the side with her butt then sticks her ear against the door.

"What're you doing?" I ask, but she scowls at me, which is a translation for, "Shut up."

Then, almost as if she only now realized she's encouraging me, she pulls herself away from the door, stands up, and dusts off the bottom of her dress.

She glares at me. "Why're you listening in on what's going on in there?"

What am I supposed to answer? I sigh. I've lied to her too many times to keep lying. She's treated me better than anyone in Eden—even better than Eve—and here I am, being dishonest with her.

"Are you spying on Eve?" she asks. She looks more upset than I've ever seen her. Her mouth hangs open, and her forehead is full of bumpy wrinkles. Nola's always nothing but smiles with me, it's hard to take in.

I swallow hard and my throat makes a toad-like sound. She turns on her heels and starts mumbling a bunch of nonsense.

What's she saying? I crane my neck, hoping to catch some of it. I hear the word *Eve* get tossed around a few times, and then the words *promise* and *loyalty*. She suddenly throws her arms over her head, and when they come back down, they slap hard against her thighs. "What am I supposed to tell Eve?"

"What?" I blurt. "Why would you tell Eve?"

Her eyes shift from side to side like I've caught her in a lie. Forget my sneaking around Eden, what's she hiding from me?

"Well?" I press. "Why would you want to get me in trouble?"

She twirls her thumbs around each other. "I don't *want* to get you in trouble."

What's she talking about? Something's up; I can see it all over her face. She reminds me of a kid who's caught taking cookies out of the cookie jar.

She scoops her bangs out of her face and holds them flat on top of her head. I've noticed she does this when she's thinking hard or when she's stressed out. And every time she does, I see that weird scar over her right eyebrow. It looks like someone took a slab of metal and jabbed her right in the face. It's square-shaped, and it's a few millimeters deep. I try not to look at it. The last time I asked her where she got it, she started blubbering her daughter's name, Gracey, and she disappeared for two days. I think she might've gotten it during the war trying to save her daughter's life.

She extends her hand palm up in my direction and her hair falls back in her face. "Well, if you hadn't been running around with that friend of yours, Eve wouldn't have asked me to keep an eye on you!"

"Keep an eye—" I say, fuming. "Why would Eve—"

"Hush!" Nola says. Her eyes look as big as those jawbreaker candies. She slaps a finger over her tight lips and makes her eyes go even bigger if that's possible.

"Okay, okay," I mouth.

She looks over her shoulder toward the storage room's door, the one I came through, then shuffles her way to me and crouches down. "You can't repeat a word of this to anyone."

"I won't," I say, but all I can think about is Emily. She's the one who told me about this storage room in the first place. I shouldn't have thought about Emily. Nola's a lot like my mom when it comes to mindreading, and she looks at me like I have my thoughts printed out all over my face.

With an inquisitive glare, she says, "Who else knows?"

Am I supposed to try to lie to get out of this one? Emily made me promise I wouldn't tell anyone. I can't betray her like that.

"N-no one," I stutter.

"Lucinda Cain," she says, and the sound of my name feels like a punch in the stomach.

"I can't tell you," I say. "I promised I wouldn't."

"And I promised I'd tell Eve everything you're up to," she hisses.

It's so weird to see Nola like this. With her eyebrows low and flat, her droopy, upside-down smile, and her finger, which she keeps sticking in front of my nose, it's almost like she's a different person entirely.

"So..." I say, rolling my eyes toward the ceiling. "Are you *not* gonna tell Eve about this?"

She crosses her arms over her big boobs and leans back against the wall, a small pocket of air escaping her lungs. "You know I can't do that."

My heart races. "Do what? Tell Eve, or keep this from her?"

She turns to me, her red face inches away from mine, and wrinkles her nose. She looks like her head could pop off at any second.

"What?" I ask.

"The situation you put me in," she says. "And I know Emily knows. It doesn't take a genius to figure it out. For the record, I figured it out, so you don't have to feel bad about breaking your promise."

Great. Emily won't be happy about this. She won't care how Nola found out; she'll care that an adult knows what we've been up to.

Nola lets out a sharp breath and slaps her knees. "Your secret's safe with me."

Without thinking, I throw my arms around her and drop my head on her shoulder. "Thanks, Nola!"

She stiffens, but only for a second. She isn't accustomed to me showing her affection. I think she's a bit confused. She reaches an arm around me and pulls me in closer until my face squishes up into her neck.

Although it's a bit awkward, I don't pull away. There's something comforting about her warmth. And by the way she presses her lips against the top of my head, I think she's feeling the same way.

CHAPTER 15 – GABRIEL

"Are you insane?" I ask, but I realize by the looks on their faces that I'm out of line.

Eve raises her chin and walks toward me, her hips swaying like a wildcat on the verge of lunging at its prey. "Am I insane?" she repeats.

Shit. I should've shut my mouth.

"Am I insane?" she repeats again, this time, laughing.

Okay, she has got to be insane.

The two witch-looking women at the back start blabbering all kinds of nonsense. The curvier of the two, the one who's sitting on the red couch, picking at its yellow buttons, keeps saying the weirdest things like, "Insane in the membrane," and "The only cocklidolis here is him." Then she points at me.

Maybe they're all insane.

Her sister, who seems a lot more soft-spoken and delicate, walks toward Eve with her hands clasped in front of her. "Eve, we're so sorry the tea didn't have the effect you wanted."

Eve's hateful eyes are aimed right at me, but then they soften so quickly it looks like a new soul has jumped into her body. She turns sideways and brushes her fingers through this woman's long, tangled hair. "Oh, Perula," she says. "Please, don't apologize. You both did everything you could."

I glance over at Freyda, who stands as stiff as a statue, her gaze fixated on the wall. Eve obviously did something right with her. She's acting like a soldier, like a shell ready to obey any command. I wish I'd get the chance to talk to her alone. I know there's something in there. There's a strong woman deep down inside.

I clear my throat. "Sorry, Eve, I didn't mean any disrespect."

She twirls on her heels until she's facing me again, this time, with her head tilted to one side and a creepy smile on her lips. I say creepy because I can tell it's fake. Why's she even smiling at me? She hates my guts. I'd rather she be looking at me like she usually does. Full of contempt and disgust. This is so much more disturbing.

"I understand," she says quietly, and that smile doesn't move. Then, she says, and much louder this time, "I'm sorry if I scared you at all, Gabriel. But my women do come first."

"Yeah, I get that—" I try, but she cuts me off.

"If the women of Eden don't trust me, who can they trust?"

This is obviously all rhetorical, so I keep my mouth shut this time. She doesn't give a damn what I think. She wants to look good in front of the women in this room.

"Freyda," she says, "take him back to the basement."

Without saying a word, Freyda gives Eve her usual obedient nod and tugs at the rope around my wrists.

"What? Why?" I ask. The last thing I want to do is go back into some dark hole with cold cement flooring. I thought she agreed to let me take them to Area 82. Or at least, a few of them. Wasn't that the plan? I even told her about the planes.

"It's only temporary," she says. "I'll come for you when it's time."

Freyda pulls on the rope, and I don't even have the chance to argue with her. She's got a lot of muscle hiding underneath that long-sleeved shirt. I trip over my boot and the room shakes, but I catch my footing in time.

We leave the weird back room we recently entered, and when we come back to the room with the stage (it looks like an auditorium or cinema room where prisoners used to get TV privileges), the metal-framed cushioned chairs are now empty and they're all neatly placed in even rows.

I wonder where all the women went. Back to their rooms? To do their chores? What do they even do around here? Does everyone work? If men ran this place, everyone would be trained for battle. But I can tell by the way Eve talks to her people that she's not into that. She doesn't want violence. I don't think any of these women even remember what violence is. They look all brainwashed and overly happy.

"How long's she gonna keep me down there?" I ask Freyda, but she doesn't answer. Her long ponytail sways from side to side with every step, and her equipment makes noise against her clothes.

I remember that. Having so much equipment on me, making it nearly impossible to be stealthy. I try not to think back to my Black Marine days. Every time I do, it reminds me of the awful things I've seen, not only during the revolution but during my mission in North Korea. All of the beheadings, the innocent women and children hung at the border, and even the nonmilitary men being shot at for no reason at all.

It was a huge massacre, thanks to President Price who couldn't swallow his ego. It all started with childish threats between the two countries, until finally, North Korea launched a missile straight for Guam, destroying half the island. After that, everything went to shit.

I see the same little girl almost every night in my sleep. As much as I try to forget her face, I can't. Her hair was as black as coal that formed wings off her shoulders and her eyes looked like little almonds. But they were open, and her face was swollen and bulging over the noose around her neck. She was hung for trying to escape, and all I remember thinking was *I hope one day soon, aliens invade planet Earth. I hope they kill us all. Human beings are too cruel of a species to deserve life.*

Well, that never happened. Instead, we went to war with our own country and destroyed ourselves.

"This way," Freyda says, and the yank around my wrists brings me back from my shitty past to my shitty reality.

* * * * * *

This can't be America's new reality.

"He isn't breathing!" the woman yells. She's kneeling in the gravel, her greasy hair masking half her face. But what gets to me is the look in her eyes. It's pure heartbreak. She keeps pulling her son tight into her arms and kissing his face. He looks like he's five, maybe six years old, with blemish-free skin and little pink lips.

I want to comfort her, but there's nothing I can do. He's dead. They're all dead.

I step my combat boot over a soldier's body and cross the street. The only reason I'm not being attacked right now is because I took off all my gear. I'm wearing cargo pants and a white T-shirt. I kept my pistols around my ankles as a precaution, but no one can see them. Right now, I'm like everyone else: lost and confused.

A thick smog floats throughout the city and dark figures appear every few minutes, searching the debris for what I can only assume are lost friends or family members. Every few minutes, a gun goes off, and I flinch.

How could this happen?

This is America.

There's nothing left.

Aside from the people screaming and pleading, there's no sound throughout the city. Cars are all over the place. Some are parked on the side of the street, but most are abandoned in the middle of roads, bumper to bumper, or crashed into each other, or crushed against electrical poles. Most of them are crumpled up at the front, their metal frames looking like nothing more than cheap plastic. Small electrical wires stick out from over some of their wheels. I'm assuming when the power went out, car engines stopped, but the cars kept rolling until they hit something. And in most cases, it was the car in front of them.

But what surprises me most are the civilians. I don't see men and women fighting. They're in a state of panic. It's almost like now that all of the anger's disappeared, everyone's realizing how bad things got. A few feet away from me, in front of an old coffee shop that has only half its store intact, two dirt-stained bearded men scoop up an injured woman and rush her inside a building. Maybe they're doctors or nurses. Either way, everyone's trying to help each other now that the military isn't involved.

I don't know how many of them survived, but if they did, there aren't many left. Not with all of the weapons they were blindsided with. Grenades, nail guns, shovels, and all kinds of military-grade guns that I can only assume came from some underground resistance led by ex-military women.

I stare inside the coffee shop. I used to come here with my mama when we'd visit downtown Washington. It didn't happen often, but the few times that it did, I was in heaven. The clerk behind the counter always gave me a free peanut butter cookie. It was their thing, and it attracted a lot of parents with kids.

The chairs, which used to be fire truck red, are now brown and black, and one of them is cut in half and its plastic back is completely melted. The smell of smoke fills my nostrils, and I turn around.

An apartment building, several stories high, is on fire. Heavy black smoke comes rushing out through one of the apartment's broken windows, and wild flames lick the exterior bricks.

An explosion blasts nearby. I instinctively reach for my gun belt, but I remember my gun is at my ankle. I wish I had all my equipment, but the military isn't exactly welcome after everything that's happened.

Something hard suddenly grabs my shoulder and spins me around.

"H-h-have you seen her?" the man asks. His eyelids are pink and his lips are shiny with slobber. "My little girl. She ran out of our apartment and came looking for her mother. P-p-please. She's this tall"—he places a hand by his waist—"has strawberry blond hair..."

He stops talking when he realizes I'm staring at him. I want to help, but I haven't seen anyone. I'm not looking for anyone, either. I don't even know what I'm doing or where I'm going.

"Please!" he shouts, and a glob of spit lands on my chin.

The last thing I want right now is to get into a fight with a civilian, so I take a step back. I don't want to hurt anyone, but if it comes down to it, I'll be the one to walk away. "No, sir," I say. "I haven't seen her. If I do, I'll send her this way."

He looks like he wants to punch me and cry on my shoulder all at the same time. I can't even imagine how many parents are going through this right now. What did the women do? Leave their kids at home with the fathers? Mind you, that view is the result of the media. The truth is, there were a lot of men fighting alongside women. Many of them, those who hadn't followed the brainwashed mindset, disagreed with what the military was doing. The news just didn't talk about that.

When all of this started, I remember hearing on the news how divorce rates skyrocketed and reached an all-new record. I was sitting at my mama's house one evening when a bald news anchor appeared on her old-school 2040 TV (the kind of TV that still had a solid screen). He kept talking about how eight out of ten married couples were splitting up. What shocked me the most was to find out that a bunch of men started segregating themselves in certain places all over the United States. So, in some neighborhoods, it was only men, and in others, only women. You can imagine how dangerous it was crossing through the opposite sex's neighborhood. I've never done it, and I wouldn't have tried it, either.

I watch as the father takes off, throwing metal debris and airplane parts into the air, looking for his daughter. It looks like a 797 passenger plane. Its nose is smashed into the pavement and its wings are in a bunch of pieces, but it's obvious they sliced through a few buildings on the way down. Glass lies everywhere, and a bunch of apartment buildings have collapsed. Bodies are piled up all over the place, and I do my best not to look at the carnage.

I can't stay here.

I know how this works. I've been trained for it.

People are panicking right now, trying to find survivors, but for the families that are still together, they'll try to find some sort of shelter and they'll wait. They'll wait for the government to step in and come to their rescue.

But that isn't going to happen.

An electromagnetic pulse attack is so unpredictable, but given the way those planes came down, I'm assuming the weapon was launched over the city. And if the blast was big enough, it probably affected a good chunk of Washington. But what scares me about all of this, and what has my heart pounding against my sweat-stained T-shirt, is how shitty America's electrical grid actually is. No one talks about it, but for those of us in the military, we know all about it. And with all the new equipment and nuclear weapons that have been exposed over the last decade, I wouldn't be surprised if this EMP's residual blast wiped out America's entire grid.

I don't know.

But what I do know is that people who stay inside the city are as good as dead. It's only a matter of hours, days, or at the most, a week, before people start acting like a bunch of savages. Killing each other for food, shelter, or water. This place is going to turn into a real shitshow, and fast.

I pull a backpack off a dead teenager's back and scavenge through its contents. A big plastic water bottle, which I keep, some music player and a bunch of school books, which I dump beside him.

Now, all I can do is try to find an analog radio somewhere to find out what's going on. Find out if this is nationwide or an isolated case. If it's nationwide, I'm going to start walking until I'm as far away from people as possible. I'll pick up supplies from bodies, even though I hate doing that. If I can find an abandoned cottage somewhere in the woods, or somewhere up on a mountain near a source of water that I can filter, I should be able to survive for a bit.

If my mama were still around, I'd do everything in my power to protect her. But now, what's the point? Who do I have? Why would anyone even want to live in a world like this?

I wish that humans' survival instincts weren't so goddamn strong. There's so much suffering around me, and it's only going to get worse. But I can't give up. Maybe after this nightmare... this hell on Earth... Maybe after all of that, I'll be able to help rebuild what's been torn to pieces.

That's what Mama would want.

* * * * * *

"You deaf?" Freyda asks.

I look back at her and realize we're back in the cold, dark basement.

"Sorry," I say. "I zoned out."

"Yeah, well, I hope you aren't this spacey when you're leading us to this oh-so-special place of yours," she says.

"Leading us?" I ask. "Are you coming?"

She drops my ropes, and I pick at the knot around my wrist. "Half these women aren't cut out for the outside world. You seriously think Eve's gonna send any of them with you?"

I'm trying hard to fight the urge to smile, but it isn't working. The corner of my lip twitches, so I clear my throat, but it comes out like a deep cough. "I don't know," I say. "I'm sure Eve knows best."

Freyda isn't buying it. She rolls her eyes, opens the big metal door, and steps behind it, leaving only a portion of her face inside the candlelit basement.

"Get some rest. I'll be back for you when it's time."

CHAPTER 16 – EVE

She walks faster at the sight of me, her fluffy hair looking like a bonnet atop her head.

"Nola," I say, and her shoes squeak against the main hall's tiles. She turns around, her shoulders hunched forward.

"Y-yes? Oh, Eve!" she says, and she lets out a laugh. "I didn't see you there."

I'm not an idiot—she was clearly trying to avoid me. But why?

"Where are you off to?" I say as softly as I can. "I saw you leave during our meeting."

She flicks her wrist as if it's no big deal. "Had a little"—she rubs at the air in front of her stomach—"belly issue, if ya know what I mean."

I tilt my head back and watch her, but I realize I'm staring when her eyes begin shifting from side to side—an obvious sign of discomfort. "Ah, yes," I say. "Of course. I understand." I let out a sharp breath through tight lips in an attempt to fluff it off. "I hope you feel better soon, Nola. When you do, could you please swing by my office?"

She plucks an invisible thread from her dress and shifts her weight.

“I want to tell you about the meeting,” I say. “The part you missed, I mean.”

“Oh,” she says, and it comes out almost too quickly. She lets out a forced laugh, bows her head, and says, “Yes, of course, Eve. I’ll head over shortly.”

I watch her as she takes short, quick steps toward Division Five. What is she up to?

“Oh, Eve,” I hear and turn around. “You were wonderful.”

It’s Madelaine, Zack’s mother. Her big brown eyes are wide open and she’s grinning from ear to ear.

“What a place,” she says, extending her arms on either side of her. “Eden, I mean. It’s… It’s incredible what you’ve done here, Eve.”

What I’ve done? I smile at her, hoping she’ll continue. I want to hear more. I want to know how she views Eden, and why she finds it so incredible. After all the work I’ve put into creating this paradise, it’s an extraordinary feeling to have someone remind me of it—to have someone express their gratitude for all I’ve done.

“How long did it take you?” she asks. “I mean… the gardens, the livestock, the solar-paneled electricity. You saved these women, Eve. Out there—” She doesn’t even give me the time to answer. Instead, the smile on her face disappears as if it were nothing more than a sticker being peeled off. “It’s horrible, Eve… There’s nothing left. I mean, aside from a few survivors who are trying to build societies, there’s nothing. The only reason I survived with Zack is that we followed a group of women…”

She's so animated, slapping the air around her. "They kept us alive. They knew what they were doing. Two of them were ex-military, and they protected us. For a while, I mean… And this place, Eden. I'd heard about it from other women. But I thought it was a myth. I can't believe you pulled this off. We'd talk about you, you know, at night, around our fire. Women cherish you, Eve. The word's spreading across America like wildfire. You're the reason so many women survived that day. I heard it myself… Someone said Bethany didn't want to attack. Is it true? Did you turn against Bethany to save the rioters? I heard they were planning on launching missiles and bombs on everyone around the White House."

There are so many thoughts rushing through my mind that I'm not sure where to begin. My name is known to women across America? Because I disobeyed Bethany, the leader of Washington's most notorious underground resistance? What else was I supposed to do? She'd intercepted military communication regarding President Price's kill order. How could anyone stand around and let that happen? Let thousands upon thousands of women be massacred at the hands of men?

"It's true," I say. "I became privy to classified information that would have killed countless women. So yes, I reacted."

Her lips stretch so wide I can see the back of her throat.

"How's your son doing?" I ask.

Truthfully, I don't care about her son. I wish

she'd come to understand that one day, he will grow up, and he will pose a threat to all of Eden. But she'll never see that—she's his mother.

The smile on her face doesn't fade one bit. "Oh, he's doing great. I mean, aside from all the looks he's getting, he seems pretty happy. He's already made a few friends—"

"Friends?" I say. "Who?"

Does she think I'm being inquisitive? Why should I, leader of Eden, care who this boy is making friends with? It must seem suspicious, but all I want is to ensure that Eden is safe.

Her eyes shift from me to a crowd of women crossing behind me, the sound of their soft shoes tapping against the tiles.

"Oh, um, some girls his age," she says. "I think he said their names were Emily and Lucy."

I clench both fists but immediately loosen my fingers and tilt my head to one side. "Oh, isn't that wonderful."

* * * * * *

"Wonderful, just fuckin' wonderful," Freyda growls. "Hello? My name is Freyda Mills. Can anyone hear me? Hello?"

She's hunched over the radio with one hand pressed on the earpiece and the other hovering over many buttons. She presses something else, and the static grows louder, filling the room with a disturbing sound.

Two women stand at the edge of the table, their eyes wide and their arms wrapped around each other. I can't tell if they're sisters or lovers, but they look terrified.

"What if there's nothing out there?" one of them asks.

The other one, a young short-haired woman with a dragon tattoo on her shoulder, squeezes her hand and says, "You can't think like that, babe. I'm sure there're people out there trying to fix this whole mess."

Freyda looks up at the couple, but her lips don't part. It seems as though she's about to say something but then decides against it and instead changes the radio's channel. Maybe she doesn't want to discourage them, but I know precisely what she's thinking—there's nothing out there and no one is coming to save us.

"This is Freyda Mills. Is anyone receiving this?"

The static sound is intermittent, crackling inches away from her face. Her fist is clenched so tight around the microphone that her knuckles look like sharp icicles. Poor Freyda. She's been doing everything in her power to find a solution to this disaster.

The problem is, there is no solution—at least not out there. I've had weeks to prepare for this, months, even. I knew a war was coming and that everything would eventually collapse. Men would rather die than submit to women's demands.

So, while these women may dread the future before them, I can't help but revel in all of this. What more could they want? The world is at our fingertips. We can rebuild a society as we see fit without the presence of men to bring about heartbreak and destruction.

"What about Canada?" says the young woman with the tattoos. She rubs her arm with her dirt-stained fingers, her thick brows slanted in despair. "Or Mexico? Or... or Europe? I mean, someone's gonna come for us, right?"

I clench my teeth and wish I could say, "You shouldn't have fought in a war if you weren't prepared for the consequences."

But I can't turn on her. Right now, we need to stick together. I understand she's afraid—everyone's afraid. Our future, or at least the future these women thought they had, has been stripped from us.

Right now, I need to be strong. I need to show these women that a better life is possible now that the corrupt society in which we once lived has been abolished. We have the power to create our own laws—to decide what's right from wrong.

I shake my head and reach for her tattooed shoulder. "There's no telling how much damage the weapon caused." I'm not about to get into the technicalities of an EMP attack based on everything Vrin explained to me. "All we know is that right now, more than ever, we need to focus on surviving. There's no telling what's going on in other countries or if anyone is coming to help."

This woman's girlfriend, or wife, winces and parts her slobbery lips. "It wasn't supposed to be like this. N-n-not this bad. How the fuck did a few marches and protests lead to the end of the fucking world?"

"A few marches?" I clear my throat when I realize

I'm about to rip her head off. "This isn't about marches and protests. It's—it was," I correct, "about everything. How long have women lived under the rulership of men? How long?" It takes everything in me not to swear, but I can't help the tone of my voice anymore. "You all heard the stories." I twirl around in a circle, eyeing the dozens of women who followed us into this room. "Your mothers, your grandmothers. They've been fighting a war against men for decades! The harassment, the abuse, the objectification! And the only reason"—I let out a short laugh, even though nothing about this is funny—"the only reason men finally got scared is because we started outnumbering them. Maybe that was God's way of telling them their time was up. And what did they do? They retaliated." I point a stiff, white-knuckled finger at the ground. "They removed women from the government, from the military, from the police force... All for what? To control us like they've always done!"

The women around me nod aggressively, and one at the back yells, "That's right!"

"So no," I continue, "this isn't about a few marches or protests. This is about all the women of America finally coming together to put a stop to the bullshit we've had to endure for centuries! We aren't objects. We're human beings. It isn't up to men to decide what we do with our bodies, or what we don't do. It isn't up to men to decide which career path a woman is allowed to follow. Men are the reason we're here today. Were you not there when they started firing?" My voice cracks and I take a deep breath. “They fucking shot down women point-blank for stepping too close to the White House. If that’s the America we once had, I want nothing to do with it.”

“Me neither!” someone shouts.

“Eve’s right,” someone else says.

The woman in front of me wipes her tears, clears her throat, and opens her mouth to say something, but an unexpected noise fills the room—the sound of a woman’s choppy voice through the radio’s speaker.

“H-h-e...o? Da...y Wy...t here from Pens... W-w-e’re f... vivors. Is an... ther—” and everything goes quiet as if the radio’s been compromised.

“Fuck!” Freyda shouts, slapping another open palm against the table’s flat surface. She twists the nob over and over again, hoping to catch the same signal.

She slowly turns around. The zippers on her pant pockets scratch the chair underneath her and her chin touches her shoulder before she lets out a long breath. “We lost the signal.”

* * * * * *

“Close the door,” I say.

Freyda slips into my office and carefully closes the door. “You okay?”

I lean on my desk, my chin on my closed fist. “Am I being crazy?”

She walks across the room, pulls the chair out from under the desk, and sits down with a soft *thump*.

“Depends on your definition of crazy,” she says, winking.

How does she always manage to lighten the mood? She's my rock. All this stress—this anxiety—would be unmanageable without her by my side. A knot sits in my stomach, and I know the reason for it. Freyda is the only woman I trust to follow Gabriel to this promised land of his. If he gets out of line, she'll straighten him out, and she'll protect my women.

But how can I ask her to leave? What will I do without her? And how long will it take? What if they're gone weeks... months?

She must sense my anxiety. She clears her throat and slides her chair a bit closer. "I don't think you're being crazy." She reaches for me across the desk. Her skin is warm and soft, and I immediately feel comforted. "What other option is there? We can't stay here. Gabriel's right. It's only a matter of time before some crazy assholes find us. And we're not prepared—"

I let out a sharp breath. "I know, Freyda, I know."

She means well, and although for the last five years, I've done everything in my power to avoid training women for combat, I'm beginning to wonder if she's been right all along.

"I'm not trying to undermine you—"

I shake my head and offer a soft smile. "I know, Freyda. You've done nothing wrong. It's me. I don't even know what I'm doing anymore."

She squeezes my hand and leans forward. "You're doing what's best for these women."

Am I? I stare at her blue eye, and then her green one. Some days, when I look at Freyda, I'm mesmerized by her beauty. Other days, especially when I'm feeling as anxious as I am right now, those eyes frustrate me beyond belief—they don't match, and I don't know which one to look at when I speak to her.

I pull away.

"You don't have to say it," she says. "I'll go with him."

I stare into her blue eye. It looks like a little galaxy filled with hundreds of planets. How does she always know what I'm thinking? Is she spying on me? I look away, guilty for having such thoughts. Freyda has always been so loyal to me. She would never betray me.

"But I have a few requests," she continues.

I raise my chin and watch her thick lips as they move.

"I know Dakota is coming with us because we need a pilot. But I'd also like to bring Jada, Miller, and Yael."

I know these names, but I can't quite seem to put a face to them.

"Jada used to be on the police force, too. K-9 unit. Miller's ex-military, and Yael, well, I don't know her history, but she's the one who's been asking to teach martial arts to the kids. She's talked about her old dojo a few—"

I lean back in my chair and offer a brief nod. "That's fine. Whatever you need."

She bows her head as a way of thanking me, something she often does.

I stare at her protruding jawline, her perfectly shaped eyebrows, her hairline, and I wonder: what if this is the last time I see her? What if she doesn't return? What if—

"Get out," I say.

She eyes me from underneath slanted eyebrows. I realize my tone came about unexpectedly, but this isn't the time for goodbyes. I can't allow myself to feel anything.

She pushes her chair back, presses her hands on her knees, and stands up.

"Is there anything—"

"You're perfectly capable of managing this yourself, Freyda," I say, staring at my fingernails. "You're in charge of this team... Of whoever you want to bring with you. I expect you and these women to go within the hour. That should give you enough time to prepare some food, water, and clothing."

I see her nod in my peripheral, but I don't look up. I clench my teeth at the sound of her footsteps as they make their way to the door. I hear her turn toward me, her vest chafing the way it always does when she rotates her body, but my eyes remain fixated on my nails, which are now digging into the desk's wood.

"We'll see each other again," she says, and my throat swells. The moment she opens the door, I look up at her, seeing only her long ponytail dangling behind her back before she disappears from sight.

I stretch my neck to the side, a loud snap filling the air around me, and lean my head back against my chair's headrest. I blink several times, my moist eyes burning as they remain fixated on the ceiling above me.

Emotions are a weakness, I remind myself.

CHAPTER 17 – LUCY

"I don't think it's a good idea you see her right now," Nola says, staring into my eyes the way my mom used to. It's a look that says, "I know better than you right now, and you have to trust me."

But I can't sit around wondering how Emily's doing. Did Dr. Lewis figure out what's wrong with her? That's all I want to know. Not knowing is what's terrifying me. Is it contagious? Or is it something else? Is she going to die? I can't lose my only friend. I haven't connected with anyone but Nola since I came to Eden, and now, for the first time, I have someone I can talk to.

I swallow hard and rub my eyes.

Please, God, if you exist, don't take my friend from me.

Maybe I'm overexaggerating. Maybe she has the flu or something. But even then… Even the flu could be fatal here. Anything could be fatal in Eden. That's the part, at least I think, Eve tries to hide from us. She doesn't like to talk about the Medical Unit much. It takes away from the idea of this perfect, paradise-like place.

But Dr. Lewis knows better. She knows that

we're living in a world without advanced medical care and that even a cut, if left untreated, can kill someone. She seems like a good doctor, though. I think she knows what she's doing. Ever since she came to Eden, people have been much healthier. She's taken all kinds of precautions, like setting up antibacterial liquid throughout the corridors and reminding people to wash their hands as often as possible. That was before we ran out of the stuff. And now, she even works with Mavis and Perula to try to create some healthy beverages to boost our immune systems.

I honestly don't know what we'd do without her. Right now, I'm placing all my trust in her, because the last time I saw Emily, she didn't look good. And by the way Nola is looking at me right now, I'm assuming Emily's doing even worse than before. Nola would know—she's always in and out of the Medical Unit, helping as much as she can.

I always forget she's a nurse.

She doesn't wear nurse clothing—scrubs, or whatever you call them. She's usually in a fluffy dress, or, when she doesn't feel like getting done up, she wears Eden's basic hemp clothes. I've noticed more and more kids are wearing hemp clothing. I guess it has to do with growing out of their old clothes—the ones they brought with them.

The only reason I still manage to wear my old pants is that they're stretchy and I lost a bunch of weight after my mom died. But they've become capris more than pants. I realize I probably look like an idiot in them, but I don't want to wear what everyone else is wearing. Sometimes I wear the pants Eve got for me, but ever since she stopped talking to me, the thought of wearing them makes me resentful.

"Lucy, are you even listening to me?" Nola says.

With her hands on her waist, she really *does* look like my mom.

"Nola," I say, and she's taken aback by the sound of her own name. Her eyes widen a bit, and she drops her arms by her sides. "How'd you know my mom?"

I don't know where this is coming from, but I need to ask. I've kept my mouth shut for five years, and every time she's ever talked about how she used to be friends with my mom, I didn't say anything. I've doubted her all this time, thinking she was only saying that to make me feel better.

But I need to know. I need to know if Nola's been honest with me because I don't know who to trust in this place. And maybe this has something to do with being sixteen. I don't feel like a kid anymore, and I don't deserve to be treated like one, either. In trying to protect me, if there's something she hasn't told me, she can tell me now.

Her honey-brown eyes stare into mine, and she scratches under her nose with her index finger. "Where's this coming from?"

I shrug. "You always compare me to Mom. Sometimes I do something, and you'll say that Mom used to do the same thing. So, how'd you know her? I never asked you."

We're standing in the middle of Division Five's

corridor. She jerks her head toward my room and leads me inside. Sitting down on my bed, she pats the spot beside her. As soon as I sit, she rests a hand on my thigh and breathes out through her nose.

"Lucy, it isn't my place to talk about it."

"Talk about what?"

I can tell she's having a hard time with this. What's she keeping from me?

"All you have to know is that I knew your mom before you were born. We met under strange circumstances."

I shake my head. "That's not enough, Nola. I want the truth. I don't care what it is. Just be honest with me. Please. I feel like everyone's lying to me all the time. I want the truth."

She tilts her head back and breathes toward the ceiling. "I knew your mom before she had you."

I don't say anything, so she looks down at me and continues. "She was pregnant with you, actually."

She bites down on her bottom lip and looks away.

"Nola, it's okay," I say. "I can handle it."

I say I can handle it, but I'd be lying if I said I wasn't afraid of what she's going to tell me. It's obvious that it's something big, and she doesn't know whether my mom would want me knowing or not. But I need to know. I'm so tired of lies.

"I used to work in an underground abortion clinic. Abortion wasn't technically illegal, but at that point, it was frowned upon. People were rioting in the streets, throwing rocks at pregnant women who went into actual clinics." She squeezes my thigh.

"Anyways, your mom walked in one evening, looking completely frantic. Her hair was all over the place, and she kept saying that he wouldn't leave her alone. I still don't know who she was talking about. She never gave me his name. But she was obviously trying to get away from him. She kept saying he'd done this to her and that she didn't want—" She pauses and breaks eye contact. "That she didn't want to keep something he'd *caused.*"

I swallow hard. Is she saying what I think she's saying? I'm sick to my stomach.

"I told her I'd seen many women in her position before, and that abortion wouldn't do any good. That she'd end up regretting it down the road... We sat there for hours, and she cried in my arms. It was the strangest thing. It was as though I knew her, you know? Really knew her." She looks at me again, her eyes narrowing in a meaningful way. "Sometimes, you just *click* with someone, you know?"

I nod. I *do* know. I've recently felt that way with Emily.

"I gave her my card that night, and she went home without booking an appointment. We stayed in touch after that. Up until you started walking and talking, that is. I think I reminded her of the mistake she almost made because I tried reaching out again a few times, and she never reached back."

I nod slowly and stare at the cement floor, which is covered in chips and scratches. Right now, I feel like if I were to slide off my bed, I'd be small enough to sink into one of them and hide from the world. I want to throw up. The thought of my mom being raped makes me want to crawl into a hole and die. I just can't...

"Honey, I'm so sorry," Nola says.

I shake my head. I don't want sympathy. "No, Nola. It's okay." I look at her, and I can tell she's about to cry. "Thank you for being so honest with me."

Her lower lip trembles and she wraps an arm around my shoulders. I want to hug her back, but I'm as stiff as a piece of wood. All I can think about is Jason. That's who it was, wasn't it? The man she kept saying was following us? It all makes sense now. Why else would someone harass our family like that? He knew I was his.

I'm so disgusted with myself. I can't believe that I come from someone like that.

"Sweetheart," Nola says, "are you okay?"

My eyes are wide and I probably have a blank look on my face as I try to take it all in. When I pull away from her, something else dawns on me.

"How'd you know who I was? I mean, you said you didn't keep in touch. So, how'd you know I was her daughter?"

She offers the sweetest smile possible, tiny wrinkles forming at the corners of her eyes, then brushes my cheek with the back of her hand. "She's all I see in you."

I'm on the verge of tears and numb at the same time. I'm probably in shock, confused by everything I've learned.

"I also knew your name," she says, winking.

She then wraps her fingers around my neck,

pulls me in again, and kisses my forehead. I close my eyes, appreciating her soft lips and warm breath against my skin.

"Do you need some time?" she asks. "You know, to take this all in?"

I'm about to say yes, but I remember why I stopped her down Division Five's corridor in the first place.

Emily.

"I want to see my friend," I say.

She must feel guilty about what she shared with me and doesn't even try to argue. She pats my thigh and stands. "All right, follow me."

She wraps her fingers around my cell's iron bars and walks out, but then, without warning, stops halfway and I bump into her.

"Nola—"

She turns around, her figure hunched and her narrowed eyes resembling sliced almonds.

I step back. "What?"

"I need to ask you something."

Why is she whispering? What's going on?

"Do you have a history with Eve?" Her eyes dart from side to side, and she hunches forward so much now that she looks like she's crippled. "I mean, did you know her before you came to Eden? I saw her holding your hand, but I assumed she was only looking out for you."

Now I'm the one whose secret is on the line. "Why're you asking me this?"

She shakes her head like she's trying to dismiss my paranoia. "It would explain a lot," she says. "Eve's been asking about you... A lot. And she wants to meet with me later. I'm assuming it's to find out what you've been up to. And now I'm thinking, why does she care so much? I don't mean this offensively, sweetheart, but there are a lot of kids in Eden, so why's she so interested in you?"

* * * * * *

"I know it's been tough, kid, but you need to hang in there, okay?" Aunty Eve says, looking at me like I'm the most interesting thing left in this world.

She leans the upper half of her body forward and holds her weight up with her hands on her knees. I've grown a few inches over the last year, and she doesn't have to go down very low. I'm guessing in a few years, I'll be as tall as her, if not taller.

Mom was taller.

She throws a suitcase in the middle of the room and starts rummaging through it. It's a big blue traveling suitcase, the kind people take with them when they go on trips, and it's full of white fabric and something that looks like red leather boots or shoes. She grabbed all of this at that wrecked store in Aticok. A lot of women filled up suitcases. The store's door was busted open and all of the windows were broken. It looked like a ghost town.

"What's that?" I ask.

She pulls out a white jacket or overcoat. It looks like a fancy top that you see successful businesswomen wearing. "Need to dress the part."

Then, she pulls out a few pairs of jeans, some T-shirts, and sneakers.

"Got these for you," she says, handing me a pair

of jeans. "They're a bit big, but that's the point. You should grow into them over the next few years."

Over the next few years? How long are we going to be here? I can't even think about that. I still don't understand how all of this is happening. I stare at the pants. I'm happy they're not white. I don't know why anyone would wear white around here. Even walking through those cities made my sneakers all yucky.

She pulls out scissors, face cloths, hairbrushes, makeup, a bunch of toothbrushes and toothpaste (like, dozens of them), a box of Band-Aids, something that looks like a small knife, packets of flower or fruit seeds, and a bunch of other stuff. I wonder if all the other women grabbed as much stuff as this. I saw some of them filling up suitcases as fast as they could.

And why would Aunty Eve grab makeup?

She's been so strange lately. Who thinks of wearing makeup when the world is coming to an end? It's like I don't even know who she is anymore.

"Oh, look at these," she says. She pulls out a pair of red leather heels, red leather boots, and then a pair of red stilettos, and hugs them with a big smile on her face.

I've never been angry with Aunty Eve before, but right now, I want to hit her on the head. My mom just died and she's excited about shoes?

She puts everything back in the suitcase and closes it, then lets out a long, relieved sigh. "I think we'll make this work just fine."

"Make what work?" I say.

My legs are killing me and my back is sore after

all of that walking. I'm happy we're finally inside of Eden. All I want is to go to sleep. Why'd she make me follow her in here? In this weird-looking room? There's dust everywhere, and the old carpet is making my allergies act up. I rub my itchy nose and blink a few times. My eyes are probably all red. I want to scratch at them, but my mom always taught me not to touch my face, especially my eyes. I could get sick.

"This place," she says, and her smile gets even bigger. It's kind of creepy. She stands up and paces back and forth in the room. "I mean, it could use a bit of handiwork. I know they didn't renovate the entire prison after the fire, but—" She walks over to the window. There are big metal bars over it, and I'm assuming that was to make sure no one was able to run away, you know, when prisoners lived here. She grabs the bars and presses her face in between them, looking outside. I don't know what she's looking at—it's all dark and gray out there. The sun's setting. We're lucky we made it here before sunset. There's nothing worse than walking around open fields, through forests, and especially through abandoned towns when all the lights are out. It's scary, but it's also dangerous. You don't know who's nearby, or how dangerous they are. Aunty Eve kept telling all of us to keep our eyes open because people become aggressive when they're scared or hungry.

She turns around and her messy ponytail dances at the back of her head. "Don't you?"

What's she talking about? Don't I what? I think

she realizes I'm confused and flicks her wrist in the air like my opinion doesn't matter anyway.

"This place has real potential," she continues. Why's she talking so much? It's almost like she's talking to herself and not me. "We'll plant gardens, flowers, trees... Ah! It'll be beautiful."

She goes back to her suitcase, unzips it, and pulls out her red boots. She then slips off her sneakers and slips them on. They're shiny, like fake leather, and they go all the way up to her knees. Well, right under them. They have a small pointed heel that makes her look a lot taller than she is. They look kind of funny with her jeans, which are full of holes, dirt, and blood.

I stare at the blood and want to throw up. What if that's my mom's blood? Was she with her when she died? Did Aunty Eve see it happen?

"What do you think?" Aunty Eve asks. She twirls her ankle from side to side, the boot's heel scratching the carpet and the leather shiny.

"It's nice," I say.

She forces a laugh. "Nice? These are four-hundred-dollar boots."

"You didn't pay for them," I say.

I'm not trying to be a smart-aleck, but I'm getting annoyed with her right now. She's acting like the only thing that matters is her and her clothes, while a lot of women out there are hurting. A lot of them are crying hard. They lost family members. Kids like me, who lost their parents are bawling. And Aunty Eve is asking me what I think about her new boots?

Her lips curve into a pout and she makes a funny

face. "Of course I didn't pay for them, silly. But I didn't steal them, either. Laws don't exist anymore."

"Why not?" I ask.

I think I'm starting to annoy her. Maybe I'm ruining her excitement.

"The world you knew doesn't exist anymore, Lucy."

My name doesn't sound too great coming from her mouth. Not like it used to, anyway. Not like when she used to bring me a cookie every time she came to visit Mom. I'm a bit old for cookies now, but the thought was still sweet. And every time she'd see me, she'd give me a big hug. She was like a second mom. She always has been. So, what's changed? Is this because she lost her sister? I mean, she has been bizarre ever since. But it's like she's getting worse every day since Mila died.

Although I'd never say this to her, it's like she's gone crazy.

She walks toward me, her boots making a soft ticking sound against the thin carpet. She then kneels without losing her balance. It's like she's walked in those boots her entire life.

"I need you to make me a promise, Lucy."

She grabs my shoulders and stares at me until I become uncomfortable.

"You can't call me Aunty Eve out loud anymore."

Why did she say it like that? *Aunty* Eve. Like it's some abominable or poisonous word. I don't say it like that.

"Can you do that? Can you keep that our little secret?"

"Why?" I ask. I'm not trying to be rude; I'm confused.

Her lips go tight and she breathes out through her nostrils. "It wouldn't be fair to the others." She brushes my cheek with her bruised-up hand, but I pull away. I'd be lying if I said I wasn't hurt. I just lost my mom, and now she wants to run away from me, too? Afraid I'm going to cry, I bite down.

"These women," she says. "All of them... They've followed me here because I promised to protect them. They see me in a certain light. I can't have you going around calling me *Aunty* Eve. It'll ruin everything."

What she means to say is I'll embarrass her. I yank myself out of her grip and start walking toward the door.

"It doesn't change anything, Lucy," she says. "I'll still be here for you."

I look back at her, and I can't help but glare. How could she do this to me after everything that's happened? We only have each other left. Why's she trying to push me away?

"Don't worry," I say, "I'll keep my big mouth shut."

* * * * * *

"Lucy?"

Poor Nola. I'm always zoning out on her when she's talking to me.

"Sorry," I say. I remember what Eve told me five years ago. I remember the day she broke my already broken heart. Eventually, I got over it. I realized that it was just a name. She still came to visit me, though not as much as I would have liked. But she hasn't been supportive at all. It's like she doesn't even care about me anymore. So why should I keep her secret? Why should I lie to Nola about Eve being my aunt? Eve doesn't deserve my loyalty.

"Eve asked me not to tell anyone," I admit.

"Tell anyone what?" Nola asks, tilting her head to the side.

If there's one person I now know I can trust, it's Nola.

I look up at her. "Eve's my godmother."

CHAPTER 18 – GABRIEL

"I don't even get to take a nap, first?" I say.

I know I'm being a smart-ass, but I can't help myself. I want to make her smile. It's not working, though. She still has that same rigid face she always has when she comes down into the basement.

"What do you need before we leave?" she asks, matter-of-factly.

Straight to the point. I like that.

"Well," I say. "It should take us about a week, give or take, if we're walking twelve hours per day."

"Twelve hours?" she asks, and for the first time, she shows some form of expression on that beautiful face of hers. Her eyes bulge out a bit and her thick bottom lip hangs open.

"What's wrong?" I ask.

"That's a lot to expect of women who've been secluded inside prison walls for the last five years."

I didn't look at it that way. I've spent the last few years traveling throughout America. Walking doesn't faze me. I've walked twenty-four hours straight more than once. It's no wonder I've had to swap my boots a few times.

"We'll start slow," I say. "Maybe four hours on the

first day."

She crosses her arms. "I don't understand. What makes you so sure this place hasn't already been taken over by a bunch of military men?"

I don't mean to laugh, but I can't help myself. "You think the few surviving military men give a shit about fulfilling their duties as soldiers? They're human, too, just so you know. I'm sure they're more preoccupied with trying to find food than they are trying to rebuild some kind of military team. And what would be the point of rebuilding an army, anyway? What're they gonna do? Storm through America and kill women? Come on. The war's over. Aside from a few savages out there, no one gives a shit about gender anymore."

She gazes up at the ceiling, an obvious sign that she's lost in thought. She must believe part of what I'm saying.

"We need a good supply of food and water," I say. "Maybe extra layers of clothing. It's getting a bit chilly out there."

She dismisses my comment and instead walks closer to me, her boots clapping against the floor. She puffs out her chest and pulls her shoulders back.

"So, is that the real plan?" she asks. "You're going to take us to some old military base and we're going to try to repair a plane? I mean, am I the only one who thinks this whole idea is fucking insane?"

I'm about to start listing off all the reasons why staying here is an even worse idea than the far-fetched possibility of getting a plane to work, but she keeps going.

"I mean, it doesn't make any sense. First of all, I highly doubt that the base is empty. If it's as protected as you say it is, I'm sure survivors have found it by now."

"It's pretty secluded. I doubt anyone has traveled that f—"

"And second, even if we somehow got a plane to work again, where would we get the fuel? You're telling me the fuel hasn't evaporated over the last five years?"

I cock an eyebrow. "It's a massive tank..."

"And what if we get lost? Who's to say you even know how to get there? It's not like you have some GPS to follow. You're going based on what, exactly? Memory? Visual cues?"

I can't help but smile. She's completely freaking out. I never thought I'd see her like this. She always looks so composed, but right now, she's having a meltdown.

"What's so funny?" she snaps.

I shake my head. "I'm not laughing." I instinctively reach for her shoulder to comfort her. Surprisingly, she doesn't pull away. "I don't know you. I'll admit that. But from what I've seen, you're a strong woman. I'm assuming you're stressed out because Eve asked you to lead the group. Trust me, I know the feeling. I've led a few missions myself, and the stress can get to you."

Her intimidating eyes narrow on me. "Missions?"

Fuck.

She pulls away and looks at me like I'm the vilest thing she's ever seen. "Oh my God. How did none of us realize this? I mean, it all makes sense. You're taking us to a goddamn base. You're fucking military."

"What? I—"

"Don't even try to smooth talk your way out of this one, Gabriel. Admit it. Fucking admit it!"

Her raspy voice carries throughout the basement and her face contorts, creating shadows around her eyes.

I raise my hands. "Hear me out."

"Oh, I'm listening, and you'd better start talking."

"It's not like I joined when all of this was happening," I say. "I didn't join the Black Marines to fight a gender war."

She throws her head back and lets out a snicker that makes me think she's losing her mind. "And on top of it, the Black Marines! Oh, this keeps getting better and better."

"No, no—it's not like that."

"Then what's it like, Gabriel?" she says with a hiss. "Because from where I'm standing, you're the enemy. Why the fuck should we follow you to your goddamn military base? Does Eve know about this? I mean, how dumb would we be to follow a Black Marine onto military territory? What're you planning, Gabriel? To make us your prisoners? Huh? Is that it?"

She has so much fury inside her that it makes me weak in the knees. I never intended for any of this. The last thing I want is for Freyda to hate me. And that's what's happening right now. She's looking at me like she wants to rip me in half with her bare hands.

"How many did you kill?" she says, but it sounds more like an accusation.

"What?"

"Women!" she snaps.

"I didn't—"

"Bull fucking shit!"

"Would you just hear me—"

"I knew this was a bad idea. I knew you were like the rest of them. I can't believe I let you convince me that—"

"Freyda!" I growl, and I immediately feel guilty for raising my voice.

But it seems to work. She stops rambling and looks at me, obviously taken aback by authoritative tone.

"I swear to God, I haven't killed a single woman during all of this." I aim a finger at the cement under my feet. "You have no idea what I've been through. No idea how bad the corruption was. I saw men being dragged away for not wanting to take part in the war. The military was wiping them out. Making them disappear. I shouldn't have stayed when I found out about the gender war, but what was I supposed to do? I'm human. I have survival instincts, too." I don't break eye contact. I need her to know how serious I'm being. "I had to blend in. You think I enjoyed hearing that my mother was nothing but a useless piece of shit? That all women deserved to be raped and beaten? You don't think it took everything in me not to want to kill my commanders where they stood? My mother meant everything to me. So no, I wasn't on *their* side. I risked my life trying to protect women during this war. You have no idea how many men I've killed. Men I considered friends… because they got brainwashed into believing that women were the root of all evil. You think that was easy for me? Watching my friends try to rape innocent women? I had no side, Freyda. What was I supposed to do? Women hated me for being a man, and my own gender started hating me for not being *hateful* enough. If I were like the rest of them, I wouldn't have killed Adam and his goons. I wouldn't have stopped them from raping your women. I would've joined in."

She wants to believe me, I can see it in her eyes. She's searching me. Analyzing every muscle on my face to detect a lie. If she was a good police officer, then she'd know I was telling the truth.

"If I could go back," I say, "I wouldn't have tried following in my father's footsteps. I became a Black Marine because of him. Because I was searching for something. If I'd known they were going to assign me to this whole nightmare against my will…"

"Okay," Freyda say. "I get it."

My heart rate slows down a bit. "So, you believe me?"

She averts her eyes. What's bothering her? It isn't about me anymore. There's something she isn't telling me.

"Freyda?"

"It's nothing," she says, but the moment her eyes meet mine, it's like something inside of her softens.

Maybe she does trust me, somewhere deep

inside. Somewhere underneath that unbreakable guard of hers.

"Eric," she says, "that was my husband's name. He was a cop, too. Masculine kind of man, but not overly, you know? Not macho. You remind me of him. He was a good cop, too. Great cop, actually. But when this whole revolution started... I don't know. Something changed. He started getting crabby after his shifts. Started raising his voice at me... Punching holes through our walls." She rubs her forehead and starts pacing back and forth like she's reliving the whole thing. "Then, when the force let me go, he said it was probably for the best. He would've never said that before. He would have fought for me, but he didn't. And it only got worse after that up until the day he got shot on duty. I never understood what happened. This whole time, I've been trying to understand where all his anger was coming from. But it all makes sense now."

She stretches her back and clears her throat. I'm assuming she's trying to get rid of a lump. Trying to mask any form of emotion from me.

"Anyways, I guess that answers it," she says.

"The brainwashing, you mean?"

She nods but doesn't say anything.

"I'm sorry," I say. I know an apology isn't much, but it's the only thing I have to offer.

"It's not your fault," she says. "I appreciate you telling me about it."

"You going to tell Eve about this?" I ask.

She scoffs like I'm a complete moron. "She'd kill you. Honestly, I don't understand how she doesn't already know—"

"Is that a no?"

"Relax, I'm not an idiot."

"What's that supposed to mean?" I ask.

"If Eve kills you, we don't stand a chance trying to find new territory."

"So, this isn't about wanting to spare my life?" I ask, and I smirk, even though it's probably not the time to be a smart-ass right now.

She pulls a knife from her belt and walks toward me. My heart skips a beat. What is she doing?

"Whoa," I say, but she rolls her eyes and grabs my wrists.

"You're a bit of a wuss for an ex-marine," she says, slicing the knife through the rope's knot.

"Maybe you intimidate me," I say, towering over her. She looks up at me, her neck craned back, and for a second, it looks like she's about to smile. She rips the broken ropes from around my wrists and steps back.

"No, Gabriel, this isn't about sparing your life. You happen to have something we want, which makes you valuable. Nothing more. And to be honest, when this is all over, I can't guarantee Eve *won't* kill you."

I swallow hard. Was that supposed to be her motivational speech? Her pep talk? If that's the case, she needs a lot of practice.

She gives me an impatient up and down and arches one eyebrow. "You ready to go, or what?"

CHAPTER 19 – EVE

It looks like an old rock you'd find by a river: matte gray with green and brown muck all over it. I rub my thumb against the green parts, trying to clean it off, then run my fingers along its cold metallic chain.

Mila loved this necklace. My mother bought this for her when she was twelve years old. It's a metallic egg that opens up, and once open, it projects a holographic screen displaying the wearer's name, address, and contact information for the family in the event the child ever gets lost. It was a huge fad back then. I remember watching Mila open it for Christmas, and the way she'd jumped up and down so hard her glasses fell off her face.

My mother bought it to make Mila happy, even though she didn't quite understand its concept. Mila, on the other hand, constantly raved about it, explaining how DDGs (short for Digital Dino Eggs) were the next best thing to replace holographic phones.

"They're solid, and... and... and," she'd said, her mouth wide open and her bright eyes bulging out behind her thick-rimmed glasses. "They can do just about anything! How're you guys not excited? I mean, look."

And then she went on to project a prepopulated video on the wall. It had something to do with a wild flock of birds—something short and cheesy. It wasn't at all interesting, but the look on her face made it worthwhile.

It was one of those things that all kids had and the kind of jewelry that was offered at different levels of quality. The real ones, golden eggs, sold at around twenty thousand dollars. Each one provided access to the internet, among hundreds of other cool functionalities, including video projection. The DDG was also virtually impossible to steal thanks to its technology. It could be found anywhere and couldn't be reprogrammed to belong to anyone else. The coolest functionality, at least in my opinion, was something called the Leash. Basically, no matter how far you distanced yourself from the DDG, it always brought itself back to you. If you were stupid about using the thing, you'd scratch it up, but kids didn't seem to mind—at least, not about the ones of midrange quality that had this functionality. Usually, the rich kids had the better ones, and you could distinguish social class by watching them throw their eggs into an open field only to watch it come rolling back.

Most kids, including Mila, didn't have a high-functioning DDG, but she didn't seem to care. It was the principle—the idea of even wearing one around her neck that made her feel important.

I'd always promised her I'd buy her a real one someday, when I had enough money to buy a car.

Even if I had to finance, I'd do it.

And now, Mila's DDG looks like it's gone through too many laundry cycles. Only one patch of it remains shiny, and it's no bigger than a pinkie nail. I crack it open and rub my index finger along its little black screen. There's no battery left and it doesn't work anymore. But what strikes me as odd is that following the EMP attack, it still worked. It may have had something to do with the metal structure.

I sigh and tuck it back into my desk.

I cannot allow myself to be reunited with feelings of grief. The best way to honor Mila's memory is to continue ruling Eden—to continue providing the best life possible for women who have endured far too much suffering.

You don't even care about these women.

I stand up and roughly brush my pant legs, even though they're clean as always.

I do care. If I didn't care, I wouldn't be allowing Freyda to leave with some man we don't even know to chase after some promised land.

Frustrated by my own uncontrolled thoughts, I storm across my office in search of something, anything to keep my mind busy, when a soft knock resonates from the door.

I quickly wipe a loose strand of hair away from my forehead and clear my throat. "Come in."

Nola's large head pops into view.

"Nola," I say, extending my arms from my waist. "Come on in, dear."

She nods, her poufy hair dancing up and down, and steps inside quickly before closing the door behind her.

"Eve," she says, her voice delicate as usual. But it's those eyes that tell me she knows something I don't. They keep shifting between mine, the floor, and the window. What's going on?

"Have a seat," I tell her, and she pulls out the chair Freyda was sitting in only moments ago.

An awkward silence fills the room as we stare at each other, waiting for the other to speak, until finally, Nola taps her fingers against the chair's armrest and clears her throat. "You wanted to see me?"

I'd been so preoccupied thinking of Freyda and Gabriel that I'd completely forgotten about Nola and Lucy. I lean back in my chair and let out a dismissive laugh. "Oh, yes, of course. Sorry, Nola. I wanted to let you know what you'd missed during our meeting. The man... Gabriel... Freyda's gone with him to find new territory."

Though I don't intend for it, my words come out sounding like I'm completely disinterested. The truth is, I don't want to talk about Freyda, or Gabriel.

Why is she looking at me like that? Her lips are sealed tight and her brows are furrowed close together. I can't tell if she's focused on what I have to say or if she's judging me, analyzing every inch of my face.

"Is something wrong, Nola?"

She straightens her posture and crosses her fingers together over her stomach. She must be taken aback by my perception. "What? No, not at all." Her lips loosen, and her dark eyes soften. "I'm just curious to know what's going on."

I nod slowly, though I can't say with full confidence that I believe her. I've known Nola for quite some time now, and over the last few years, I've come to see her develop an attachment like no other to Lucy. There is a bond between them, but I assumed my rulership would triumph over their relationship.

Perhaps I was wrong.

She shifts uncomfortably in her chair and scratches the top of her head. "What did I miss?"

If she is hiding something, she is out of control. Women should know by now that they can trust me. I bite the inside of my cheek, infuriated at the thought of her choosing Lucy over me. I didn't expect this from her. I would expect her to place Lucy's well-being above all else, and if Lucy is acting out in a way she shouldn't be, it's important that I know about it. How can I help her if I don't know what's going on?

I break eye contact when I realize I've been staring at her this whole time.

"Oh, there's a big change coming, Nola," I say, scratching at the groove on my desk again. I've managed to scrape out half an inch of wood, and although I hate any form of damage on furniture, it's the only thing that relaxes me. "Gabriel will be leading some of our women toward a safer territory. The goal is to have them inspect it before we start a mass migration. We're hoping to make use of certain technology to simplify transportation..."

"A mass migration?" Nola says.

I stare at her but don't respond.

"Can I ask why, Eve? We've built such a paradise here."

Why is she questioning me? Is this where Lucy is obtaining her inquisitive, disobedient ways? Perhaps I had it wrong all along. Nola's sweet and loving demeanor—maybe it's all a charade. What lies has she been telling Lucy? I scratch even harder at the chipped wood, and the corner of my nail bends backward.

"Eve?"

I force a smile, though I'm growing tired of having to smile all the time. What reason do I have to smile? My Eden is falling apart. Everything I dreamed of is crashing down—drowning in a flood of impurities.

When I look back up at her, she's halfway across my office.

"I'll come another time," she says. "I'm so sorry if I intruded on anything."

I've allowed myself to be seen.

"No, no, sit," I say, my lips stretching so wide my cheeks ache.

"Are you sure?" she asks. "You seem to have a lot on your—"

I shake my head hard enough to throw my stubborn strand of hair away from my forehead. "I'm sorry, Nola. I just—"

I bow my head and take a sharp breath. "I'm just worried."

She seems intrigued. She hunches her shoulders forward as if limiting the space between us will allow her to hear me better. I have her right where I want her.

"It's Lucy," I say.

"What about her?" Nola asks.

I tap my fingers on my lips to give off the appearance of deep contemplation. "I… I don't know what to do anymore." Then, I quickly slide to the edge of my seat and lean my elbows on the desk. "Nola, I have to tell you something."

"O-of course, Eve. Anything."

She sits back down again, her eyes never leaving mine. My mother always taught me that if you give someone a little, be it information or a gift, they will, in turn, want to give back. It's human nature. And I know Nola is a good woman—she only wants what's best for Lucy, which, if approached correctly, may serve me advantageously.

"No one knows this," I say, "so please, can you keep it between us?"

She nods.

I pause for effect, then say, "Lucy and I knew each other before we arrived in Eden. I was her mother's best friend."

I can't quite read her reaction. She looks both confused and shocked, but I'm not certain why. Is it because I revealed a secret? Or is it the secret itself?

She parts her dark lips and scratches her temple. "Why are you telling me this?"

I fight off the urge to glower at her. Her reaction isn't what I was anticipating. I opened up to her about something I've kept secret from everyone in Eden, and all she can do is ask me why I've told her?

I swallow my rage and reach for her hand, even though the thought of touching her repulses me. “Because, my sweet Nola, I need you to understand why I’ve asked you about her. I mean, you must have thought I was being a little crazy”—I let out a forced laugh—“asking about some little girl in Eden and all.”

She stares at me and I squeeze her hand.

“Nola, please look out for her. I trust you more than I trust anyone.”

This seems to have caught her attention. Her lip twitches at one corner and she shrugs with one shoulder, clearly embarrassed by my compliment.

“I know you love Lucy as much as I do,” I say. “I also know how rebellious her mother was, and some days, I fear Lucy might turn out the same way. I only want what’s best for her.”

She pulls away from me. Why is the smile on her face disappearing?

“Her mother? Rebellious?” she asks.

She’s staring at me as if she’s caught me in my lie—as if she knows that Ophelia was a woman who followed rules and avoided conflict at all costs, that Ophelia wasn’t rebellious in the slightest. Did Nola know Ophelia? That’s impossible. How on Earth would they have known each other?

I clear my throat. “Y-yes. In the last few years,” I say, hoping to save myself. If she knew Ophelia, which is highly unlikely, she knows that describing her as rebellious couldn’t be further from the truth. “She used to be such sweet woman. She never disobeyed the law. But before her death—before her tragic accident—she changed.”

Nola nods slowly, looking almost heartbroken.

"Lucy can't know this," I say, shifting my eyes from side to side. "But Ophelia's behavior is what got her killed. I tried to save her—"

I pinch the skin between my eyebrows and lower my head until my chin almost touches my shoulder. I let out a whimper. "Oh, Ophelia."

"Eve, I'm so sorry," Nola says. "But you don't have to worry about Lucy. I don't think she's getting herself in harm's way. She's just a teenager. You know? She likes to question things."

But the moment I look up, Nola looks away.

"What I mean is," she rambles on, "is that Lucy isn't causing any trouble."

But she's questioning things? I wipe the excess moisture from my eyes—something I've always known how to produce voluntarily—and clear my throat. "Oh, goodness. I hope she isn't questioning me. After everything I've done for her and Ophelia. After—" And I turn away again, waving a hand in front of my face as if trying to erase my emotions with a gust of air.

It's apparent Nola's uncomfortable, and with good reason. Never once have I shown any form of emotion to the women of Eden. But I need answers, and if emotion is the way to Nola's heart, then that's precisely what I must show her.

"I'm so sorry, Nola." I blink repeatedly and look up at the ceiling. "I don't know what's come over me. It's only, I knew Ophelia better than anyone. Lucy wasn't around when Ophelia spoke of being spied on by hidden cameras in her walls... When she spoke of voices telling her that her doctor was part of some big conspiracy to have her killed. She did everything in her power to keep that from Lucy."

I don't know where I'm coming up with these ideas, but they're flowing out so easily.

"I-I don't want Lucy developing the same... *problem*," I say.

Nola's lip curls up over her teeth. "Are you saying she suffered from schizophrenia?"

I arch an eyebrow. "I don't know. She never got a diagnosis... You know how it was, Nola. Doctors stopped wanting to treat women." I sniffle up excess moisture from my nose. "I loved Ophelia like a sister and Lucy like a daughter. I still do. I don't visit her as often because I want her to have her own life with her own friends. If she's seen being favored by me, it won't go over well with the other children."

Nola nods and brushes the back of her fingers along her jawline. It's working. Those eyes are searching for something.

"I know you're looking out for her," I continue, "and I can't thank you enough, Nola. You've become like a mother to her."

Her cheeks darken a shade and she averts her eyes. I maintain a look of distress—slanted eyebrows, droopy lips, and tear-filled eyes—though what I want to do is smile from ear to ear. I can't believe how easy she is to manipulate.

"You don't have to tell me anything. I understand you two have a special bond. All I ask, Nola, is that if Lucy is coming up with wacky ideas about certain people being evil, or if she's snooping around, listening for voices… Keep an eye on her. Don't encourage the behavior. That's how it all started with Ophelia. It all started with conspiracy theories."

Nola doesn't respond, but it's obvious she's mulling this over, which means Lucy has in fact been exhibiting this behavior. Why is she so keen on digging for answers? She doesn't need to understand my methods. Is she hoping to find out what happened to her mother? No one knows that but me and a few other women who were present in the Oval Office, but they didn't follow me to Eden.

What is she looking for?

Nola scrapes her chair backward and stands up. "Don't worry, Eve. I'll watch out for her."

CHAPTER 20 – LUCY

"Is everything okay?" I ask, but Nola shakes her head and offers a fake smile. I know it's fake—her eyes don't get all small and shiny like they do when she's genuinely happy to see me.

"Are you ready?" she asks.

I've been ready this whole time. She's the one who said she had to talk to Eve to *get it over with* before she brought me to visit Emily. I probably have a face full of attitude because she wiggles her fingers at me and says, "All right, let's go."

"What happened?" I ask. "What did Eve want? Was it about the man? Or... the boy? Zack? What's she planning, Nola? No one tells me anything around here."

Nola stops walking almost too briskly and wraps her fingers around mine, pulling me back.

Why's she being weird all of a sudden? She's looking at me funny, too. Like I'm back to being my young twelve-year-old self. Like I'm too young to be involved in matters discussed by adults. This is ridiculous. Fifteen minutes ago, she was on my side. And now she's looking at me like I'm too dumb to understand anything.

What's her problem? I frown and pull away from her. "What's up with you?"

"Oh, sweetheart," she says. "Nothing's wrong. I simply want you to stop stressing so much about everything."

I glare at her. "Eve put you up to this, didn't she? She turned you against me!"

Maybe I'm making things worse. She tilts her head and pets my shoulder like I'm precisely that: a pet.

"No one's turning anyone against anyone, Lucy. I'm on your side. I always have been."

"Then what's this about? Why won't you tell me what Eve talked to you about?"

She guides me out of Division Five's corridor, probably because my voice is getting loud and it's carrying throughout every cell.

"There's nothing to get all worked up over. You don't need to know everything, Lucy," she hisses, and her eyes dart from side to side. A few women give her an awkward look, but they keep walking. She straightens her posture and brushes her dress with her hands like she's trying to flatten out the ruffles. "Would you like to go see Emily, or not?"

I don't know what Eve said to her, but it had an impact. The more I ask, the more she gets upset, so I'm going to shut my mouth and act like everything's fine.

"Yes, I would," I say, and without a word, Nola turns on her heels and takes me through the main hall and toward the Medical Unit. I watch her shoes as they click hard on the tiles.

What the heck did Eve tell her? She's even walking differently. I don't know if she's upset with me or she's stressed out. Nola's never acted like this before. Did I do something wrong? Maybe I shouldn't have told her about everything… About Emily, and about what we overheard in the storage room.

And why'd she go see Eve so quickly, anyway? She could have taken me to see Emily first. Was it to tell her what I've been up to? Maybe I can't trust her like I thought I could. Maybe Eve truly is up to no good and Nola's in on it, too.

I hate this feeling. I feel like I'm going crazy. Everything is making me paranoid and I can't stop thinking. My mind keeps racing all over the place, trying to figure out what Eve is up to if she *is* up to anything. Just the other day, I decided to give up on this… To have faith that Eve would do what was best for everyone.

But there's a feeling in my stomach that I can't seem to shake. It's a gut feeling, and Mom always told me that gut feelings pretty much always mean something. They might not be right, but they mean something.

Nola turns around to make sure I'm following. I don't look up at her. To be honest, I'm a little hurt right now. An hour ago, she was sitting by my side in the secret storage room bonding with me. For the first time, it seemed like we were on the same page.

And now she's being all weird. I think of Emily and a lump forms in my throat. She's the person I need right now, but there's no telling how she's going to look when I get there. What if she got worse?

I follow Nola's heavy footsteps down the Medical Unit's narrow hallway. The room that I saw earlier, the one with the four women staring at me through the window, is still blacked out with the same curtain over the window.

I don't bother trying to understand what's going on. Every time I question things, I get myself in trouble. I look up at Nola's frizzy hair as she knocks on Dr. Lewis's door. A few wild curls are sticking out over her ear, and some strands are stuck to the sweat on her neck. Mom's hair was always perfectly combed. It was nothing like Nola's.

Right now, I miss Mom more than anything. She'd be on my side. She wouldn't be basically telling me to shut up about my crazy ideas. That's what it felt like when Nola was glaring at me. Like she was telling me to keep my mouth shut and stop questioning everything. Like she didn't want to hear about any more of my stories or adventures with Emily.

The door creeps open, and Dr. Lewis's dark, glistening forehead is the first thing I see. Her bright, chocolatey eyes follow and she looks confused when she sees Nola.

"Nola," she says. "I thought you were taking the day off."

"I am," Nola says, and she must have shot her eyes in my direction because Dr. Lewis's attention turns to me. The second she looks at me, I can see every single one of her teeth.

"Little Lucy," she says. "How're you doing?"

“I’m not that little anymore,” I say, smirking.

“I bet you’re here to see your friend,” she says.

I nod.

Barely cracking the door open, she slips her slender body through the small space and closes the door behind her. The doorknob makes a soft clicking noise. Why’s she stepping out into the hallway? What’s going on? Why isn’t she letting us in? My heart starts racing, and I swallow hard when I notice the smile on her face disappear. She slants her dark eyebrows the way a worried mother does when their child is hurting.

“Emily’s okay,” she says quickly. Maybe she noticed I was panicking. “But she isn’t doing well.”

“What?” I say. “What does that even mean? How’s she okay if she isn’t doing well?”

I’m not trying to be rude, but she’s not making any sense. If she isn’t doing well, she obviously isn’t okay. I think what she meant to say was, “She’s alive, but I don’t know for how long.”

“Lucy,” Dr. Lewis says, resting her long bony fingers on my shoulder.

I yank away.

“I’m not a kid!” I say, my voice carrying down the hallway. “Tell me what’s going on.”

I’m so sick of this. So sick of being treated like I can’t handle anything. This is bullshit. I clench my fists and breathe out through my nostrils. It’s not Dr. Lewis’s fault. She’s only trying to help. But I can’t stop the rage that’s building inside.

Everything’s falling apart. There are secrets inside Eden, my best friend is super sick, and now

Nola is distancing herself from me.

I don't know how much more of this I can take.

"Lucy," Nola says, her voice back to being as smooth as it always is.

"I don't wanna hear it, Nola," I say. "Honestly, I don't even want you here."

Her eyes expand like little balloons and she pulls her chin back, rolls forming on her neck. She wasn't expecting that. I wasn't either, but I can't stop.

"You're supposed to be here for me, and you're acting so f—" I'm about to start swearing, so I stop myself. Nola's never heard me swear. "You're being all weird, Nola. And it's ever since you talked to Eve. I should've listened to my gut in the first place. I knew she was up to no good, and I couldn't trust her. If it wasn't for Eve, my mom would still be alive."

I've never said that aloud before, but it feels good coming out.

Nola cocks an eyebrow, looking more intrigued than shocked now. Dr. Lewis is right in front of me, and I know I should shut my mouth. I shouldn't be talking badly about Eve in front of her, but I don't care anymore.

"Eve's the reason my mom went to the White House!" I say, smashing the side of my fist against the concrete wall. "My mom didn't want anything to do with it. She didn't want to stick her nose in the war. She wanted a quiet life with me!"

"Lucy, what're you talking—" Nola tries.

"Whatever Eve told you, you seem to believe her. I'm not an idiot, Nola. I've spent every day with you for the last five years. I know you. And I can tell you have something in your head. Probably a bunch of bullshit!"

"Lucy!" Nola hisses.

"Just leave me alone," I say. "It's obvious I can't trust you."

"That's enough talking like—" Nola tries, but then, the words come flying out of my mouth.

"Fuck off!"

If her eyes weren't attached to her skull, I think they would fall to the floor. Her mouth hangs wide open, and she looks at Dr. Lewis, who lets out a soft breath.

"Lucy," Dr. Lewis says, "why don't you come inside?" She then tightens her lips and glances at Nola. "I think it's best you leave for now."

I'm still fuming when Nola finally walks away. Dr. Lewis presses a warm hand against my upper back and guides me inside her clinic. Everything is so quiet and I'm calm the moment I step inside. She looks down at me, presses a finger over her lips, and points to the back of the clinic where two massive windows make up most of the wall. They're protected by metal bars, of course, but the lighting makes it feel a little less dreary in here.

Then, I see her.

She's lying on a stretcher-like bed with a thin cotton sheet over her curled body, all the way up to her neck. She looks like a caterpillar cocooned in the sheet. It's even wrapped around her legs and feet.

"She's running a high fever," Dr. Lewis says.

Emily doesn't even seem to hear her. Her eyes are sealed shut and her lips are a light shade of gray—almost blue.

Oh God, Emily.

"What's wrong with her?" I ask.

Dr. Lewis lets out a solemn breath. She hasn't even started talking and the room is already spinning around me. I want to know, but at the same time, I'm terrified of what she's going to say.

"Without proper medical equipment, I can't be sure. I gave her some acetaminophen to reduce the fever," she says.

Now I know it's bad. Her fever must be pretty high for Dr. Lewis to try to reduce it. Everyone in Eden knows that acetaminophen isn't handed out lightly. There's a limited supply, which means anyone with a headache is told to lie down or seek out help from one of Eden's therapists. There are three of them, as far as I know, who do massage therapy and physiotherapy. But they also don't get paid for their services. Eden has no currency system. It's one of those things where everyone's happy that it's free, but at the same time, it makes many reluctant to ask for the favor.

Dr. Lewis picks up a bottle of pills and reads the back. "Do you know how long she's had the cough?"

I glance up at the ceiling, trying to recall. "Um... Maybe a few weeks."

I feel like such an idiot. I can't even say for sure how long she's had it. I mean, I noticed it a while ago, but it didn't seem that bad. I guess I figured it was allergies. I was so preoccupied with myself that I didn't even think to tell Emily to see Dr. Lewis. Even the smallest of infections need to be addressed right away here in Eden.

Dr. Lewis nods knowingly. "It progressed rather quickly, then. I didn't want to scare you, Lucy, but it sounds like pneumonia."

Pneumonia? What is that, anyway? I've never had it. I think she realizes that I'm confused. She smiles, even though there's nothing to smile about, and places the bottle of pills on one of her medical tables.

"It's a lung infection," she says. "It can sometimes be mild, which is known as walking pneumonia. Some people aren't even aware they have it. They think it's a chest cold. But the congestion in her lungs..." She makes a face and shakes her head from side to side. "It sounds severe."

"But it's treatable, right?" I ask. That's all I want to know. I need to know she'll be okay.

She stares at me with a terrifying sadness in her big brown eyes, and my stomach wants to climb out of my throat.

"All we can do is wait," she says. "I've started her on some antibiotics—"

"Antibiotics!" I say.

I don't mean to raise my voice, but now I know it's *really* bad. Antibiotics are only given as a last resort in Eden. A few women have died because Dr. Lewis didn't want to give them antibiotics right away. She wanted to wait it out, not realizing how bad the infection had spread. She also rarely ever gives it to adults. It's one of her rules. Kids always come first; they have weaker immune systems.

Some women resent her for this, and I don't

blame them, but at the same time, there's only so much she can do. She doesn't have any fancy equipment like the hospitals had. And she's a great doctor, but she isn't perfect. She makes mistakes like anyone else.

"She needs help fighting the infection," she says. "They're strong antibiotics, so if they're working, we'll know within the next twenty-four hours."

My mind's racing all over the place. This can't be happening, can it? Only a few weeks ago, Emily started popping up into my cell to chat. And now, almost as if out of nowhere, she's lying on her deathbed.

"You should let her rest," Dr. Lewis says. She forces a big white smile. "I'll keep an eye on her. Don't you worry."

How can I not worry? I am worried.

I'm beyond terrified to lose my new best friend.

CHAPTER 21 – GABRIEL

The shortest of the bunch looks like she wants to either kill me or have her way with me. I can't tell which. I swallow hard and throw my bag over my shoulder. Freyda gave it to me. There's a knife in there, a blanket, some medical supplies, a lot of water, which is making it heavy, and a lot of food. Mostly fruits, vegetables, and nuts. I'll have to manage how I eat them carefully, so they don't spoil.

It looks like a military bag or a giant hiking bag. The women, including the shortest, all have bags too, but theirs don't look as heavy. I don't blame them for taking advantage of my size. Besides, these women probably haven't walked more than a mile in the last five years.

I look down at their feet. They all did as told and found comfortable pairs of waterproof boots, either from storage or from friends in Eden. I also asked them to bring a set of sneakers to keep in their bags. Weather is unpredictable, and so is life. If something happens to their boots, they need a backup plan.

"Can we do a little roundtable kind of thing?" I ask.

No one looks impressed with me. There're four of

them forming a crescent moon beside Freyda. *The best of the best*, Freyda told me.

Freyda lets out a soft breath and points at the shortest one first, the one who was giving me the *look*. She has dirty blond hair with a few gray strands pulled into a tight ponytail, blue eyes that look grayer than stone, and prominent blotchy freckles that run across both her cheeks. She looks like the short and feisty kind. She's sporting a black vest with wide pockets (something that looks like it came off a man) and baggy cargo pants.

"This is Dakota," Freyda says, and Dakota crosses her arms over her chest and raises her chin.

I try to smile, but my lips barely move. There isn't much I can do about getting these women to like me, and to be honest, I don't much care to. I'm here to bring them to Area 82. Not to make friends.

"She's our pilot," Freyda adds. "Thirty years of experience flying anything and everything. And this right here"—she sticks a thumb out sideways—"is Miller. She's ex-military."

She looks ex-military, too, and is wearing what I assume is her old gear: camouflage pants and a thick cargo jacket with black stitching. Her hair is shorter than everyone else's, and it suits her. It's light brown with shaggy waves that hang right above her eyebrows and over her ears. Although she's thin, she also looks tall and strong. She could probably take someone out with one swing. She places two veiny hands on her waist and gives me a proud grin.

"Sixteen years of service," she says.

I don't know what to say, so I don't say anything

and move my attention over to the next woman.

"That's Jada," Freyda says. "She was on the police force with me." She reaches out and squeezes Jada's shoulder.

The woman doesn't look much older than Freyda. She has smooth dark skin, short fuzzy brown hair, and piercing eyes that look like roasted almonds. She smirks, her plush lips curving up under her small nose, but I know the smile was intended for Freyda.

"And that right there," Freyda says, pointing at the woman at the end of the line, "is Yael."

I can't tell what nationality she is. She's tall, almost as tall as me, with thick curly black hair that reaches the middle of her back and angular eyes that are a yellowish green and look like snake eyes. They complement her rich, olive complexion. Her face, too, is stunning and perfectly symmetrical with thick red lips and nicely arched eyebrows. Her jeans look like they've been worn a thousand times, and her shirt is full of dirt stains. Over it, she wears a brown leather jacket that hangs open in the middle. She stares at me, her lips sealed shut. I'm assuming she's the strong, silent type.

I want to ask her what her background is because she isn't saying anything, but every time I open my mouth, I piss someone off. It's best I focus on the mission rather than the team.

Freyda reaches for the door switch, the one that opens Eden's front gates, I'm assuming, then glances back at all of us. "Everyone ready?"

* * * * * *

"Are you ready?"

The little boy nods with tears streaming down his face. Even though he says he's ready, I know he isn't. No one's ready for pain. Not to this level, anyway. The kid looks like he's six, maybe seven years old. His cheeks are bright red, probably due to the pain, and his black hair is covered in God knows what. It looks like blood, dirt, and ash from a burning building.

I look up at the boy's father. His eyes, which are far apart on his face, are wide open and he's nodding along with his son, almost as if trying to absorb some of his pain. That's what it looks like: he'd do about anything to take away his son's pain.

"There's no other way," I tell him. "Electricity is out, and whether you believe me or not, help isn't coming. If you wait for an ambulance, he'll die."

The father nods, and the little black hairs from his bangs dance on his forehead.

"Is okay, Akeno," he says. His voice sounds like gravel being dumped onto cement. Like he hasn't had a lick of water in days. "Papa right here."

Akeno, the little boy, squints his narrow eyes and squeezes his dad's index finger. I let out a long breath through my nostrils and push away one of the plastic chairs beside me. We're crouched in the middle of a sushi restaurant with a missing roof. At the back of the place, near the kitchen, what I assume were once two massive chrome fridges look like silver puddles of water. Grenades and gunfire likely tore this place apart.

"H-h-he was with me. Today only," the father says. "His mother went to protest. He taken out of school because he a boy. I-I-I don't know how this happened."

He sniffles and wipes his nose with the back of his torn sleeve. He has a sangria-colored apron on, so I'm assuming he's the cook or the owner.

"This isn't your fault," I say, staring the father in the eyes. I then pull at the bottom of his apron and turn my attention to the boy. "Akeno, I want you to put this in your mouth, okay?"

The boy doesn't question anything I say. He knows I'm trying to help. He nods again so fast that it's hard to tell if he moved or if he's shaking. The father looks confused, but he doesn't say anything either as his son bites down on the end of his apron. Instead, he runs his hands over his face and through his hair.

I glance down at the boy's leg, which is now turning a deep shade of purple. I managed to wrap some rope around his thigh to cut off circulation to control the bleeding. I firmly rest my fingers on his knee and apply a bit of pressure, so his leg doesn't kick up when I go in to get what's left of the bullet. It looks like it split inside. There's a hole right through the boy's thigh, which is no bigger than my forearm, but inside this hole, I can see a piece of bullet fragment beside his femur bone, which is also damaged.

"This is going to hurt," I tell the boy, but all he does is keep nodding. His eyes are so full of tears I can barely see the shape of his iris, and his red-lipped mouth looks like a slimy piece of raw salmon. I look up at the father again. "Make sure you hold him down."

I reach for the bright green bottle of sake beside me. I grabbed it from the kitchen before laying the boy down. There's Japanese writing on its white label, and although I can't tell what the alcohol percentage is, I'm sure it's high enough. I'd have preferred vodka or whiskey, but this Japanese wine will do.

Most people associate wound disinfection with strong booze, but Sabin, one of our military medics, is the one who taught me that even wine serves its purpose. I didn't believe him until he told me Hippocrates, one of the most celebrated Greek physicians of all time, believed this, too.

If some famous Greek guy believed it, then so do I.

I crack the seal and twist the cap off, and a cool mist licks the bottle's lip and collar before slithering its way into the air. I reposition myself so that my weight rests on my other knee, then apply even more pressure to the boy's leg because I know he's going to kick.

There's no point counting down, either. In one rapid motion, I tilt the bottle nearly upside down and the fluid pours all over his leg, mixing with the blood and creating a pink layer on his skin.

He lets out a scream so loud that even his father flinches. He looks so helpless, fidgeting where he sits, wanting to save his boy but knowing that there's no easy way out. A few voices erupt behind me, but I pay no attention to them. I'm assuming people are watching through the restaurant's busted windows.

I don't even realize the boy stopped screaming until the father starts shouting in Japanese. I can't understand anything he's saying, but he's no longer holding his song, and he's making sporadic gestures around his face. He keeps pointing at his son, who looks dead with his chalky white face and now colorless lips that are parted a bit and forming a small black crack.

"It's okay," I say, and I raise a flat palm in the air as the universal sign of submission or peace. "He's alive."

This seems to work. The father starts to calm down, his breaths short and shallow.

"It was too much pain," I say. "He passed out."

The father cocks a curly-haired eyebrow, so I place my two sake-soaked hands together and rest my face on them as the universal symbol for sleep.

"He okay!" the father shouts.

"Yes," I say. "Yes, he's okay. But I need to move fast before he wakes up."

I don't think he understood me. He's too panicked right now, so without wasting any more time, I rinse my finger off with some more of the sake, then stick my wine-soaked finger into the wound, feeling around for any metal shards. I'd much have preferred a nice clean pair of tweezers, but I'm not exactly in a medical facility. I'm doing the best I can.

I feel his femur bone, then some nerves and warm muscle tissue, until finally, something hard and sharp-edged pokes the tip of my finger.

"Got it!"

I reposition myself on both my knees now, my back hunched and my face nearly touching the boy's leg. I can't seem to pull it up with my finger. It's too big, and the wound is too small, so instead, I push. If I can get it out through the wound, I'm happy with that.

Then, I hear it. It ticks against the floor underneath his leg.

"You got it!" the father exclaims.

I pour what's left of the sake into the boy's gunshot wound and sit back, my bloody hands dangling over my knees. A few people start entering the restaurant looking like a pack of wild deer, their eyes bulging, their stances cautious.

I look up at the curious crowd. "I need one of you to find me a needle and some thread."

CHAPTER 22 – EVE

"How're my lovely ladies doing?" I ask, stepping foot inside Mavis and Perula's Herb Shack. I despise being in here—it always smells of moisture and dirt. To make matters worse, Mavis and Perula aren't known for their cleanliness. I glance at the ceiling, observing the dozens of spiderwebs that have accumulated this summer alone.

Would it kill them to take a broomstick to it once in a while?

I inhale deeply and focus on the present moment before me. I need to be here. If I sit in my room, overthinking that Freyda is gone, and the way I told her to leave, I'll fall into a depression so deep I fear I may never come out of it.

I know myself, and I know what my mind is capable of.

"Eve!" Mavis shouts, resembling a five-year-old girl welcoming her friends to her at-home birthday party. She wiggles her fingers at me. "Come, come!"

Perula, always the more rational of the two, rolls her eyes and smirks. I'm certain that whatever Mavis is about to show me, Perula has had to hear about it hundreds of times.

I join Mavis at her giant pot—it looks a bit like a witch's cauldron now that I think of it.

"Just came in from its daily dose of sunshine," she says, gently rubbing her fingers along its leaves. She's being so cautious as if it were a newborn baby in need of special care.

Although I could care less about plants, I force a smile, letting it linger on my face longer than necessary. "What is it?"

Her eyes widen at me and her nostrils double in size. Mavis isn't a model to begin with, but when she makes ugly faces, she looks exactly like a witch found in children's books. All she's missing is a wart on her nose or her chin.

"It's for your tea, you silly crackle-pot!"

"My tea—" But I cut myself short when I realize what she's talking about. I was so preoccupied with Freyda that I completely forgot about my Devil's tea, and how Mavis warned me that our supply was running extremely low. The whole point of letting Gretchin and those women out of Eden—the whole reason they were attacked—was in part because I wanted more of this plant.

I take a step forward, the fake smile on my face stretching into a genuine grin. "We have more?"

She throws a protective arm around her plant and bares her teeth at me. "Careful!" she hisses. "It isn't ready."

"How long?" I ask.

"A few more weeks," Perula says from the comfort of her wooden rocking chair. She taps her fingers over her knees, then leans back and places both arms on the armrests.

It's hard to believe these two are twins. They're not only complete opposites, they barely look alike in their older age, which I'm assuming is the result of life: scars, skincare, weight. Perula's frail figure looks like it might break if she tries to stand.

"Maybe a month," Mavis adds. "One long trickidity month of babyin' this thing and we'll have Devil's tea up to our yang-yangs!" She then smacks the table and lets out a loathsome laugh, her front teeth sticking over her lower jaw. "We'll be floatin' in tea!"

I glance back at Perula, who has that same smirk on her face—the one that says "Mavis will be Mavis." I never understand Mavis's jokes, but I do my best to laugh whenever possible, even though it drains me every time.

* * * * * *

This is draining. How much longer is she going to keep rummaging through everything?

"What did you expect? A five-star hotel?" Freyda asks, slouching forward as she searches through the desk's drawers in what is apparently going to be my new office.

"I didn't expect anything," I say.

She glances up at me and blows a breath up into the air when a scraggly hair falls out of her ponytail, tickling her lip. I don't think she realizes how uncertain I am about this entire thing. And for some reason, I'm not afraid to admit it to Freyda. Out of everyone I've led to Eden, she's the one person who won't judge me for being human.

"You're scared, huh?" she asks.

I can admit uncertainty, but I'll never admit fear. I cock an eyebrow at her, almost as if to say, "How dare you insinuate that I'm afraid... I, the one who murdered the president of the United States."

She closes the door and raises her hands, palms facing me. "All right, all right, you're not scared."

She straightens her posture and tucks her thumbs into her belt, letting her hands dangle over her hips. She does this often, and I'm not quite sure why. It's a posture of pure confidence, though.

"Can I ask how old you are?" she says.

I nearly glare at her, but I bottle my emotions instead and plop myself down onto the office chair.

"What does it matter how old I am?" I ask.

I'm not trying to be defensive, but the last thing I need is for someone to undermine me because of my age.

"I'm just curious," she says. "You look young, and to be honest, I'm surprised you're able to be so levelheaded about everything that's happened. What's your past? What'd you do before all of this?"

She's searching through another drawer now as if she thinks she'll find something other than cobwebs or old chips of paint.

"You ask a lot of questions," I say.

She rests her arms over her puffed-out chest and looks at me with her nose high in the air. "And you don't answer any of them."

I hate the way she's looking at me—as if I'm a lesser being than her. Who does she think she is?

"What're you, a cop? Am I being interrogated, or

something?"

She scoffs and closes the drawer, its wheels scraping against the old track. "Actually, yeah, I am—well, I used to be. You know... Before all of this."

I part my lips to speak, but nothing comes out. I wasn't expecting for her to *actually* be a cop. Is that why she's following me around? Does she know what I did? Am I under investigation? All I wanted was a bit of space to myself, away from all the women who are waiting for my guidance.

I don't know what I'm doing. I thought I did, but I don't.

"What's up with you?" she asks. "You look all sketched out." She smirks up at me. "Are you hiding drugs?"

"What? No," I blurt.

"Relax," she says. "Do you honestly think the law matters anymore?"

She moves toward the window—a translucent glass caked with dust and covered with black iron bars. There's barely any sunlight coming through, so I don't know what she's looking at.

"We're screwed, Eve," she says without looking back at me. Letting out a sigh, she wraps her fingers around the filthy metal and turns her head sideways to see me from her peripheral—from her one blue eye that looks gray due to the natural light shining in. "I heard some rumors... About what happened in the White House."

I swallow hard, my gaze never leaving her one bright eye.

"Rumors are rumors, Eve, but if what I heard is

true, you're the only one who can save these women."

She turns around and places her thumbs into her belt again and stares at me. "I asked your age because you look pretty young. You look like someone who isn't equipped to lead hundreds of women. I don't know what your background is, but I doubt it's extensive. Maybe you were studying in university… Maybe you had some part-time job. I don't know. But honestly, it doesn't matter. Whether or not you see it yet, there's a leader inside of you who hasn't come out yet. At least not entirely." She lets out a chuckle and scratches her eyebrow. "You didn't even know where you were going, and you convinced hundreds of women to follow you. That says something. So whatever doubt you're feeling… whatever is draining you emotionally… let it go. Be the leader you think these women want, and with time, that's exactly who you'll become."

* * * * * *

"Ain't she a beaut?" Mavis says.

I shoot her a glance—is she still talking?

"Where'd ya go, your scrumptious majesty?" she asks.

I let out a soft laugh and wince. "Majesty, huh?"

"What else ya want me to call you? Queen?"

"How about Eve?" I ask.

Any other day, I'd have become enthralled by her casual use of the term majesty. But today, as I think of Freyda and how terrified I was when we first arrived in Eden, I'm reminded that I'm nothing more than a human being.

I'm reminded that I'm Eve Malum—Mila's big sister.

"It is beautiful, Mavis," I say, returning my attention to her sprouting plant. I gently touch her rounded shoulder. "Thank you."

She parts her rotten-toothed mouth and stares at me with big bug eyes. "Uh, y-you're welcome."

Am I so cruel to her that she's taken aback when I show her kindness?

"Really," I add, gazing around the Herb Shack. For the first time, the humid scent of live plants and dirt does not repulse me. I admire every inch of this cabin—all the work and dedication that has been put into creating such a healing space. "You ladies are doing such a wonderful job here."

Neither one responds. They're obviously taken aback by my change in behavior. But everything is so clear to me now. Why haven't I shown them the love they deserve?

Then, I hear my mother's voice creep in. "Eve, have you taken your medication? You're going manic again."

I shake these thoughts away. This isn't my mood disorder—it can't be. This feeling is far too real to be something produced by a chemical imbalance in my brain. When Gabriel and Freyda get back, everything will change. Everything...

A loud knock at the Herb Shack's big wooden door shakes me from my trance.

CHAPTER 23 – LUCY

Perula's eyeball is the first thing I see in the crack of the door. Within seconds, she pulls the door wide open and lets out a chuckle.

"Oh, goodness, it's just you, Lucy. Why did you knock?"

"Why did I knock?" I ask. "You locked the—" but I can't even finish my sentence. I can't believe what I'm seeing. In the middle of the Herb Shack, standing beside Mavis at her cauldron is Eve.

What the hell is Eve doing here? I want to hate her, to glare at her until she walks away without saying a word, but I can't. Why can't I be mad at her? It's... It's that smile.

"Oh, my sweet little Lucy!" she shouts, rushing her way around the table and joining me at the front door.

I almost step back outside, freaked out by her over-the-top happiness, but I can't move. I'm stuck, almost as if I've made eye contact with Medusa.

"Where have you been?" she asks, wrapping a cold arm around my shoulder. I wince as she pulls me into her chest and my cheek presses up against her soft breast. I don't even know what to say.

What the heck does she expect from me? She's acting like the last five years never happened. In fact, she's acting like she used to before Mom died, or even before Mila died. After her sister died, that's when she changed.

But right now, with that big goofy grin on her face, she looks like Aunty Eve. A lump forms in my throat. Am I dreaming? This is who I've always wanted… the same Aunty Eve who was there for me like she used to be. The Aunty Eve who was happy to see me and tell me jokes when no one was around, even though they weren't age-appropriate. She never viewed me as "just a kid."

I was always equal.

So, who is she now? Why is this happening? A person doesn't go from being dark and cold to rainbows and sunshine overnight. What happened? Mom told me about her mood disorder when I was young. She only told me because sometimes I wouldn't see Aunty Eve for weeks at a time, and Mom had to explain to me that Eve was *depressed*.

I didn't understand it at that age, but when Mom died, I finally understood what it meant to be depressed.

"Oh God, Lucy, you've gotten so big."

I want to cry, scream, and hug her all at the same time. She's genuinely happy to see me; I can see it in her eyes, a look I never thought I'd see again. And although part of me hates her for what she's put me through, for whatever she said to Nola, deep down, I miss her.

I've always missed my Aunty Eve.

I glance over at Perula who seems as perplexed as me. She doesn't know that Eve's my godmother—all they know is that Eve led me to Eden, hand in hand, which means we have a special bond. And although Perula knows something is up, she doesn't know what. It's like she wants to give me the answers I need, but she doesn't have them. So instead, she offers me a meek smile.

Eve's warm lips suddenly kiss me on the forehead; then she pulls away and lets out an excited laugh.

"I've been so caught up in my own head, Lucy." She leans forward, her bright eyes inches away from mine. They look like crystal marbles soaked in water. Her nose is pink, and she sniffles. "Oh God, Lucy... I'm so sorry."

My jaw hangs open. I've never been so speechless before. I can't say anything. I can barely even think.

She squeezes my shoulders, then wipes a tear away from the corner of her eye.

"How do you like it here?" she asks, her gaze shifting to the ceiling and around the Herb Shack. "Are you happy? Are you learning new things? If this isn't the job you want—"

"I like it," I blurt out.

I honestly don't know what to think. Is this some sort of mind game? I know Eve didn't want me to become a Healer. Is that why she's so eager to push me out? Or is she genuinely checking up on me? Why else would she be crying? There's real emotion in there. I can see it. I can see her: Aunty Eve.

I want to wrap my arms around her so badly, but

I'm scared that if I do, she'll evaporate into nothingness because none of this is even real. Then, I'll wake up alone in my room, with specks of dust floating around me.

"What's the matter, Lucy?" she asks.

I can't talk.

"I know this is a bit of a shock," she says, "but it's me." She narrows her eyes and her lips form a thin, flat line. She's staring into me so intently, wanting me to believe every word she says. "I see things differently now, Lucy. I've been... I've been so depressed."

My defense begins to crumble. Is Eve honestly admitting to being depressed? Eve Malum, leader of Eden, wouldn't admit to that. Aunty Eve, though, would. At least to me, or to people she feels safe with.

"I know it doesn't excuse how I've treated you," she says, "but I want to make things right. I want to be the caregiver Ophelia would've wanted me to be."

The tears are trying to squeeze their way out of my eyes, and I swallow hard. I don't want to cry... I won't cry. I'm not letting her manipulate me again.

"Take all the time you need, Lucy Doll," she says, and my heart shatters. She hasn't called me Lucy Doll since I was seven or eight years old. She always used to call me that. "I'll be around," she continues. "If you ever need anything at all, come to me. You can come see me anytime, okay?"

That smile is back on her face, revealing a set of surprisingly white teeth. I'm sure she's been busy keeping up with personal hygiene. If she can manage to keep her suits looking so white, she can keep her teeth clean. I breathe in, and a fresh powdery smell fills my nose.

"You two," she adds, standing up as though she's about to scold them for something. That's what she always does. "Thank you again for all your hard work. You're both amazing."

I'm left standing stiff as Aunty Eve walks around me, the tips of her fingers brushing along my neck and through the back of my hair. Right before walking out, she leans over me, and her hot breath warms the top of my head. I pull my shoulders back and stare straight ahead, my eyes probably looking like they're on the verge of falling out.

But she doesn't hurt or threaten me. Instead, she presses her lips against my head and lets out a long breath that sends goose bumps down my back. "I love you, Lucy."

I'm too shocked to say it back. So instead, I stare at the back wall of the Herb Shack feeling like my wide eyes are going to crisp into little raisins. The sound of her heels stepping off the wood and onto the grass outside the cabin lets me know she's gone.

The atmosphere is so oppressive and surreal that I have to inhale deeply to make sure I'm still breathing. Perula doesn't say anything, either. It's like she's waiting for me to explain what happened.

"Well, hotcakes in a toaster!" Mavis blurts out, and my shoulders flinch forward.

I glare at her. Why does she always open her big mouth like that when everything is so quiet?

"Now where's ma mixelator?" she continues,

huffing and puffing around the table. She ducks, pops back up, then disappears again, her pointed nose nearly hitting the tabletop every time.

I glance at Perula who's now sewing what looks like a wrist or ankle support made out of hemp and wooden slabs. She doesn't have to do that. Make medical equipment, I mean. But Perula likes to help with anything she can, and the other day, she overheard Dr. Lewis saying we had run out of support bands for the kids. Technically, the responsibility falls on Sahana, since she's the one who makes all the clothes, blankets, and whatever else requires material. But she's been way too busy.

Kids are either outgrowing their clothes or ripping them when playing outside. I've asked her for a favor once or twice myself, but it wasn't for new clothing, it was to fix a hole I'd found in my jeans. Some people do that, too. Ask her to fix outsider clothes.

I can't even remember why I came here, to the Herb Shack. I'm too caught up in my own head about what happened a moment ago.

"I-I'm gonna get some air," I say.

Perula nods but doesn't look up, and Mavis is still storming around the Herb Shack looking for something she lost. That woman is always losing something. I'd say she often loses her mind, too, but I think she lost that a long time ago.

I creak the big wooden door open and step out onto the fluffy grass like I'm floating with clouds beneath my sneakers. I cast my eyes toward the ground. Although the grass is thick and soft-looking, it's turning a dark shade of green. It isn't bright like it usually is in the summer—a neon green, almost.

Then, something tickles the side of my cheek and lands on my shoulder, covering it entirely. I pluck it off and twirl it in between my thumb and index finger. It's a bright red big-leaf maple leaf, and its edges have already started to crisp.

I close my eyes tight and breathe in the cool, late-summer air. It smells of moist grass, blossomed flowers, and an unidentifiable sweetness, all in combination with the subtle scent of manure. The unusual part is, I don't mind it at all. I kind of enjoy it. Besides, I love Pearl, Freyda's horse. Everyone loves her. It's cute how she actually looks like a Pearl, too, with her shiny white-and-cream coat and gold mane. Freyda told me what she was once, but I can't remember... A teke-something.

Where is Freyda, anyways? I haven't seen her today. She's usually always by Eve's side. I wonder if this has to do with the man hiding in the basement. Or, is something else going on? I did overhear Mavis and Perula talking about moving to a new Eden. Is that where Freyda is? Looking for new territory? And if so, why didn't she take Pearl?

Maybe she didn't want to take her away from Eden because they're using her manure as organic fertilizer, and Pearl also keeps the grass short. Or, maybe I'm completely paranoid, and Freyda's still inside Eden somewhere.

I'm about to go back into the Herb Shack when I hear something I haven't heard in a long time—a crowd laughing. Not just one or two people, but an entire crowd. I turn my head toward the noise and spot dozens of women and children gathered around one of the garden beds.

But in the middle of this group is one person who is impossible to miss. Her bright white overcoat and white pants shine right through, like a highlighter in a pile of black and blue pens. She's waving her arms animatedly over her head, and her face is glowing so much she doesn't even look like herself.

From where I'm standing, it looks like she's telling a joke. I step a bit closer, trying to catch what's going on.

"And rumor has it..." Eve says. She's shouting for everyone to hear her, and the crowd is getting bigger. "That the monster turned into a fairy!"

Everyone bursts out laughing again, and some of the kids are so excited they wrap their arms around their mothers' waists and tug on their clothes. A few years ago, some of these kids were only reaching their mothers' legs.

I don't realize how close I've gotten until Eve's bright eyes turn my way and I stop moving entirely.

"Lucy, my love," she shouts with a grin so wide I can see every single one of her teeth. "Come join us!" She waves excitedly toward herself.

Although part of me is screaming to run the other way, the other part is yearning to stay.

She looks so happy.

Everyone looks so happy, and all I want to do is be happy with them.

"Coming," I say.

CHAPTER 24 – GABRIEL

"How far is this place, exactly?" Freyda asks.

I look away from my compass and stretch my neck to the side until I hear a soothing crack. "Close to three hundred miles, give or take. I thought Eve caught you up on this whole thing."

She avoids eye contact, which I'm assuming means something happened between her and Eve.

"Don't worry," I say. "We'll take breaks as often as possible."

She doesn't look convinced. I know Freyda's a strong woman, but realizing we have to walk for over a week is probably sinking in for her at last. And it's not because she's lazy or unfit, either. It's because it fucking hurts. I know the drill. Your feet start to ache, then your heels and ankles start to burn and chafe, but you keep walking. And the more you walk, the more blisters you get. It's when those nasty things start popping and peeling that the real fun starts.

My feet are so full of callouses it doesn't faze me anymore, but after the war, I walked more than I did in my entire military career. I can't even remember how long I walked before finally sleeping. I'm sure I did, otherwise, I'd be dead, but everything is one big blur. There were so many people crying out for help, and all I wanted to do was get away from it all.

I stare straight ahead and wince. The sun is strong and hot, making me sweat like crazy in my heavy boots. The wind is cool though, so it balances things out nicely. If we were in the middle of the summer, we'd be covered from head to toe, making our trip even more uncomfortable. I've seen some of the most disgusting sunburns over the last few years. It's like people think that being unable to find sunscreen means their bodies will adjust to the rays.

It doesn't work that way.

It's sad how so many lives have been lost because people simply don't know. They don't have the internet to guide them anymore. Hell, I was guilty of that, too. Mama used to make fun of me for always researching everything online. Didn't believe something? You'd look it up. When Bill E-02 was passed, though, everyone trusted the internet. Why? It became illegal to post anything that wasn't true without clearly stating that it was meant to be irony or a joke. The government even designed banners for people to use on their fake news sites, and if they didn't use them, they'd be shut down within a matter of twenty-four hours. Not only that, but they'd be charged for it.

I'm glad the internet's gone. It pissed me off that the government stepped in like that, took control over everything. Big sites, the ones generating money, had to pay "rent" to be online. I don't remember how much it was or how many people were affected. It pissed off a lot of people. The worst part of it, though, was having to use your PI Chip to maintain any kind of online space. That's short for Personal Identification Chip. We weren't allowed PI Chips in the military, but most of the population ended up getting one. Why not? It was implanted in your wrist, so no one could see it (aside from the tiny white scar), and you could use it for payments, identification, starting your car, unlocking your house door... Pretty much anything and everything. The only thing people didn't know was that the chip had a hidden location sensor in it. In other words, it could track anyone at any time. Rumors got out like they always do, but both the manufacturer and the government kept denying it. But we knew... The military, I mean.

So, the idea of restricting online maintenance and page creation to people registered with these Chips was pretty smart if you ask me. Online fraud and crime went down by 98 percent. The only people who were able to bypass this whole Chip thing were the crazy hackers, and let's face it, hackers are too smart to be wasting their time sending out fake emails from financial institutions. They had better things to do, like trying to hack the White House's security system.

I turn around when I hear someone breathing loud. It's Dakota, the short one with blond hair and gray strands. She stretches her neck from side to side until something cracks, then aggressively wipes the sweat from her heavily freckled face. We've only been walking for three hours. What's her problem?

“We’re not all ex-military,” she says, her face barely moving. It’s obvious she takes herself seriously.

I look at her boots, a pair of brown leather ones she must have plucked off someone on her way to Eden. They kind of look like men’s boots, too. They probably aren’t as comfortable as she thought they’d be, and they were probably sitting in some dusty closet for the last five years, up until today.

“You guys do realize I’m not an engineer, right?” she says. She looks like she wants to smack someone across the face. Her neck is blotchy and red, and her round nostrils flare out so wide her nose looks like its twice its usual size.

“I have some background,” Yael says. It’s the first time I hear her voice. It’s deep, but the attractive kind of deep, and she has an accent that rolls off the tip of her tongue. It suits that perfectly symmetrical face of hers.

Dakota cocks a blond, barely visible eyebrow. “Some background?” she sneers.

Obviously, Dakota was voluntold into coming along on this trek. She doesn’t want to be here. She probably thinks this whole thing is a waste of time, or that she’s been asked to sacrifice her life, which is understandable. We’re going into this blind for the most part (well, they are), and she hasn’t left Eden for five years. I can see why she’d be reluctant to follow along.

Yael stares at her but doesn’t answer. It’s like she doesn’t have to justify herself to anyone, which is pretty admirable.

Dakota shakes her head and whips a hand in the air as if to say, "Whatever, doesn't matter."

She starts searching through the pockets in her black vest and cargo pants like a smoker looking for their pack of cigarettes. Now that I think of it, it looks like her entire wardrobe was taken off a dead guy. There's absolutely nothing feminine about her. Not that I care. Clothes are clothes.

And now that I think of cigarettes. Jesus Christ. How did Eve manage to keep an entire society of women sane after the revolution? I mean, realistically, some of them had to be smokers. Last I heard, smokers in America made up something like 20 percent of the population. And I know what withdrawal does to people, let alone a group of women stuck together. Emotions were probably already high. Then again, I'm sure a bunch of men together wouldn't be any better. They'd probably fight like a bunch of anxious chimpanzees. Funny how that works... We're so primitive by nature, which serves a purpose, and women are sensitive and empathetic, which also serves a purpose. Together, we can be pretty great, but all we do is point out each other's flaws or try to prove which gender is better than the other.

No wonder our world's gone to shit. Men and women have always been at war in some way, and things finally blew up. It was bound to happen.

"What're you looking for?" Miller asks. She stretches her neck over Dakota's shoulder, her short shaggy brown hair dancing over her dark eyebrows.

Dakota swings a shoulder away from Miller,

who's so much taller, she towers over her. "None of your business."

Miller smiles and salutes her. "All right, pilot."

I take it she's the patient type. It's funny how the stereotypes are usually true. Not always, but often. Short and feisty, then there's your gentle giant. I smirk at this because I like to see myself as a gentle giant. Don't get me wrong, I'll tear someone's throat out if it's deserved, but for the most part, I'm pretty patient, and I'm a nice guy. Then, I think of my mama. I can't think of anyone feistier than her, and she was so petite her forehead came up to my chest.

I can't think of her too long, or I'll picture her body lying in her living room, underneath a bunch of rubble. That thought destroys me, so I've been doing everything I can to pretend it never happened. Maybe if I keep lying to myself, I'll start to believe that Mama is somewhere safe and her house didn't crumble on top of her because of this war.

Dakota lets out a sigh, and I look up in time to catch her smudging what looks like lip balm on her lips. I say lip balm, but it looks more like a container of beeswax or something.

"All that panic for lip balm?" Jada chimes in. She purses her thick dark lips and smirks, revealing a sharp canine tooth that looks like something out of a vampire movie. The sun is beaming down hard on her face, casting a smooth warm brown color on her cheeks, and she squints.

Dakota glares at Jada like she's a complete moron who's too stupid to understand anything in life. What's her deal, anyway? I get that she doesn't want to be here, but why's she so damn cranky?

"Look," I cut in, and Freyda seems relieved. It's like she wanted to take charge, but at the same time, didn't have the energy to get involved in a petty argument. "I know some of you don't want to be here—"

"Not with you," Dakota cuts in.

"Give the man a break," Miller says. "He's trying to help."

Dakota spins around and fastens her stubby hands on her waist. "How the fuck you do you know?"

"Eve told us," Freyda says, and everyone goes quiet.

Eve's name seems to be a powerful thing among these women. It's like whenever she's mentioned or even thought about, people listen. They follow like a bunch of sheep.

"We're doing this for Eve, and for Eden," Freyda continues. "I'm tired too, okay? It's not like I've been running marathons, preparing for some week-long trip. My legs are killing me, and my back is getting sore. We're human. That's going to happen."

"Should've brought your horse," Dakota mutters through a scoff.

Freyda crosses her arms. It's obvious she's pretty defensive about her horse. "Pearl wouldn't have handled this any more than any of you. She's not built for traveling long distances."

"All right, all right," I say, hoping to ease some of the tension. "We're stuck with each other for the next few days, whether you like it or not. No one said this would be easy or that we'd come out of it in one piece. We're taking a chance, here. You heard Eve yourself. Eden isn't going to survive much longer. You're limited on resources and running out of space."

No one says anything, so I'm assuming they agree with me.

"Like I said," I continue, "we'll stop whenever we can and try to make this as comfortable as possible."

To my surprise, Dakota doesn't scoff this time. She nods and wipes a line of sweat from her freckled face. "You're right. I'm sorry. I'm just... I'm so tired, you know? Fuck. I'm tired of everything. This is such a nightmare. I try to put a smile on for Eve, for everyone... But I'm fucking miserable. Aren't you?" She eyes the other women, and although they seem to understand exactly what she's saying, they don't respond. "Eve's not around," she adds as if this will somehow make them open up. But when they still don't say anything, she lets out a long breath. "I think we can do better. And I do want to go to this place." She looks up at me, her head completely tilted back." But I don't want to get my hopes up." She turns her attention back to the women. "Some man appears in Eden, and all of a sudden, we're going to some new place? Some safe location? It doesn't add up, I'm sorry."

She shakes her head and raises a stiff hand in the air like she's getting ready to slap away any argument we might have.

"And to be honest," she cuts in before anyone can say something, "I don't fucking trust you." Now, she points at my face. “For all I know, you’re taking us to some group of men, and we’re going to spend the rest of our lives being fucking beaten and raped. I’d rather suffer in Eden.”

I part my lips, but Freyda steps in. “Dakota, it isn’t like that. You have my word.”

“Your word?” Dakota spits. “How’s your *word*”—she makes air quotes—“going to protect us?”

“Freyda’s always protected us,” Jada says. Her soft-eyed look is gone now, and her eyebrows almost touch over that black button nose of hers.

I can tell she and Freyda are good friends. Two seconds ago, she looked like the most gentle out of the bunch, but now she’s ready to kick some ass. There’s that police side. She must’ve made a good cop.

Dakota throws her arms in the air, obviously too flustered to deal with any of this. She storms off past me like she knows where she’s going and mutters, “Nightmare... A fucking nightmare.”

* * * * * *

What a fucking nightmare.

I squeeze my way through the crowd, wincing as elbows and shoulders hit me in the chest and back. I need to get the hell out of here. I push through one final wave of people and rush into an old cobblestone alleyway. The stones are shiny, almost black, due to the downpour.

People are shouting over one another, trying to get an answer, while others are trying to maintain order. There’s no order, and there won’t be. Not anymore. People (men, women, and children) are crowded around a group of female police officers who are standing in front of their cruisers.

"Please, everyone, return to your homes and wait for help to arrive!" one of them shouts, but the officer's voice barely carries through the shouts and rainfall.

Doesn't she know what's going on? Wasn't she informed about the EMP attack? That power isn't coming back at all? I get that radio communication is off the table now, but you'd think as a woman, she'd have known about... Well, now that I think of it, the women... The ones I saw in the White House, were probably part of some underground resistance. It's not like they communicated their plan to the whole nation. If they had, maybe some sense would've been knocked into them. Maybe the women of America (like this police officer who's doing all she can to keep everyone calm) would have put a stop to it. There's no way that all women wanted this to happen. No one wants to go back to the dark ages.

On the other hand, groups of enraged individuals can cause a lot of damage. Especially big groups that operate on such an advanced level. I wonder how many people were involved in the resistance.

"We're working on getting the power grid back up," the police officer says. Poor woman. She looks like she's ready for retirement with her short gray hair and pudgy belly. She's trying as hard as she can to make things right, but there's no way she'll be able to.

Not now. Things are too far gone.

The other cop, a younger woman with a nose

ring and tattoos on her fingers, raises an arm in the air to try to silence everyone. It works, for the most part, and the rain sounds louder. It's splashing on stalled cars and slipping into the city sewers.

Why aren't the cars working, anyway? Anyone who's done research on EMP (I did after we learned about them during training) knows that tests were run and proved that this whole idea of everything shutting down might be a myth. But who knows the real answer? I mean, tests can't replicate the real thing. At least not perfectly. How powerful was this damn thing?

I watch the water trickle down into the sewer drain.

Shit.

The drains.

It's only a matter of time before garbage and debris pile up against them and blocks all water from going in. With no garbage collection, people are going to start tossing their junk outside. Nothing's going to be maintained and the more rain the city gets, the faster it'll start flooding.

"We need to stay strong together," the police officer says with her arm still straight above her head.

For a second, it looks like everyone's considering her words, until someone shouts, "People are dying all around us, and you want us to fucking stay strong? Why aren't the ambulances coming? Why isn't there any help? What the fuck are you—"

But the woman breaks off into uncontrollable sobbing.

"There are children!" a man shouts, his voice carrying over the crowd.

Everyone starts yelling again, but not at him... at the police officers. Like they aren't doing enough.

I wonder if male officers will show up. I doubt it if I'm being honest. After everything that's happened, any male authority figure is probably going to be attacked by the citizens. So, these women, even though they probably hate their jobs because of all the bullshit they've had to face over the last year, are still standing here, trying to help people.

"I understand your concern," the young officer says, "but—"

"But what?" a woman shouts. "Hours ago, our city was at war! Where's the fucking president now? What are the authorities doing to make this right? Or is this it? Are we living in some third world country now? Are we still at war? Should we be finding weapons? What the fuck—"

I'm not sticking around to watch this.

I need to get the hell out of here. Turning, I rush down the alleyway, my boots making a slapping noise against the wet cobblestones when I hear a window shatter behind me.

"Hey! You!" the police officer shouts. Her voice sounds croaky and strained, and I can tell it's the older one.

"What're you gonna do?" someone says. "Shoot me? Go ahead!"

Then, more glass shatters and I see people, their clothes like a bunch of jumbled colors, run down the street.

People scream and more glass breaks.

"Family before law!" someone shouts, and it starts a chant.

"Family before law!"

"Family before law!"

Across the road, a man and three women break into what looks like a drug store. The owner, a middle-aged Arab man who looks like he wouldn't harm a fly, is waving his gun at them, but it's obvious he doesn't want to shoot.

Only a few hours into this nightmare, and people are already looting.

* * * * * *

"You trust her to fly a plane?" Yael asks, pulling her thick wavy black hair over one shoulder.

Dakota is at least a yard away from us now, which is pretty stupid. She shouldn't be distancing herself from us. It takes two seconds for someone to fire a shot at her. And if she's seen alone, she's a walking target.

"She's going through a lot," Freyda says.

"We're all going through a lot," Yael says.

Freyda shakes her head. "Not like her. Camille, the young woman who died last month?" she says, and everyone nods. "That was Dakota's daughter. Twenty-six years old. Something to do with an infection of the kidneys."

Yael looks away, probably feeling like an ass for having compared her hardships to a grieving mother's.

"And what she said about being unhappy," Freyda adds. "What's said here, stays here."

I'm about to make some stupid joke about "What's said in a postapocalyptic world stays in a postapocalyptic world," but I don't have time. A loud gunshot suddenly blasts nearby, and I'm pulled back to North Korea. I'm standing behind an electrically engineered blockade, surrounded by a dozen men who smell like three-month-old sweat and dry piss.

We're about to attack, but something's wrong.

"Gabriel!" James shouts.

His ginger hair looks brown and his yellow eyes almost black behind his tinted glass mask. I know it's James because he wears a red emblem on his onyx-colored BIO-8 Skin—a skin-textured armor that engulfs a soldier from the neck and below with the press of a button, providing bulletproof and knife-proof protection. From behind the glass shield over his face, his mouth flaps open and closed. He's yelling at me and pointing behind me. I don't even have the time to turn around when an explosion goes off and I'm propelled in his direction, my body knocking hard against the mud wall beside me. I blink, my ears ringing, and the next thing I know, I'm being dragged through the mud.

I'm assuming it's James and that he's saving my ass, but I can't see anything. There's debris in my eyes and all I smell is burning... Burning wood, burning flesh, burning hair.

"Gabriel!"

I blink hard again and find myself being shoved by Freyda. Her eyes are so big that I panic, thinking another explosion is about to go off.

"Snap the fuck out of it!" she shouts, shoving me

again.

What happened? Where am I?

The gunshot.

Fuck.

I take a few rushed steps toward Dakota, even though I have no idea what I'm running into. I can only assume that someone tried to shoot at her, but I stop myself short when I see Yael coming out of the forest beside us. Her jeans and T-shirt are covered in bloodstains, and she's walking toward us like she just came back from a hike, her shoulders drawn back and her boots kicking through the tall grass. By her hips hang two pointed blades, blood dripping from their tips. She wipes them on her jeans before slipping them back into their holsters.

I glare at her. Not because I'm pissed off, but because I have no idea what the fuck just happened.

"Thanks for the help, Gabriel," she says, her dark eyes aimed my way.

She's barely made any eye contact since I met her, and now she's looking at me like I'm nothing but some piece of shit.

I glance at Freyda and then toward Dakota, who's walking back toward us, fingers pressed firmly against the side of her neck. Was she shot? Is she hurt?

"What happened?" I ask.

"What are you, blind?" Miller says.

That's the first time Miller shows any form of aggression. I took her for the gentle giant kind of woman when I first met her, but it looks to me like she's willing to stand up when the safety of these women is involved.

Jada runs a hand through her dark fuzzy hair and gives me the stink-eye.

I really fucked up.

I'm supposed to be protecting these women and I disappeared on them.

"Three male rebels," Yael says, matter-of-factly. She throws her chin out at Dakota. "They took a shot, but luckily, only nicked her in the neck. We'll have to get that cleaned up."

Dakota's now standing beside me looking pretty unimpressed. It's the kind of look that says, "You're totally useless."

"And what," I say, eyeing Yael, "you took care of it?"

She gives me a full up and down, her chin angle with the ground, and says, "Someone had to."

I shoot Freyda a look, but all she does is glance away and slide her pistol into her holster. I don't even know if she fired shots. I fucking hate this feeling. I hate blacking out.

Who is this Yael? How'd she manage to take on three rebels on her own? She isn't even hurt.

"Where'd you train? You military?" I ask, returning my attention to her.

She cocks an eyebrow, almost in a condescending way, then wipes a speck of blood from her chin. "Was," she says plainly. "Israeli special forces."

CHAPTER 25 – EVE

"Don't be afraid, sweetheart," I say. "She's gentle."

Little Scarlet reaches toward Pearl's muzzle, her mother by her side. She giggles the moment she touches its nostrils and turns around, her big honey-brown eyes glued to her mother with fascination.

The children of Eden know that Pearl is designed for assisting Georgia, the woman responsible for Eden's primary garden, and the horse is not to be approached at any time. She's a wonderful animal and would never harm anyone, but the idea of children frolicking around her isn't something I encourage. When Freyda first introduced Pearl into Eden, a little girl nearly lost her finger, having tried to feed Pearl a bundle of grass when no one was watching.

Now, the children know that unless Freyda or myself are nearby, they should look at Pearl from a distance.

"Beautiful, isn't she?" her mother says, now brushing her fingers against the tip of Pearl's fuzzy, pearl-colored nose.

Scarlet nods then turns her attention to me. "How old is she?"

I smile because I'm reminded of our mornings spent discussing how Eden came to be. Scarlet has always been the most lively and inquisitive child, posing questions about anything she is curious about.

I pet Pearl down her neck and plant a soft kiss on the side of her muzzle. It's warm and softer than a freshly washed fleece blanket. "I don't know all that much about horses," I admit, my words coming out with such liveliness as if I were eighteen years old again and telling little Lucy a story, "but Freyda seems to think Pearl's about eight years old." I stick out two hands, one with all five fingers stretched out, and the other with only three.

The other little girls gasp, and Scarlet turns to her mother again, this time, with a red-lipped grin on her porcelain face. "She's older than me!" she says to her mother.

Her mother smiles, more at me then at Scarlet, and another little girl steps forward.

"And me!" the girl shouts. She smiles so much that her beautiful angular eyes turn into little black lines.

I let out a laugh, and for the first time in a long time, I have nothing but love for these little girls. They are becoming such bright young ladies, and the thought of their development warms my heart. These girls are our future.

They will be the ones to rebuild America years from now—they will be part of something bigger than themselves. This overwhelming feeling of pride causes my throat to swell.

"Did you know that Pearl's grandparents used to be a unicorn?" I say, changing the subject entirely.

Scarlet's eyes widen and her mouth hangs open. "A unicorn?"

"Well," I say, smirking. "There are myths."

"What'th a myth?" asks the little girl standing near Scarlet. She has a lisp that makes her look even more adorable than she already does.

I let out a laugh, and a few of the mothers join in with me.

"A myth," I say, "is a story from a long time ago. Sometimes, these stories even have magic in them."

"Magic!" a few of the girls shout.

I reach for the nearest seat—the side of one of Georgia's garden beds—and sit down. The children circle me and plop themselves down onto the grass. I glance up at Lucy, who is standing uncomfortably with her fingers in her hand, pulling and playing with them.

"Lucy here knows a myth or two," I say, and their little heads move from side to side as they look for Lucy. "I'm sure she'd be happy to share one of her stories."

Seeming uncertain, she stares at me then gazes down at the children as if attempting to assess their level of interest.

I wave toward Lucy and offer her a sweet smile. "Come on, love."

She offers me a brief nod and steps quickly toward me.

I pat the wood by my lap. "You can sit here."

She still seems uncertain. She looks at me as if

I'm a stranger. It's upsetting, though I know this isn't her fault. I've spent the last few years distancing myself from her. It's only natural for her to doubt my intentions.

If only she could read my mind; if only she could see how truly sorry I am for the way I've behaved.

I pat the wood again and give her my Aunty Eve smile—a crooked smirk that playfully says, "Get over here, kid."

It seems to work. The corners of her lips twitch and she joins me on the garden bed. I wrap my arm around her shoulder, and even though she stiffens the moment I touch her, this is the warmest feeling I've had in a long time.

Nothing is going to take this away from me.

* * * * * *

"Still nothing?" I ask.

Freyda shakes her head and slouches against the wall. For the last few days, Freyda and I have been secluding ourselves in this room—this office—to discuss what is happening and how we intend to move forward. Every day, she keeps me posted on her attempts to communicate with the outside world.

Do I regret what's happened? Do I regret taking part in an underground resistance that is responsible for America's collapse?

Not for one second.

I understand that the life ahead of us is going to be difficult, but the life we once knew was poisoned with corruption and greed. Our primary goal right now isn't to focus on what's been lost, but rather on what remains.

"Are you sure this is for real?" Freyda asks. "I mean, it sounds like something out of a movie… The *Binaries*," she scoffs.

I scratch my nail into a small indent on the desk in front of me. "This isn't some joke for your amusement."

She quickly clears her throat and straightens her back. "I'm sorry… I didn't mean any disrespect. If you'd like me to keep looking into it—"

I cock my head to one side and smirk. While I oddly enjoy how quickly she backed down, I don't understand where this is coming from. Only a few days ago, Freyda was lecturing me on how to become a stronger leader. Now, the moment I show her any form of anger or aggravation, she withdraws like a submissive dog, prepared to obey any order I give.

Is this what she was trained for? Was she programmed to follow orders? I rub my chin and stare at her, admiring her new demeanor. Perhaps this is what she's been pushing for all along—a leader to follow.

"I would like you to keep looking into it," I say, and she offers me a brief nod. "The Binaries are out there, Freyda. I realize it may sound like some fictitious delusion, but doesn't it all?" I laugh, even though there is nothing funny about the situation we're in. "We're living in a goddamn prison. I don't see how it gets any crazier than that. So no, the Binaries aren't some *joke*. Bethany spent years researching"—I pause, realizing she has no idea who

Bethany is. "Bethany Lee," I add, "the most notorious leader of Washington's underground resistance."

Freyda offers a brief nod but doesn't cut in.

"She spent years," I continue, "building this team… this group of women with incredible knowledge. Neuroscientists, engineers, surgeons, programmers… and they knew what was at stake. They knew this was coming. They agreed to find a safe haven until the dust settled. I don't know where they went, and I don't know how long it will be until they resurface. But we have to keep trying. I need you to keep trying, Freyda."

She nods again, her lips tight and her eyes glued to mine. "I will."

I offer a genuine smile. For the first time in a long time, it seems like I have someone by my side—someone I can count on.

* * * * * *

"And now," Lucy says, her arms exaggeratedly stretched out into the air, "they say she lives under the water… in the Pacific Ocean."

The little girls gasp and slap hands over their mouths.

Though I do enjoy watching their expressions during story time, I much prefer watching Lucy deliver the story. She is so animated, so full of life and excitement. The last time I saw her like this, she was seven years old. I'd gone to visit her and Ophelia. As I always did, I brought Lucy a cookie. She ate it so fast that crumbs flew out of her mouth and onto the floor as she spoke. I remember laughing because Ophelia got upset. She kept mumbling about how she'd just cleaned the entire apartment. But little Lucy was so excited to tell me about her day, to explain to me how she'd won first place in a race at school.

Watching her talk was one of the best feelings in the world. I could feel the excitement and joy bursting out of her, and it warmed me inside. That was the last time she smiled so big. A few months later, everything started going to shit.

But now, to watch my little Lucy tell a story to a group of children... I can't even begin to describe the joy it brings me. My throat tightens, and I take a deep breath.

I have her again. I have my little Lucy.

She looks at me from the corner of her eye and the grin on her face shortens into a subtle smile.

"What a story!" I say, bulging my eyes out at the children. I slap my knees and lean forward, my gaze moving from one child to another. "I have an idea—"

But then, a silence so heavy fills the air that for a moment, I think I've gone deaf. I follow everyone's eyes to find Zack standing at the back of the crowd, his fingers tucked into the front pockets of his pants. He looks uncomfortable. It's apparent he wasn't expecting everyone to look at him, almost as if he thought he could join in on the amusement without being spotted.

The crowd of women separates even further, and he stands alone in the open. He keeps jerking his head to the side as if trying to get his wavy locks to mask his face. I can sense Lucy staring at me, but I don't look back. I know she admires this boy. I've seen the two of them together.

Who does he think he is, intruding on our story time like this?

My back stiffens and I elevate my chin.

He's only a boy, Eve. He deserves love and kindness like every other child here.

"Zack," I say sweetly, and he focuses his dark eyes on me. "Come join us. Lucy here was telling us about the myth of Octopula, and I was about to assign some homework."

"Homework!" says a little girl. She frowns and pouts so much so that her little chin sticks out farther than her lips.

"This is fun homework," I say.

I notice him staring at Lucy more than anyone else. I'm assuming she comforts him somehow.

He takes a step forward, and the crowd of women and children start to murmur. It sounds like a thousand insects buzzing around my head.

"Everyone," I say, but the whispering only grows louder. Why aren't they listening to me?

"Enough!" I shout, and the heavy silence returns. I brush my fingers along my eyebrow and stretch my lips back into their smiling position. "Please, everyone... Children. I know it might feel funny having a boy around, but Zack here is part of our family now. He's a person like each and every one of you."

I can tell some of the mothers aren't impressed with the message I'm delivering. Some have crossed their arms over their chests and others are avoiding eye contact altogether, but most are receptive.

"He has a heart," I say, pointing to my chest. "It beats same as yours—" I point at little Scarlet's chest. "And yours and yours." The children giggle when my finger nearly tickles their stomachs. "He breathes the same air as us, doesn't he?" They nod. "And he's also been nice to all of you, hasn't he?" They nod again. "So, it's important that we be nice back, okay?"

"Okay," says a soft voice.

A few others join in, and I notice several of the older kids—those older than eight years old—move toward the crowd, followed by Mrs. Lewenburg. Her dark hair is pulled back into a tight, greasy ponytail, and her bright eyes look flat over that big veiny nose of hers. She always looks like she's in a bad mood. I wonder if that's why the older kids and teenagers call her Mrs. *Lewenturd*.

I suppose even in a paradise like Eden, children will be children.

"Hey, Zack," says one of the girls.

He scratches his thick-haired head and smirks up at her uncomfortably. "Hey, Sophia."

"Now, everyone," I say, breaking the awkward atmosphere. "I have a task for all of you." Their eyes are fixated on me as if I'm about to announce the winner of some lottery draw. "I want you to draw your version of Octopula."

Their delicate faces light up and everyone starts bouncing around on the grass. The children love to draw, and it isn't often that they're allowed to do so. Although we have several dozen packets of printing paper here in Eden, we reserve it for important matters such as note-taking for the Medical Unit or important notices Freyda sometimes hangs in the main hall.

Only last month, I asked Freyda to leave a note reminding the mothers to supervise their children at all times—especially after curfew. The moment nighttime is declared—which is when the sun sets entirely—everyone is to return to their rooms where they are to remain for the night unless, of course, they require the bathroom.

This rule was set in place to ensure everyone obtains adequate sleep. Poor sleep weakens the immune system, which in turn increases one's odds of developing certain illnesses. Only several weeks after arriving in Eden, women complained of being kept up all night by children wandering the halls.

But today, I am deciding to allow each child one piece of paper.

"Can we use color?" Scarlet asks, jumping to her feet.

I brush the tips of my fingers along her fuzzy cheek. "Of course you can, sweetheart."

CHAPTER 26 – LUCY

"Inside, inside, inside!" Mrs. Greensmith shouts.

Children come rushing inside their Division with clothing drenched and water dripping from hair, noses, and fingertips. It isn't the enjoyable kind of rain, either. Not the kind that makes you want to tilt your head back and stick your tongue out. It's the opposite of that. Like little knives are poking you in the back because the water's so cold. The kind of rain that makes people sick.

It came pouring down without warning, too. First, it was cloudy, but then out of nowhere, the clouds turned a dark gray, almost black, and it dumped on us. I have to admit, watching Eve run inside with her heels was funny. I honestly don't know why she wears those, but they seem to make her feel important.

My wet shoes squeak against the tiled floor as I make my way toward my cell for a change of clothes. I stare at my own feet as I walk. They're so wet they look dark, but they'll dry. I feel worse for whoever's responsible for cleaning this week. Every week, it changes. It's some kind of rotation among the adults of each Division.

I leave Division Three and cross the main hall, trying to step down on muddy footprints. I'd rather not create new prints if I can help it. Maybe Nola's responsible for cleaning our Division this week. I can't remember the last time she did it, so it must be her turn.

Good.

I glare at nothing just thinking about her. I still can't believe how quickly she believed whatever Eve told her. But then I think of Eve, and my anger starts to disappear. I want to believe so badly that she's here to stay... That she's changing her ways and she'll be the same old Aunty Eve she was before we came to Eden. Before my mom died.

But then I wonder: why would Nola get all weird with me unless Eve told her something bad? Or something that isn't true? Does that mean I still can't trust Eve? I'm so sick of having to try to understand everyone. Why can't it be simple? Why are there always lies and secrets and mind games?

I wish people were more transparent.

How hard is it to be open and honest about things?

Yet then again, I guess Mom kept things from me, too. She wasn't doing it to be mean, or to be secretive. She was trying to protect me. Is Eve trying to protect me? What about Nola? The difference is I trusted Mom more than anyone in the world. I knew that in the end, she'd do whatever she had to protect me.

But Eve isn't my mom, and neither is Nola. As much as I want to trust them, I can't.

There is someone I can trust, though. Someone who's trusted me to keep her secrets, too.

Emily.

Oh God… How is she doing now? I know it's only been a few hours, but I can't stop worrying. I feel sick to my stomach. What if she dies? What if seeing her in that bed… Her lips blue and sweat sliding down her hairline… What if that's the last image of her I have in my head? What if I wake up tomorrow and she's… gone?

"Eve!" someone calls out and I turn around. I hadn't even realized she was behind me.

A young woman rushes to Eve, who's laughing and squeezing rain from her overcoat. Why is she laughing? She's acting like getting caught in the rain is the most fun she's had in years. It's not a fake laugh, either. Because Eve lets out a lot of fake laughs. I don't think the women in Eden know the difference, but I do.

"The children are so excited about drawing Octopula," the woman says. "Would it be all right if we pushed curfew a bit this evening?"

I know it's none of my business, but I can't walk away. No one's ever asked Eve to push curfew, not for anything. And because evening is here, the children will soon be asked to go to bed. Eve isn't saying anything. Why isn't she answering her? She looks like she's either gone brain-dead or she's on the verge of snapping.

But then, as if someone hit the power switch in her head, she flicks her wrist and grins from ear to ear, her perfectly straight teeth taking up a big portion of her face. “Of course!”

The woman doesn’t smile right away. Instead, she pulls her head back and her chin disappears. It’s almost like she was asked to ask Eve on behalf of someone else, and she wasn’t expecting to receive a *yes* for an answer.

“Oh... uh,” she says. “Th-thank you, Eve. That’s wonderful.” She balls two fists and excitedly shakes them in front of her. “The children will be so excited!”

“Do you know where the paper is stored?” Eve asks.

The woman’s eyes dart from side to side like she’s trying to remember something she doesn’t even know.

Eve lets out a soft laugh. “In room D-12. Head down toward the main entrance and you’ll find it. It isn’t locked.”

“Thank you!” the woman says, her bony fists still balled in the air.

A few women wearing Eden’s hemp dresses stand at the back of the main hall, near Division Three’s entrance. They stare at Eve as though she took off all her clothes, their mouths hanging open. It’s almost like they placed a bet on whether or not Eve would say yes, and they all bet she wouldn’t.

The young woman, the one who asked Eve about the curfew, spins around and offers two thumbs-up to her group of friends. She then rushes toward the main entrance, her shoes squeaking loudly throughout the entire hall.

* * * * * *

There are too many women talking loudly in the hall, and I don't know where to go.

"You look lost, honey," comes someone's voice.

I turn around to find an amicable-looking woman standing tall with frizzy brownish hair and a smile that makes me want to hug her. She looks like the kind of person who truly cares about others. I can see it all over her face. It's the way she's looking at me. Aunty Eve was supposed to care, but she doesn't... This lady, though, looks like she cares. And she's a total stranger.

"Come here, sweetheart," she says, wiggling her fingers at me.

I grab her hand and she walks me down the big hall. There are entrances everywhere. I have no idea where I am or where I'm supposed to go. Everyone else has their mom or an aunt or even a friend of a friend who seems to be showing them where they're supposed to be.

But I have no one.

No one except this lady.

As she walks forward, all I can smell is hot cinnamon. Maybe she's chewing gum. How much of it does she have? One day soon, I don't think she'll be able to get any more. I'm not stupid. I saw those cities. The stores were all broken into it and there was glass everywhere. So, if stores aren't going to exist soon, then that means people won't be able to buy things anymore.

Like gum.

She makes a popping sound, so now I know she's chewing gum.

“You look familiar,” she says, looking back at me.

I guess she kind of does, too. I don’t know her, though. I stare at her face, trying to figure out where I saw her, and then I remember. She’s the lady who tried to help that dying girl. She’s the nurse.

“You’re the nurse,” I say.

She gives me a big smile. “That’s right. I am. My name’s Nola. What’s your name, sweetheart?”

“Lu-Lucinda,” I say. “Cain. But I like Lucy.”

Her smile disappears like she saw a ghost. I turn around to see if maybe something’s happening behind me, but there’s nothing. Only a few kids dragging suitcases across the floor.

Her lips twitch and her smile reappears on her face. But it looks like she’s forcing it now. “Well, it’s a pleasure to meet you, Lucy. I’d shake your hand, but I’m already holding it.” She laughs this time, and it reminds me of my mom’s laugh. It’s not too loud but not quiet, either. It’s the kind of laugh that makes you want to laugh, too.

Now, all I can think about is Mom again, and my throat starts to hurt. I don’t have her here with me, and now Aunty Eve has abandoned me. What am I supposed to do? How am I—

“Oh, honey,” the woman, Nola, says.

She looks at me like I broke her heart. My lip must be trembling.

“Come here.” She pulls me into her arms.

I don’t even know this woman, but I can’t let go of her. I press my face into her neck, squeeze her tight, and burst out crying.

I don’t know how long I cry, but she doesn’t let

me go.

* * * * * *

I look up when I hear something ticking against my cell's iron bars. It's Nola, and her face is pressed up against the cold metal, making her cheek look even more plump than usual.

"I see you got caught outside," she says playfully.

I want to be friendly with her, but it's so hard. She betrayed me.

"Can I come in?"

Nola never asks to come in. She simply comes in. She must know I'm pretty pissed off.

I shrug.

She must take this as a yes because she steps inside with her fingers wrapped around one of the gate's bars.

"Mind if we talk?"

I don't answer. Instead, I plop myself down on my bed, pull my knees up to my chest, and wrap my arms around my legs.

She lets out a long breath, pulls the back hem of her orange dress to the front of her and slowly sits at the end of my bed. She sounds like Mom right now. That long breath. Mom used to do that when she had something difficult to tell me. Something she thought I was too young to understand. Kind of like when I asked her about why people were turning on each other. Why people were killing each other based on something as stupid as gender.

She had to explain to me that things weren't so black and white. War wasn't happening because someone was a boy, a girl, a man, or a woman. It was caused by the abuse of power that came from being a certain gender. I never did understand what she was trying to tell me. It didn't make sense. People are people. Why would you hurt someone because they're the opposite sex? They're still a human being. They still have feelings, a heart that beats... Human beings are friggin' ridiculous.

Then she told me how women were being made to do things they didn't want to do. That, I already knew about. I heard it on the news when Mom thought I wasn't listening. I was too young then to get what she was saying, but now I know. I know about the rapes. The thought makes me sick to my stomach. And apparently, it happened a lot. It's almost like men knew the best way to hurt a woman was to rape her.

I don't know... I don't know anything anymore. When I think of these things... of everything my mom tried to warn me about, I'm reminded of how sick people are. Then, I'm reminded of all the men who turned on their wives, their children, their mothers after the government brainwashed them into believing that women were the cause of this war.

How do you turn on your own family? Because someone in power tells you to? I guess it's more complicated than that. I still don't understand it. But the more I think about how bad America got... How despicable people became, the more I realize that maybe Eve has every reason to do the things she does.

I can only imagine what she's gone through, trying to keep this place intact. I mean, it probably isn't easy to keep hundreds of women happy and remind them that men aren't needed for our survival. Well, not yet, anyway. I'm sure as the years go by, she'll have to figure out how we're going to reproduce. But maybe that's why she let Zack in. Not that I want to think about Zack being a tool for reproduction, but from what I've seen of Eve, she doesn't do anything without a good reason. At least not anymore.

"I'm sorry," Nola breathes, and I'm so caught up in my own head that I flinch at the interruption.

I look up at her, but I don't say anything.

"I shouldn't have doubted you," she says. She looks sad, her thin eyebrows slanting over her eyes.

So, she's admitting she doubted me. Why did she doubt me? What did Eve tell her?

"Eve's been worried about you," she says.

Worried about me? A few hours ago, I'd have jumped down Nola's throat for saying something like that, but now... Now that I've seen Eve, and the way she's been acting with everyone, maybe this isn't so farfetched.

Maybe Aunty... Maybe Eve *is* worried about me. For some odd reason, I want to smile. The idea of Eve actually caring about me means more to me than anything. I know that deep down, despite my resentment and bitterness, I still love her. I'd never admit it, but I do. And I miss her, more than anything.

"What's she so worried about?" I ask.

Nola cranes her neck back and rolls her eyes toward the ceiling. The kind of look that says, "Oh, it's no big deal." But that's exactly the kind of look that *is* a big deal. It means she's holding something back.

"She wants you to be safe, that's all," she says.

The skeptical side of me still exists and I scoff. "Safe? How am I not being safe? What could I possibly do that would be unsafe here in Eden? In my prison cell?" I don't mean to rant, but now that I've started, I can't stop. "I mean, that's what this is, isn't it? A prison sentence? It's not like we're even allowed to go out and explore. It's too *dangerous*"—I make air quotes—"so we have to stay in here where it's *safe*—" and I make the same gesture.

I'm sure she can sense that I've grown a little sick of having absolutely nothing to look forward to in this life. I never talk about it. There's no point. We're always reminded to keep our mouths shut about anything negative. But this world isn't all rainbows and butterflies. There's negativity whether we like it or not. Like Emily. She's sick, and she's probably going to die. How the hell is anyone supposed to stay happy in a situation like that? And what about those women I saw cooped up in one of those medical rooms? I bet you they're the ones who went outside and got attacked. It would make perfect sense. Now they're being held in the Medical Unit until they can get over their trauma. God forbid they bring their *negativity* into Eden.

"And you know what," I start again before she has the chance to say anything, "we're not that safe if you think about it. It's pretty damn stupid that we're staying in a place where people are looking for us. I mean, those men out there found us. We're lucky that man was around, but what happens next time, huh?" My eyes bulge as I glare at her, and she looks a bit scared. She looks like she's watching Dr. Jekyll turn into Mr. Hyde. "Is that why the adults had that meeting? To talk about finding a new place? Is that where the man went? He isn't in the Medical Unit, so he's either being kept a prisoner, or he's gone on some mission—"

Her eyebrows drop low and she shakes her head vigorously from side to side, so I stop talking. Obviously, I shouldn't be talking about this out loud. I don't see what the big deal is, though. What does it matter if anyone hears me? They had a meeting about it.

"It's not our place to talk about that," she says in a whisper. "Eve doesn't want the kids getting all worked up until we have a definitive answer. We don't know what's going on yet. And yes, that's where Gabriel went. He's gone with Freyda and a few other women. I don't have all the details, but the plan is for us to migrate somewhere safer..." She rolls her eyes, probably because she knows I'm sick of hearing the word *safe*. "Somewhere bigger and better."

I cross my arms even tighter across my chest and stare at the wall behind her. I still don't get why she's in here or what's going on.

"I understand why she was worried," Nola continues. Is she seriously going to take Eve's side right now, after trying to apologize to me? "You know how she felt about graduates taking on the role of Healer. But you chose it—"

"Yeah, why is she so opposed to it?" I cut in. "Maybe she wanted to hide the fact that she drugs people."

Her nostrils flare and her eyes go huge. I slouch against the wall at the head of my bed and shut my mouth.

"All I'm trying to say here is I think you're right," she says.

What? What's she talking about? I perk up. This was the last thing I expected to hear from Nola.

Her eyes shift from me to the entrance of my room. Squeaky footsteps echo from down the hall, but for the most part, it's quiet no doubt because the kids are in one of the classrooms drawing their version of Octopula.

She leans in closer, her grip fastened gently around my shin. "About Eve, I mean. She said a few things about your mom that didn't add up. I knew your mom, but Eve doesn't know that... Earlier, you said Eve was the reason your mom was killed."

That's exactly what I said, and I nod. I said it out of anger, but at the same time, part of me believes that to be true. Mom didn't want to go to the White House. She only went because of Eve.

"That's not what she told me," Nola says. She lets out another long breath and stares at me, her hazel eyes looking like little glass balls. "I don't think we can trust her, Lucy."

CHAPTER 27 – GABRIEL

"I'm not gonna force you to eat," I say, crunching down on the rabbit's crisp leg, "but if you plan on surviving out here, you'd better get used to meat."

Jada looks like she's about to throw up, her cheeks ballooned and her hand pressed so tightly over her mouth that her knuckles have gone white.

Yael, though, doesn't seem to care. She grabs at the rabbit and tears off whatever she can. I'm assuming most of these women have been living off a plant-based diet. It makes sense if you think about it. It's not like they've been going out hunting. From what I've heard, Eve's been keeping them inside the walls for the last few years.

I pull a long piece of meat off the rabbit's back and wiggle it in the air, under Miller's nose. She hesitates, her dark eyes darting between Freyda and the other women. But the second she gets a whiff of it, something that would typically make any meat eater hungry, she turns her head away. "I'll pass."

"You guys don't—" I correct myself. "You women don't eat meat at all?" I probably look like a barbaric caveman. My beard's already starting to grow back out. It's prickly, but it grows fast, and I'm hunched forward with my back round and my greasy fingers in my mouth. They must think I'm repulsive.

"Some women do," Freyda says, "but not many. We've been trying to maintain some livestock, but we can't keep up with the reproduction. Not only that, but the kids get attached to the animals. They give them names." She smiles, and I stop chewing. I want to see every second of it. "Can you imagine how hard it is to slaughter an animal for meat after that? After these kids think of them as their best friends?"

"Sammy was my favorite," Dakota says, biting down on what looks like a piece of bread. She pulled it out of the bag I'm carrying. It won't sustain her, but it'll do until she's starving enough to eat what I catch.

The women laugh, and I feel like I missed out on a joke.

"Sammy the Piggy," Miller says, shaking her wavy locks away from over her eyes. "Poor guy."

"Did you kill it?" I say, my mouth full of food.

"We couldn't," Jada says. "Everyone loved him. He used to chase some of the kids to play." She stares toward the darkening sky. It looks like clouds are moving toward us, and a nasty breeze is following them. "So, he grew old until he died. Never wanted to reproduce, either."

I chuckle and a small piece of meat flies out of my mouth.

I don't like the way the sky looks right now. Seems like a nasty storm is on the way. Thankfully, we're sitting beside an abandoned camper parked on the side of some old campground. The sign's been shot and part of its corner is missing, but it's a big green sign that reads, "Watercrest Campground."

I won't go inside the campground to rest. God knows who's in there. What a shame. It's the perfect place to hide out and build a shelter. But the side of the road will have to do for us, for now. We could keep walking, but if we get stuck in the rain, it won't be pleasant for anyone. There's nothing worse (well, okay, there's a lot that could be worse) than traveling with drenched clothes. And wet boots... I won't even get started.

The camper looks like it's a 2040-something model. With its cylindrical shape, it seems like a giant bullet, and it's an all-in-one, meaning, there's no vehicle attached to it. It runs on all four wheels. It's black and blue, for the most part, with chrome plates running along its side. I guess if I look back at the old campers they used to have in my mama's time, this one would look like a spaceship in comparison.

I had to shoot at the door to get inside, but it's big enough for all of us. There are two beds in there, so I'm sure if some of us need to rest, we can figure out how to take turns. I'd be scared to lie down in it, though. I don't even want to imagine how many dried-up insects are hiding in there, waiting to be crunched under the weight of someone's body. Or mold... I stood in there for five minutes and my throat started hurting. I have allergies, like most people on this planet, but they're not severe. But with my reaction to this place, it must be bad. I'm sure it was once nice, though. There's even a little kitchenette with metallic counters and glass appliances. I don't know how glass appliances became a fad in the forties, but they did. And, most important of all, there's a bathroom. So, I can't complain. I think, for now, this will do. At least until the storm passes.

It would've been awesome to get the thing working, but there was no key inside, so I'm pretty much fucked. Not only that, but I doubt there's any fuel in here. And if there was, that whole hot-wiring thing you see in the old movies, well, it doesn't work. At least not on new cars. They're too advanced for that. The biggest problem my generation has, or, had, with cars, was when they were hacked because the whole thing ran on a computer.

Often, when someone's car was stolen, it happened when someone else knew how to break through its security and start the car from either an H-Cap, a plain old computer, or even those freaky, super-advanced eggs: DDGs.

And even if we had electricity, it's not like I have hacking skills.

"Shit," Miller says, and she reaches for the top of her head.

I'm about to ask her what's wrong when I feel a big cold droplet land flat on the tip of my nose. It explodes into even smaller droplets, and then more start coming down.

* * * * * *

I wipe the cold water from my face and blink hard.

I'm not the kind of person who enjoys taking a

life. It isn't something anyone enjoys, really. The only ones who do are sociopaths or people who are fucked in the head. If I have to, or if it's part of my job, I'll do it, as I did in North Korea, and I hated it every time. But after a while, you get used to it. Well, not used to it, but it becomes easier.

Now, I don't have a job. The only reason I'd have to kill someone is to defend myself.

This man is probably thinking the same thing, but he's being an idiot. The short-muzzled shotgun in his grasp is shaking from side to side while heavy raindrops splash off its metal. Every time he opens his mouth to talk, he spits out a bunch of water. The rain's coming down so hard, it's hard to hear him, too.

"G-give me everythin' you have!" he shouts.

There's so much running through my mind. We're all struggling in this. I think of my mama and the way I found her lifeless body, and a rage starts to build inside me until all I can think about is killing this son of a bitch.

It wouldn't be hard, either.

But that's not who I am. My life is not at risk, and it would be senseless. If he wanted to shoot me, he'd have done it already. He'd have shot me and taken everything I have. There's a reason he's trembling, too. He's probably never shot a gun before.

He looks like a typical hillbilly. I don't mean that in a condescending way, but I don't know how else to describe him. He's thin... really thin. He doesn't look much older than thirty. He's wearing a white tank that's gone transparent because of the rain, and two dark nipples are visible under the cotton. He has a bit of a beard growing in, but it appears he has a hard time growing it. There are patches here and there, and it looks prickly. His head is shaved on both sides, but not the top. It's probably blond, but it looks brown now that it's wet, and its folded over his head likely in a hawk style.

His jeans are ripped and there's a big hole in his left pant leg. A long cut runs down his knee.

I wonder how long he's been out here or if this is where he lives. It looks more like a hunting cabin than a home, though. Maybe he got stuck out here. We're standing in the middle of some forest off the highway. It's a pretty big forest. I've been here before. A lot of hunters come out this way, so it doesn't surprise me that there's a cabin here.

Hell, there could be a bunch of them.

"Daddy?" comes someone's voice.

The man snaps his head toward the cabin, to where the voice came from, but his gun stays pointed at me. A little girl's head sticks out the front door. Her eyes look like something on a toy doll. They're big and bright like she's seen a ghost. The poor kid is probably terrified.

"Madison, get back inside!" the man yells, his country accent obvious.

The last thing I want to do is traumatize a kid, but I have no choice. This is my best chance. I run up to him and grab the muzzle of his gun, tearing it right out of his hands. I'm about to smack him in the nose with the stock, but that little girl's eyes are even bigger now.

I can't make her watch me break her dad's nose, even if he is being a dick.

So instead, I snap the gun open and pull out the shells. He probably has a spare pistol hiding in his belt, but he'd be a complete moron to take it out. Unless he wants his kid to watch him die, he'll cooperate.

"There's no need for this," I shout.

"Look, man," the guy says, throwing two arms in the air as if I'm pointing a gun at him. But I'm not. I'm standing there with his unloaded gun. "I-I'm sorry. I'm just tryin' to take care o' my little girl."

"I know," I growl, and I stand there staring at him.

My feet are killing me and my boots are drenched inside. I know he tried to kill me, but all I can think about is getting inside that cabin. I need shelter. I've been out here for a few days trying to build a shelter, but then the rain started and it wouldn't stop. It's fucking cold, too, and I'm shivering. I can barely feel my fingers.

The rule of thumb is that a person can survive three hours without shelter in harsh conditions... I'm not too sure this would count as harsh conditions, being that we aren't in the dead of winter, but I know my body, and I'm reaching my limit.

He must see me eyeing his cabin or me shaking. Hesitating for a moment, he says, "Uh... You wanna come in and warm up? I got us a fire goin'." He grins, revealing a set of crooked teeth. "I promise I won't try ta shoot ya."

It's almost like the animal side of him

disappeared and he's back to being a decent human being. I suppose that's what happens when people are scared... When their survival instincts kick in and all they can think about is themselves and their family. They'll do anything to protect what's theirs.

He must know I'm not a bad guy. If I were, I'd have shot him the second I took the gun from him.

I nod, and he takes me inside.

* * * * * *

"Looks like this place has been empty for years," Miller says, lifting one of the bed's thin sheets. It's brown, but it looks like it used to be blue.

"Well, what d'you expect?" Dakota says, scrunching her freckled face. "Everyone's dead."

"Not everyone," I say, but Dakota gives me a dirty look. She was obviously exaggerating, and I didn't catch on.

She lets out a rough breath through her nostrils. "Well, no one's been here in ages. Hopefully, the rain stops soon, 'cause this place is disgusting."

"At least it's shelter," Jada says. She sits down against the side table beside the bed, probably too freaked out to sit on the actual bed. I don't blame her. She rubs her thin legs, stretches her neck, and sighs.

She looks exhausted. They all do. Except for Freyda, who's good at holding herself together. She's probably tired as hell, but she'd never show it. She stands at the front of the camper, gazing out through the windshield. The rain makes the glass look wet, but on the inside, the camper is caked with dust. I can barely see the road from here.

"How often did you find survivors?" she asks, turning her head sideways. She doesn't make eye contact, but she's looking at me.

"What do you mean?" I ask.

"What are the chances we'll run into someone?" she asks.

They all stare at me like I hold the answers to everything. In this case, I guess I do. At least if I'm comparing myself to them. They've spent years locked up inside of Eden. They have no idea what's out here.

"The first year," I say, "a lot of people died. I mean a lot." I stare out through the camper's windshield. I can almost see it all again. People screaming at each other, guns going off, glass shattering in the cities. It's like the rain is recreating a scene in the road. "The second year felt eerie. Everything was empty. Running into someone was rare, and if you did, more often than not only one person came out of it alive. It's a dog-eat-dog world out there." I lean back against one of the kitchenette's cupboards and bow my head. "It's been downhill from there." I glance up at Freyda who's staring at me now, almost like she can see exactly what I'm thinking. Like she's experiencing all of the pain, too. "I can't give you an exact formula." I rub my forehead. "Sometimes, I went months without seeing a single person. Other times, I saw a few families within the same week. It depends where you are. All I can say is that if you do come across someone, don't trust them. The first year, maybe. But everyone's grasping at straws now, trying to survive this shitty life. Most people have probably already killed someone else by now. They won't hesitate to do it again."

I might have just traumatized them all. What have they been doing in there? In Eden? Living in some delusional paradise? Pretending the world around them wasn't a complete hellhole?

Freyda clears her throat and glances at the others. "We knew it was bad, but we didn't realize it was *that* bad."

"That's why we're doing this, isn't it?" Yael cuts in. Her accent is so interesting, it's hard not to want to listen to her talk. "Trying to find a better Eden? Imagine the lives we could save." She brushes her long black hair over one shoulder and her green eyes dart my way, but she doesn't look at me. I can't tell if she's freaked out because I'm a man, or if she doesn't trust me.

"Yael's right," Jada says leaning the upper half of her body forward, her fingers wrapped around the side table's ledge. "If we succeed, we could be saving countless lives."

"So, what aren't you telling us, Gabriel?" Dakota asks. She crosses her arms over her chest and leans against the fridge's glass doors.

Not understanding what she's getting at, I stare at her.

"You're obviously taking us to Area 82," she says.

My heart almost stops. I look at Freyda in a panic. How does Dakota know where we're going? The plan was to get there first and then explain. They knew we were heading somewhere safe, but

Freyda's the only other person, aside from Eve, who knows it's a military base.

"What's Area 82?" Miller asks.

I'm surprised it's Miller who doesn't know about it. She's the one with the military background. Dakota, though, is the pilot. What kind of shit was she involved in? How does she know about Area 82?

She smirks, but it isn't a happy kind of smirk. It's a cocky one. It's like she has me right where she wants me. I part my lips, though I have no idea how I'm supposed to explain all of this right now, but I don't have time to say anything.

She jumps forward with what looks like a kitchen knife and pushes the blade hard against my neck. I look down at her without moving my face and she's looking up at me like a wild animal. Her yellow teeth are visible, and her skin pulls so tightly across her face that her freckles seem to expand.

"Who the fuck are you, really?" she says.

CHAPTER 28 – EVE

The sound of children laughing fills the main hall as I make my way toward Division Five, where Lucy sleeps. I may be pushing my luck with her, but I need her to know how serious I am about everything I said—about feeling reborn and wanting a connection with my godchild.

Surely, she must sense it. She must know that all I want is to have her back in my life. Something's changed inside me; something has shifted. I tilt my head back and gaze up at the ceiling, admiring every design, every cobweb, every color.

I'm alive.

I've never felt more wonderful.

The rain pours down hard overhead, hitting the glass windows in the ceiling, but the sound doesn't depress me. It relaxes me, makes me feel whole.

I breathe in the scent of cool humidity and exhale a long breath, my lungs deflating. I bend forward and remove my heels to feel the cold tile against my skin.

I want to keep feeling alive.

"Eve, is that you?" comes someone's voice.

I turn to the side to find Agatha sitting on the

same bench she does every day. A smile splits her wrinkled face, and her glazed eyes are narrowed on me as if she's having a difficult time seeing me.

Poor Agatha lost her glasses last year after a few children bumped into her while playing. Her glasses shattered the moment they landed on the tiles, and little pieces of glass slid underneath her bench. I suppose that's what happens during the winter months—children become restless and climb on anything they can find.

She must have heard my heels against the tile before I took them off.

"It's me, Agatha," I say sweetly.

I approach her, making absolutely no noise as I walk. It's a strange feeling to move about silently. I enjoy the loud clicking—it's a powerful sound. But at this moment, all I want is my skin against the cold surface. I can't remember the last time my feet touched anything other than the insides of my heels or the sheets on my bed.

"Oh," Agatha says with a cute chuckle. "I didn't see you."

I smile, but she probably doesn't see it even though I'm merely a few feet away from her now.

"That's all right, Agatha." I sit down beside her and place my palm against her tiny thigh. She looks so frail, it breaks my heart. I've never had the courage to ask her age, but if I had to guess, I would say she's in her mid-eighties. Her skin is loose, her white hair is curly atop her head, and her nose and ears have grown twice the size they presumably were when she was young. When looking at her profile, she has a bit of a bird's face—a long, pointed nose with a lump on its bridge and a chin that protrudes farther than her lips. But despite her less than aesthetically pleasing appearance, Agatha is one of the sweetest women I know.

She is always smiling, even though she has no teeth. And her smile is so contagious it warms my heart.

"How have you been, my dear?" I ask.

She purses her lips, her chin moving forward and backward, and gazes at me with her gray, glazed eyes. It almost looks as if she's going blind. She blinks a few times, then finally makes eye contact, and her smile grows even wider as if she'd laid eyes on an angel.

"Oh, you know," she says, her voice croaky. "Hanging in there."

I gently squeeze her thigh. "Is there anything at all I can do for you, Agatha? Anything to make you more comfortable?"

She shakes her head, her little white curls wiggling at the top. "Oh, don't you worry about me, my sweet, sweet Eve. I'm doing just fine. You keep doing what you do..." Her crusted eyes aim toward the main hall. It probably all looks like a giant white blur to her. "You're a hero, Eve. Don't you—don't you ever forget that."

She pats my hand on her lap, but her arm is shaking. In fact, her entire body is trembling a little bit. This isn't the first time Agatha trembles—she often does. But it seems as though it's getting worse.

"I hope—" she continues, "I hope you don't think

you can force my bony little ass to follow you... To follow you to this place you're goin' to."

She's referring to Area 82. I should have known that Agatha wouldn't follow. She'd never make it. I wonder how many other women will refuse to migrate.

I gently hold the back of her wrinkled neck and press my lips on her forehead.

"You do whatever you want to do, sweetheart."

She pats down on my knuckles again as a way of saying thank you, and I stand.

"I mean it, Agatha," I say. "If you need anything," and I pause for effect to make sure she understands how serious I am, "you tell me. Okay?"

She sticks a finger in the air, and it trembles from side to side. "Oh, I will, my sweet Eve, I will."

My chest tightens and I turn away. The idea of leaving Agatha behind destroys me. I love that woman. If I focus on that... If I focus on losing people I care about...

Freyda's face suddenly appears in my mind and I nearly burst out crying.

I swallow hard and clear my throat.

I'm stronger than this.

I'm stronger than this.

Everything is just fine.

* * * * * *

Everything's fine, I tell myself, though I feel like it's all falling apart.

"How is this supposed to work, Eve?" someone asks.

I glance at Freyda, who stands at the edge of the

crowd that's accumulated in the hall, or, as I've decided to call it, the main hall. She's my rock—she grounds me when I'm uncertain of myself.

These women are all still terrified.

What more do they want from me?

I've taken them away from Washington and toward safety. Don't they see that? If they had stayed behind, they would be dead within a matter of days, maybe weeks. I can only imagine how bad things have gotten in the city. Vrin warned me about all of it. She warned me that criminals would be the first to start damaging property being that cameras wouldn't be working anymore and police cruisers wouldn't function.

"People will be in denial during the first twenty-four hours, maybe even the first week," she told me. "Criminals will want to take advantage of the situation, so they'll surface first. But it won't be long before regular citizens panic... They'll start looting to collect supplies for their families, and, well, that will eventually lead to violence."

I remember wondering if an EMP was the best approach. As Vrin explained to me the mechanics of it along with its impact, I had my doubts. But then, the more I thought of President Price and the army of men he'd built for himself, the more I remembered why we were doing this in the first place.

A clean start.

Sometimes sacrifices must be made for the greater good.

"How long are we staying here?" another woman asks.

The bickering spreads across the hall and a multitude of voices bounce off the beautiful white-and-gold-trimmed walls.

I raise a stiff arm in the air, and to my surprise, everyone goes quiet. Is this how Bethany Lee felt during her underground meetings? Immediately, I'm filled with a sense of power and influence. These women look up to me. I can tell they're terrified, but inside each of them, there's a sheep waiting to follow its shepherd.

That's all they want, isn't it? Guidance?

My eyes shift toward Freyda again. She gives me a brief nod, one that says, "You can do this."

I have to do this.

Bethany isn't here, and I saved them—I'm the reason these women are even alive.

I raise my chin with pride and an unfamiliar confidence washes over me.

It's true. Most of them would be on the verge of death or stuck inside a city filled with violence.

I am their salvation.

"I know you're all scared," I say, and my voice echoes down a few of the dark corridors at the back. "But trust me when I say that everything is going to be okay."

"How do you know?" someone shouts.

But then someone nudges the woman in the ribs and whispering breaks out. Most of these women know that I'm the reason we attacked the White House in the first place—I'm the reason they weren't slaughtered by men.

They should know better than to question me.

"Because I know," I say, and a heavy silence fills the room.

No one questions me.

* * * * * *

A little girl comes blasting out of Division Five, her arms flailing in every direction. I'm pulled out of my trance and completely enthralled by the contagious grin on her face. She's having the time of her life, and I have no idea why. The wet floors make her feet slip all over the place, but she seems to be enjoying this.

I smile as I brush past her and continue my way toward Lucy's cell. My dear Lucy. I hope she's weighing everything I've said—I hope she's willing to forgive the way I've behaved.

All I want is to sit by her side and talk.

Surely, she'll allow this, won't she?

She did appear to be a bit reluctant in the courtyard.

I breathe deeply through my nose and make my way toward her cell. The floors have slowly begun to dry and the pads of my feet feel sticky.

I see her cell, and my heart beats faster. Although I haven't been in Division Five in quite some time, I know where Lucy's cell is, in part because it's approximately halfway down the corridor, but also because a braid of sweetgrass hangs over her doorway.

Ophelia was always into that—crystals and herbs. I thought it was all nonsense at the time, but now that I've seen what Mavis and Perula are capable of, I feel terrible for having poked fun at her all those years.

As I stare at the small bundle of hanging grass, I realize it's no wonder Lucy chose to become a Healer. It's in her blood. With the way she's turning out to look so much like Ophelia, it would only make sense that her mind resembles her mother's.

The only difference between the two is that Ophelia wasn't rebellious—she wasn't the type to question authority or take a stand against corruption. She was a follower. Lucy, contrarily, seems to be paving her own road in life.

This would normally upset me. The last thing I need in Eden is a young girl to question my ways. But today, I am seeing things in a different light. What I see in Lucy is what I see in myself; it's what I see when I think of Mila—a strong woman capable of creating a positive change in this world.

With the right guidance, my little Lucy could accomplish great things.

I move toward her cell, and my lips spread with excitement when I hear something I wasn't expecting—Nola's voice. Not wanting to interrupt, I step sideways and press my back against the wall along Lucy's neighboring cell.

Why are they whispering?

"So, what's your plan?" Lucy says, her voice sharp and excited. She sounds so passionate, it reminds me of Mila. Even though I can't see her, I can picture her perfectly—sitting on her bed with her posture slouched forward and her elbows resting on her knees. Her eyes are probably wide open and fixated on Nola.

"We just have to be careful," Nola says.

"Careful how?" Lucy says. "She seems different, Nola. She's been really nice to everyone."

They're talking about me.

My eyes dart from side to side and my heart pounds hard against my rib cage. I shouldn't be here, but at the same time, I need to know what they're saying.

"That doesn't mean anything," Nola says.

Why is she trying to turn Lucy against me? Did she not listen to a word I told her? Who the fuck does she think—

"You know how she is," Nola continues. "One day she's smiling, the next she wants to kill anyone who gets in her way. This little mood of hers won't last. Something's not right up there."

A soft tap fills Lucy's cell, and I can only assume Nola is tapping her temple.

I bite down hard and my jaw pops. How dare she—

"Maybe she does mean well, Lucy," Nola continues, "but all I ask is that you be careful. I know you miss her, and I know you want to reconnect—"

Lucy scoffs. "Relax, Nola. After everything she's done, I don't miss her, okay? I don't care about her anymore. But I'll play along and see where this goes, okay? Now can we please stop talking about this?"

She doesn't mean that. She can't possibly mean that. I'm still her godmother. I'm still the one who came back for her, the one who saved her. How could she...

The skin on my face heats as though it's on the verge of melting off and landing on the tiled floor at my feet. My hands become clammy and it feels as if my heart has climbed into my throat, where it sits, pumping.

I want to cry, scream, and hide all at the same time.

But I don't make a sound.

I stand still, unable to move. They continue to talk, but I can't hear what they're saying. It all sounds like words jumbled to create a meaningless language.

Is this what heartbreak feels like?

I haven't felt anything for so long.

I swallow hard. I won't allow it. I won't allow myself to be hurt—not by Lucy. Not by this little ungrateful bitch.

I glance up and stare at the stone wall in front of me.

I won't allow myself to hurt.

I clench my fists so hard my nails bend backward.

CHAPTER 29 – LUCY

Nola means well.

I get that she's trying to keep me safe, and honestly, after today, that's a huge relief. To know that she's on my side means everything to me. But, I don't know. After seeing Eve act the way she did, it's hard to think she's up to no good. I know I keep flip-flopping, but I don't know what to believe.

What I do know, though, is that I want to see where this is going with Eve. She seemed genuine. I'd never admit that to Nola, though. I think part of her might be jealous. I mean, she's been caring for me this entire time, and now, out of nowhere, Nola learns that Eve's my godmother and wants me back in her life. So, I can understand how that would be threatening to a mother figure.

I feel terrible for saying I don't care about Eve. It's not true. And it's not like anyone but Nola heard it, but vocalizing it made me feel bad. I've always cared about her. That doesn't go away, even if she's done things to hurt me.

"Okay, okay," Nola says, and she raises both hands in front of her, causing her big golden bracelets to make a clinging noise. She's always wearing jewelry. It looks cheap, but she seems to like it. I guess even though she isn't trying to impress a man, she still likes to look good for her own self-worth. That's how it should be, anyway.

I wonder if I'll ever meet a guy. Considering the life I'm living, I haven't given it much thought. Now that Zack's entered Eden, though, it's got me thinking a bit. I don't find him attractive, but being around him still does something to me. He's the first guy I've seen in years, and I'm not a kid anymore. He makes me feel special. Maybe Eve will let other boys enter Eden, and then, who knows? Maybe one day I'll find the man of my dreams.

Mom always told me that when I met the right one, I would know. I'd feel it in my stomach, in my legs, in my arms… Everywhere. He'd make me weak and strong all at the same time. And he'd treat me like his queen.

"Have you checked on Emily?" Nola asks, and my cheeks get hot.

I didn't mean to daydream about my future husband. That's if marriage even exists by the time I'm an adult. Kind of hard to get married when there aren't laws anymore.

I shake these thoughts away and clear my throat. "Y-yeah, I did."

Nola knows me, and she knows something is up. She leans toward me with that motherly look on her face: a combination of seriousness and tenderness all at the same time, the kind of look that says, "Talk to me, kiddo, I'm here for you."

I shake my head. Not because I don't want to

talk, but because I'm scared that if I open my mouth, I'll start crying. Nola knows that, too. She knows I hate getting emotional or even talking about my feelings. That's why she let it go when I said I didn't care about Eve. She knows I don't want to talk about it.

Instead of pulling me in for a hug, which would only make things worse, she gently smacks my thigh with an open palm and says, "Dr. Lewis is a great doctor. I'm sure she'll fix her up fine."

Nola's trying to cheer me up, and I want to smile but can't. I also want to believe her, but if I did, I'd be delusional. Dr. Lewis has lost tons of patients. Those deaths weren't her fault. She isn't properly equipped, and we lost people.

What if she isn't prepared to handle Emily's condition.

Nola reaches for my chin and tickles the underneath with her long fingernails. "I wouldn't worry too much, Lucy. Dr. Lewis doesn't take risks with the young ones. She'll use antibiotics."

I already know she is using them, but hearing it does make me feel a bit better. I roll my eyes up at Nola's bright orange dress and at her shadowed face. "Can you check on her?" I ask.

She parts her lips, but I cut in to add something else. "I don't want Dr. Lewis to get annoyed with me. She told me to let her rest, but it's been a few hours now, and I want to know that she's okay. I can't go in there again. Dr. Lewis will tell me—"

Nola offers a consoling smile. "Say no more. I'll check up on her."

All I want to do is hug Nola. I don't know how I'm feeling. I'm sad, terrified, excited, and freaked out all at once. This whole thing with Eve has me all messed up. And then my best friend... I hate having so many feelings. So instead of hugging her and telling her how nice she's been and how much I appreciate having her by my side in all of this... Instead of showing any of my emotions, I say, "Thanks, Nola."

******

She seems nice.

"I'm gonna count to three," the doctor says. I stare at her curly brown hair and wonder if she has to put gel in it to keep it looking that way. It's fuzzy-looking, and I want to touch it. It smells nice, too. Kind of like soap you used to find in shopping mall bathrooms. Only stronger and more clean-smelling. Like freshness mixed with mint and ice.

I'm not describing it too well, but that's what it smells like.

"One," she says, and I glance at Nola.

She's looking at me like I'm making her so proud. Her palms are flat together in front of her face, and her fingertips are touching the tip of her nose. I don't get it. It's just a vaccine. All the kids in Eden are getting it. So why does she care about me? There are tons of other kids out there who don't have their moms.

The doctor is about to say "Two," but then she sticks the needle in. It's a little pinch, and it does hurt, but I don't make any noise. Mom always taught me that no one likes someone who whines or complains. That the best way to get through in life is to be positive and to focus on the good.

Right now, there's no good. I feel guilty for being so hateful, but I can't help it. Everything makes me angry. In a peculiar way, I kind of enjoy the pain of the needle. At least I feel something other than hopeless and lost.

Without Mom, that's exactly what I am. I'm lost. And I don't know who this Nola lady thinks she is, but she'll never replace Mom. She can't just walk into my life and think I need her to protect me. I don't need protection.

And even if she wants to try, it's not like it matters. Tomorrow, a week from now, maybe a month from now, she'll leave. She'll get fed up and leave me to be alone again. That's what always happens. First, I lost my mom, and now Aunty Eve has left. If I can't even trust my own godmother, how can I trust some nurse lady?

"You did great!" she says, her eyes so wide they remind me of oversized marshmallows.

Dr. Lewis sticks a little Band-Aid over the hole. "All done, kiddo."

I try to smile at her, but my lips don't even move.

I glance back at Nola, who seems like she's about to break out into a song. She's so expressive. It's like anything she feels or thinks, she shows it right away. I'd be scared to see what she looks like if she's upset. She probably wouldn't even look like herself. I bet her face would get all twisted and she'd yell. But then again, Nola doesn't seem like the type of person who gets upset.

That reminds me of Mom.

Mom barely ever got upset. She always liked things to be peaceful. And they were, up until that Jason guy started following us more and more. Then she got stressed out, and it showed. I was scared, too, but Mom was so stressed, I didn't want to make things worse. I didn't want to tell her I was scared. It would only stress her more.

"Why don't we go find you something to eat?" Nola asks. She wiggles her fingers at me like I'm four years old. Doesn't she know how old I am? I might be a kid, but I'm not a toddler. I can walk myself.

I slide off the stool and stand up. She stops wiggling her fingers when she notices that I don't want to hold her hand, but the smile on her face doesn't go away.

I want to tell her to leave me alone, but at the same time, I don't want to be alone. I don't know how to feel.

"Come on in," Dr. Lewis calls out, and a lady comes in with a baby in her arms. It's crying and she keeps bouncing it against her chest. It must be a girl. Before we left the city, Eve said that anyone with little boys had to stay behind.

A lot of people got upset about that, but obviously, those were the ones who had little boys. The moms with girls still followed Eve.

A nasty feeling sits in the bottom of my stomach. I'm so angry I want to tear the baby out of her arms, and I feel guilty for even thinking this. I'd never do that. But I'm so mad. Why does this little girl get to have her mom and I don't?

"Come on, sweetheart," Nola says. She wraps a

warm arm around my shoulder, and although I want to pull away, I don't. Because at the same time, I need the comfort.

I don't even know this lady, but if I'm lucky, maybe she understands me.

* * * * * *

"Shhhh," someone says, and a young girl giggles.

It's pretty dark in the corridors at night, so it's hard to imagine anyone walking around and knowing where they're going. And why is everyone up so late, anyway?

Another voice carries throughout the hall, and a few more giggles echo.

Is this Eve's doing? Did she let everyone stay up past curfew?

"Hi, Lucy," I hear.

I turn my head to the side to see a black silhouette of a little girl with pigtails. I recognize the voice. It's June, Eden's youngest girl. Everyone calls her the miracle child because when we first got to Eden, she was only three months old and still breastfeeding. Most babies that young died.

"Hi, June," I whisper, unsure who's asleep and who isn't.

"Wanna see my Octolololo?" she says, and I smile.

She's such a cute kid.

"Not now June-bear," her mother says. Her tall, dark silhouette gently pushes on her daughter's back to get her to keep moving. "It's bedtime."

"But—"

"June, what did Mommy tell you earlier?"

A little sigh comes out of June's lungs. "I can show it tomorrow."

"That's right," the mother says, her voice disappearing as she moves past my cell.

The sound of little bodies plopping down into their beds fills Division Five's corridor, and the older kids start entering their cells.

Someone scoffs and I hear a nudge, or a punch, I can't tell which. "He hasn't even talked to you. But he talked to *me* this morning."

"That doesn't mean anything, Mal. You can't assume you'll get the only boy in Eden to fall for you because you have gorgeous long hair."

"It's not about my hair," Malory says. "It's about these bad girls."

I roll my eyes in the darkness.

It has to be Malory—she has this Barbie-like way about her. She talks like she's the best thing that ever happened to this world, and all she does is flaunt her body. She may be only fifteen years old, but she already has the body of a twenty-year-old with long golden locks that always make her look like she's stepped out of a hair salon.

There aren't many people like that in Eden. Most people here have suffered so much that they're down-to-earth. They're genuine, and they don't care about the stupid little things in life anymore. They want a simple, happy life.

I guess some people don't change even after the end of the world. Or, maybe it's because she's a teenager and eventually, she'll grow out of it.

The other girl laughs. It's probably Stacey, her

best friend. She follows her around like a puppy dog. I close my eyes and wait for the voices and footsteps to stop.

All I want is sleep.

But how am I supposed to sleep when Nola hasn't come back? She said she was going to check on Emily and that she'd be back to tell me all about it. Is there terrible news to share? Is that why she didn't come back? I let out a long breath, hoping it'll take my anxiety of out my body along with it.

This is torture.

I can't wait until morning.

I throw my legs out from underneath the sheets and slap my bare feet against the cement floor. I consider changing into my regular clothes, but a lot of people walk around in their pajamas before bed. It's not a big deal.

What is a big deal, though, is that it's pretty late. Eve must have made an exception tonight, but that doesn't mean I can abuse that. If I get caught walking around while everyone's gone to bed, I'll never hear the end of it.

Those people (the ones who get caught walking around) get called Prison Ghosts.

It started as a joke to scare the kids, but it's gotten rather annoying. And it's kind of spooky, too. A few women started saying that anyone who walked around the prison halls after curfew attracted the spirits of dead prisoners.

In other words, they'd be haunted for a long time after they broke the rule.

It sounds like a bunch of hocus-pocus, but I'd be

lying if I said this place didn't freak me out at night. Every time I hear a voice in the middle of the night, I think it's a spirit, and then I lay there for an hour, convincing myself that it's only someone having a nightmare.

Nightmares: those happen a lot, too. Especially night terrors with the younger ones. There's nothing worse than being woken up by the sound of someone screaming.

I stick my head out of my cell, look from side to side, and step out into the corridor.

"Hey, where's she going?" someone says.

"Shhh, honey."

I won't be gone long.

I need to know what's going on with Emily, and why Nola hasn't come back.

CHAPTER 30 - GABRIEL

"Dakota, calm down," Freyda says, holding up a hand.

But Dakota's like a dog with a bone. She won't let it go. And even though I could tear that knife right out of her hands, I don't do it. I don't want these women to think I'm a threat to them. I need to convince them that I'm on their side.

"Number 98425," I say.

Dakota curls her lip over her yellow canine tooth that sticks out farther than the rest of her teeth. It kind of makes her look like a vampire, especially given her pale skin.

"The fuck is that supposed to mean?" she says.

"Dakota," Freyda tries again. "Put the knife down and we can talk about this."

Dakota leans her head to the side, but her grip around the knife doesn't loosen. If anything, it gets tighter, and the blade digs even farther into my skin.

"You know about this?" she growls.

Freyda's eyes shift between Dakota and me.

Shit.

I didn't mean to get Freyda involved.

"I'm ex-marine," I say, trying to take the heat off Freyda. The last thing she needs is for these women to turn on her. "That's why I know about Area 82. I've been there."

"So, it actually exists?" Miller says. Her big brown eyes wide, she looks like a kid who's heard that someone saw Santa Claus fly through the sky. But then she catches Dakota glaring at her and the smile disappears. "We just—we only heard of it when I was in the military."

Dakota scoffs and turns her hateful eyes on me. "Is it even *real*, Gabriel? Or is this some plan to get us to follow you, you sick piece of—"

"Dakota!" Freyda says. "Put the knife down." When Dakota doesn't listen, Freyda jabs a finger toward the ground and her multicolored eyes widen. "Right now."

I don't know what to think. Freyda's defending me. Me, a man, of all people. I've never seen her upset before, and it's hard to look away.

Dakota drops the arm that's holding the knife, but her knuckles are still all white around the black handle. When Freyda sees that Dakota is still prepared to stab me in the gut, she raises her eyebrows and says, "Put it away."

Dakota mumbles something, but it sounds like a growl.

"Does Eve know about this?" Jada asks. She looks a bit worried, too, but she's calm and collected. She doesn't seem like the type to pull out a knife and stick it against someone's throat without having all the facts. That's a good thing, considering she used to be a cop.

Freyda looks down like she's embarrassed about

the whole thing. Either that, or she's scared to tell them the truth because deep down, she knows that Eve should have dug up more information about me. That's what scares me about Eve. She's quick and impulsive and acts on her emotions. That's not what a strong leader should do. But on the other hand, she must be doing something right if she's managed to keep these women safe for the last five years.

Miller takes a step forward, her shoulders drawn back. Obviously, her military background is kicking in. "Why wouldn't Eve know about this? What's going on here?"

Everyone looks worried, aside from Yael, who's sitting at the edge of one of the beds with her legs crossed in front of her. Looks like she's reading an old magazine. Some techno-science thing about the latest technological advancements. My mama used to love reading those even though she never understood half of it.

"It's not as bad as it looks," Freyda says.

* * * * * *

"That looks bad," the young girl says.

She looks like she's eleven, maybe twelve years old.

"It's not so bad," I say, looking down at my swollen, blistered ankles. "Could be worse."

The girl's dad, Cash, he said his name was, crushes his cigarette in the sink and blows out one last puff. "Don't look so great to me, man. You're welcome to stay the night, but after that, you gotta go."

I nod. The last thing I'm going to do is argue with

a guy who's brought me into his home. And I get it, too. If I were him, I wouldn't want some stranger living with me. Not because of the unknown, but an extra mouth to feed takes away from his resources.

"I appreciate this," I say, leaning back into the recliner chair. It's not as comfortable as my mama's old couch, but it's something, and it lets me keep my feet up.

"What's your name?" I ask the girl.

"Callie," she says with a smile on her face.

She looks like a sweet kid. She isn't shy at all, something she probably gets from her dad. She looks like him, too, with blond hair and light eyes. They both have overly thick eyebrows, which is both peculiar and charming at the same time, and they both have a bit of an underbite. I wonder if she looks anything like her mother, wherever she is. This girl looks like she was cloned using her dad's DNA.

Not that it would be possible, mind you. That kind of technology was being perfected inside the military only. I probably shouldn't be talking about that, though, considering my clearance. Then again, it's not like I have a clearance anymore.

"That's a nice name," I say, and her smile doesn't even twitch. She's resting her chin in her palms on the side of my recliner chair, looking up at me like I'm some new shiny toy.

How long have they been out here? This attack only happened recently, but she's acting like she hasn't seen another human being in forever.

My curiosity gets the best of me.

"How long have you two been out here?"

Cash shrugs his bony shoulders. “A year and a half, roughly. We knew this was comin’.”

I lean forward and my recliner shortens. “Knew what was coming?”

He laughs, but I can tell he doesn’t find any of it funny. “The end o’ the world.”

“Well, it isn’t technically the end of the world. I mean, as far as we know—”

“Daddy heard it all on the radio,” Callie says.

“Radio?” I ask. I almost stand up, but then I remember how badly my feet are hurting me.

“Yeah,” Cash says, all proud, “got ourselves an analog radio in here. Been catchin’ a few stations.”

“American stations?”

He laughs. “See that, right there?” He points a red finger toward the radio, then up along the wall where wires seem to be running. “That goes all the way up to the roof, and then even higher.”

“You’re catching international signals?” I ask. I jump to my feet and wince when my pads hit the wooden floor. But I can’t help myself. I need to hear what’s going on. I need to know how bad this is. “Is that an S-Viper model?”

Those things came out in 2045, and only a few people ever knew about it. Mostly military men and women or conspiracy theorists who believed the world would come to an end. Apparently, analog radios are supposed to survive any kind of power outage. Guess those so-called “crazies” weren’t so crazy after all.

“Sure is,” Cash says, patting the top of his radio. “Only choppy signal I get is in Australia, but then again"—he rubs his bony-fingered hand back and forth over his head—"everythin's gonna be choppy real soon."

I don't know what he's talking about, so I limp my way to the radio. I can't believe I'm looking at one. It's sleek and black with silver buttons, and the antenna looks like a long thin piece of black rubber. It's matte, not shiny, so you'd never even know it was an antenna without seeing the source.

I slide the tips of my fingers on top of it and form traces in the grimy layer that's accumulated on it.

These things have no shelf life. They don't die. At least not for several centuries, which is what makes them so damn cool.

"Daddy's talked to people in France! They had funny accents. Especially when they tried to say—"

Cash smiles sweetly at his daughter and gives her a nod like he's trying to say, "The stranger doesn't know what words French people have a hard time with."

She plops her chin against the back of the recliner chair where I previously sat and watches us.

"I could tell you," he says, "but how's 'bout I show you instead?"

He reaches to the front of the radio and turns the dial. It makes a faint clicking noise, and then the static kicks in. He turns the volume down, so it isn't too overpowering.

As he scans through the channels, a few choppy voices jump out, but barely anything audible. With an advanced radio like this, he should be able to catch thousands of stations. What the hell is going on?

At last, a man's voice comes on the radio. It's not too deep, and if I had to put a face on him, it would be a terrified face no older than thirty years old. He has an elegant British accent, so I'm assuming he's somewhere in Europe. He's breathing hard into the microphone, and he keeps swallowing which makes a sticky noise in the speakers.

"... talking about this for several months now, but it's a surprise to all of us here in England how quickly this is all happening. America has gone completely dark, and it's only a matter of days, weeks, before we join them."

"What did you expect, Charlie?" comes another man's voice. This one sounds much deeper and aggressive. "These women are creating a war."

"To anyone tuning in," says the younger one, Charlie, "we, Charlie and Archie, will be keeping you informed during all of this. And if you don't know what is going on, please get informed."

Archie, the bigger-sounding of the two, scoffs into the microphone. "Either that, or keep your women in line, men. We can't let the same thing that's happened in America happen here. These women have gone insane since America's disappeared off the grid. It's like they've become inspired to do the same. We're being shot at and bombed every day by these groups of women. Is that what you want for Great Britain? A world ruled by crazy, hateful w—"

"We can't generalize, Archie," Charlie says. He's obviously the kind of guy who likes to keep the peace. It also sounds like he's been a radio host with

Archie for a long time, but now that this war's happening on their territory, Archie's opinions are coming out. The hatred, the bitterness... All of it.

Archie laughs and it sounds like a bear coughing. "Can't generalize? How are you being so blind? Do you not see what's happened in America?" A loud smacking sound booms out of the speaker, and I'm assuming he smacked a fist against the table in front of him. "We can't let this happen in Europe. Not here. Not on my watch!"

Charlie breathes out, almost in a whistle. "We're outnumbered, Arch. There's nothing we can—"

Another smack against the table and Archie's growl of a voice comes back on. "Nothing we can do? Get armed, men! We are not letting these bitches launch EMP attacks on our homeland! And if you don't know what an EMP is, get fuckin' educated, you fuckin' twits!"

"What Archie means," Charlie cuts in, "is that we have to take this seriously. An EMP stands for Electro Magnetic Pulse. Attacks such as these are destroying electronics around the world. Following America's revolution, which everyone had eyes on, women around the world seem to have become inspired to create their own. Wait. What—what's that?"

What's going on? I lean in toward the radio, my eyes wide and my back hunched.

"Jesus Christ," Charlie says. "R-reports... Reports are showing—I can't believe this."

What are they seeing? Spit it out, already!

Archie approaches the microphone and a bubbly

rumble fills the air around the radio. “There you have it, gentlemen.” He sounds amused in a sick way. Cocky, even, like he knew this was going to happen. “France has gone dark.”

I pull away and place a hand on my forehead. How… how is this possible? How is our war affecting other countries of the world? I knew that our gender imbalance wasn’t only affecting America, but this?

Cash turns off the radio and bows his head. “I suggest you find someplace safe to stay. Nothin’s ever gon’ be the same again.”

* * * * * *

“Well it looks pretty fuckin’ bad,” Dakota says. She looks like she wants to swing a fist at Freyda.

I know that anger. That feeling of not giving a shit what happens to you, so long as you hurt the other guy. Mama would be ashamed of me if she knew the thoughts I’d had when I was on missions… The graphic images I fantasized about… ways I wanted to make some sick sons of bitches pay for the things they’d done to innocent families.

So, I get it. This woman has a lot of anger inside, and now that she feels betrayed by the people who are supposed to be guiding this mission, she wants to hurt someone.

“Gabriel’s ex-marine,” Freyda says. Her hands are back down now, resting on her waist.

It almost looks like she’s decided that she’s running this shop, and the others will have to listen to what she has to say. I think her cop side is coming out. It suits her. I wonder if being Eve’s little follower caused her to lose this side of herself.

"Great, that's fuckin'—" Dakota starts, but Freyda sticks a finger in the air like she's trying to cut the air with it.

Her nostrils flare and she sucks in a loud breath. "You know what? We all have a past, Dakota. We've all done things we're ashamed of. What happened five years ago was a shitshow caused by a few, and a lot of people suffered for it.

"Yeah, the underground rebellions," Jada says, rolling her eyes.

I can't believe what I'm hearing. Is Jada actually turning on everything that Eve stands for?

Freyda clenches a fist. "I don't agree with some of the things those underground groups did, but they also stood up for our rights. They're the only ones who were willing to put up an actual fight. You think protesting at the White House would have gotten us anywhere? No, all that did was lead to riots and property damage until the feds started lashing back and hurting women."

I swallow hard. The heat's on me now. I'm part of the so-called "feds." I sense Dakota's hateful eyes on me, but I don't look at her. I don't need to aggravate the situation.

"No, the blame doesn't fall on the underground feminists." She's closed her fist again, and her stiff finger moves from side to side, pointing at each of us, one at a time. "The blame falls on everyone. Men and women."

Dakota crosses her arms over her chest. She's not responding, which is probably a good sign, but she isn't happy about this, either.

A heavy silence fills the camper as everyone thinks about what Freyda said. I've never heard her talk this much. It's obvious that she has a lot to say but feels smothered for one reason or another. Maybe Eve's rulership is too much, and it pushes her to the side. Eve doesn't seem like the type of woman who wants to share the spotlight.

Yael suddenly clears her throat, the most noise she's made over the last few hours, and stands up. It looks like she's about to say something, but then the strangest sound fills the air around us. It's a deep rumbling, a growling, almost. It's so loud that it overpowers the sound of the heavy rainfall. It sounds like it's far away and moving toward us fast.

I haven't heard any noise bigger than myself, other than gunfire, in years.

What the fuck is that?

I brush past Freyda and run outside into the pouring rain.

The other women follow, aside from Jada and Yael who stay inside with their heads poking out. Miller wipes a thick layer of water off her face and brushes her bangs up on top of her head so she can see better.

That sound… I know that sound.

It's coming from the sky.

I crane my neck and look up in time to see its huge shape fly overhead.

Holy shit.

It's a fighter jet. There's an actual plane flying in the fucking sky!

It looks like one of the newest models, too. One

of the drone crossovers. I know exactly where these models are held, and that's Area 82. No one else has them.

Yael and Jada come running out with smiles on their faces.

"That's a plane!" Jada shouts in the rain. "A real-life, flying mother-fucking plane!"

I look at Freyda, who's smiling from ear to ear.

"Someone has technology back up and running!" she says.

Everything feels so surreal. In any other circumstances, we would be terrified to know who's flying this jet. But right now, after years without electricity, all that matters is that someone is *flying* a plane.

We don't care who it is. I don't even care to think that someone's in Area 82 because there's something more important here. They already have technology back up and running, and that means something. Something huge.

It's a symbol of hope.

I blink hard and stare up at the sky. "And I know where it's headed."

Dakota uncrosses her arms for the first time and looks up at me. "All right, Gabriel. I'll follow."

CHAPTER 31 – EVE

They're acting like they've been best friends for years. I've never even seen Nola talk to Betsy before. The woman likes to keep to herself. She is always out in the courtyards, plucking fresh apples and pears from the trees for the children. But she doesn't talk to anyone—at least not to say anything other than, "Would you like an apple, dear?"

Her large ears and scraggly gray hair, which always sticks to the sides of her face, make her look like a mouse. She also has severe seasonal and environmental allergies, which doesn't help her look—her small pointed nose turns a bright pink nearly every day.

Perhaps I should have stayed in my room. The sight of Nola right now is making me want to punch a hole in the wall. I thought after a few hours of solitude, I would have calmed down by now, but as I watch them make energetic gestures in the air and talk about what I'm sure are trivial things, I can't help but hate her.

How dare she turn Lucy against me? Things were finally turning around. I could see it on Lucy's face—there was a curiosity in her eyes; there was a desire to want to have me in her life.

And what is Nola doing up so late? The children were all sent to bed after I allowed them to stay up past their curfew.

Nola lets out a soft laugh that sounds strained and takes a step away from Betsy. But Betsy takes a step with her and keeps talking. She's grinning and looks excited about something. I wonder if this has to do with leaving Eden. I've seen a change in some women ever since we held our meeting.

While some women are resistant to the idea of change, the possibility of an entirely new life must be exciting for others.

Betsy throws her arms in the air like she just performed a circus act and lets out a giggle. Nola laughs again, and this time, it's quite obvious that she's trying to get away.

I smile, my face pressed against the doorframe of my room, my eye hovering behind the small door crack.

Nola nods and takes a step back, but Betsy starts rambling again. What is Nola doing here, anyway? Why is she in the main corridor? The only reason anyone would come down this way is for supplies, to see me, or to visit the Medical Unit. She certainly wasn't on her way to see me.

I pull away from the doorframe. If I keep looking at her any longer, I don't know what I might do.

Fucking traitor.

I clench my fists, a familiar rage building inside me.

Lucy is mine.

* * * * * *

"It's mine!" cries a young girl.

She looks to be no older than four years old. I don't know her name, nor her mother's, but their faces are familiar to me. I must have seen them in the crowd of women as we migrated.

The little girl tugs on what appears to be an old teddy bear. One of its eyes are missing and its ear has been ripped off.

Another young girl claws the air with tears streaming down her face. "No, it's mine!"

"Girls," the mother says, obviously trying to stop her daughters from making a scene.

It's too late. Several other children are staring wide-eyed and a few of the adults, who are trying to make their cells a comfortable living space, keep giving the mother strange looks. Everyone is exhausted, and surely, the last thing they want to listen to are two young girls screaming.

"Are you okay here?" I ask Lucy, eyeing her through her new room's iron bars.

She nods but doesn't look up at me. She's probably still upset about what I told her in private—that I did not want her telling others she's my godchild.

I want to console her, but at the same time, I'm too irritated to bother, both by her and by the screaming children. I'm not her mother, and she can't possibly expect me to take over Ophelia's place. That's not my job. I don't have the time or energy to offer any child love.

Not now.

Haven't I done enough? I brought her to safety. She should be grateful. Instead, she sits there, pouting.

I roll my eyes when she isn't looking and focus my attention on the little girls. The mother is now trying to tear the teddy bear out of the first girl's hands, but the little girl squeezes it tight against her chest and gives her mother a hateful stare with giant brown eyes.

Her sister, who looks even younger than her, starts screaming.

I walk toward the mother and her girls, my new heels ticking against the hard floor. As soon as the girls hear me approaching, their cries subside, and they turn around to look at me.

"Now, now, girls," I say.

They almost seem afraid of me. Perhaps they're not accustomed to being disciplined by anyone other than their mother—and she isn't doing a very good job, either.

I kneel on one knee and stare at the older sister—the one who's holding on to her teddy bear for dear life.

"What's your name?" I ask.

She sniffles and blinks hard. "L-L-Lilly."

I force a smile and turn to the younger one. "And what's yours?"

She just stares at me, probably too young to understand what I'm saying.

"Her name's Bailey," Lilly says.

"Lilly and Bailey," I say, my smile never fading.

The corridor has gone silent, and I feel several

eyes on me.

"May I see this?" I ask, pointing at Lilly's teddy bear.

She looks up at her mom, visibly confused about what's going on. She nods slowly, hesitates, then gives me her cherished toy.

"Where's this little guy from?" I ask.

"Daddy gave it to me," she says.

I clench my teeth. Why would they miss their father? After everything—

They don't know any better. They're too young to understand.

I take a deep breath, careful not to let my anger show. I turn my head sideways to see the mother, but she tightens her lips and turns away, sobbing.

"Who did your daddy give this to?" I ask, eyeing them both carefully.

Lilly looks at her feet but doesn't say anything.

"Lilly, sweetheart, please look at me when I speak to you," I say.

Her big eyes roll up at me and her bottom lip trembles. "Bailey."

I give Bailey the teddy bear without hesitation. "It's important to share, girls, but it's also important that you learn to respect the belongings of others."

Both of their little jaws drop. They have no clue what I'm trying to teach them.

"One day," I say softly, "you'll realize that it's important to think of other people's feelings."

* * * * * *

I stare at the wall, listening to Nola and Betsy's bickering until finally, their footsteps begin to fade into the main hall.

A heavy silence fills my room and I find myself standing still, staring into nothingness. There are so many thoughts rushing through my mind, yet, I can't seem to focus on a single one. What am I supposed to do about Lucy? All I want is to have her back in my life.

She's mine.

I turn and catch a glimpse of my stiff figure in my mirror's reflection. I look pale today—paler than usual, with puffy bags under my eyes. I haven't been sleeping well at all. My lips are beige, white, almost, and they've begun to crack.

What am I doing to myself?

What have I become?

What you need to be, Eve. What these women need you to be.

I shift my body until I am facing the mirror and tug on my overcoat to straighten my attire. I raise my chin and stare at the woman before me.

Fucking bitch.

This isn't Lucy's fault. She's been brainwashed.

No, she hasn't.

She hates you.

She fucking hates you.

I scowl at my own reflection.

"You don't know what you're talking about," I say aloud.

I'm torn between anger and love, desire and heartbreak. Did she mean what she said? Does she no longer care about me? Why else would she have said it?

God, I miss Freyda.

Love is a weakness.

I squeeze my fists until two of my fingers pop, pull my shoulders back, and gaze at myself—Eden's leader. I've come so far and changed so many lives.

How could I possibly allow one little bitch to get in the way of that? Love and happiness are blinding me. Perhaps this sort of life was never intended for me.

What matters most of all is Eden, and no one will ever get in the way of that.

CHAPTER 32 – LUCY

"Lucy, sweetheart, what're you doing up so late?" Nola hisses, moving toward me like a cat on the hunt.

I point an accusatory finger at her. "What're *you* doing up so late? Why didn't you come see me? What is it, Nola? Is she dead? Is that it? Just tell me!"

"Whoa, love," she says, and wraps two firm hands around my shaking shoulders. She brushes my hair out of my face and smiles at me. "Emily's doing just fine—great, actually. Dr. Lewis says there's improvement. That it's almost miraculous."

I sigh, all of the oxygen in my body pouring out into one breath.

"I'm sorry I didn't get back sooner," Nola says, rolling her eyes but then looking around to make sure no one saw her do it. "She means well, but she's so chatty." I have no idea who she's talking about. "Anywho, my dear Lucy. Where do you think you're going? The girls have already been sent to bed."

"I was coming to find you," I say. Although I'm not lying, I'm not being entirely honest, either. I also wanted to talk to Eve. I can't stop feeling guilty for the way I talked about her, even though she wasn't around. That's like if someone called my mom stupid. It's like the time I got mad at Mom for taking my H-Cap away from me. I was young, but I remember storming off to my room and calling her a "poopy-fart-face." Looking back, that's pretty funny. At the time, though, I was so angry, and I hated her at that moment. But after my anger went away, I felt so guilty that I told her what I'd said. I needed her forgiveness, even though she hadn't heard me.

I don't like talking about people behind their backs, especially when I'm saying how much I don't care about that person. It's not true at all, and I need to get it off my chest in some way. So, that's why I'm going to talk to Eve. To make myself feel better.

"Well, I'm here," she says. She starts shooing me with her hands like I'm a toddler. "Let's hurry along now."

I look over her shoulder, then back at the main hall. Everything is dim and cool, and the only sounds to be heard are faint whispers coming from each Division as mothers try to put their girls to sleep. I wonder where Zack ended up and if they're treating him like a real prisoner. I bet some of the mothers feel the need to watch their girls.

Nola angles her head from side to side like she's trying to land her face in my focus. "Hellooo?"

I force a laugh that could barely even be called a laugh. "Sorry, Nola. Um, listen, I'll meet you there, okay?"

She draws back and glowers at me. "What's going on with you?"

"What? Nothing. I need to use the washroom."

Her lips turn into one flat line. She's not buying it. "There's a washroom in your Division."

"Yeah, but it's at the far back," I say, surprised by my quick thinking, "and the mothers are trying to put the girls to sleep."

She relaxes her lips and gives me a slow nod. "Don't take too long."

I smile at her and walk away, but when I realize she isn't budging, I turn back around. "Hey, Nola?"

She stares at me.

"Thanks for checking on Emily for me..."

She gives me a warm smile. "You're welcome, love."

And with that, she turns away and starts ticking her way down toward our Division.

I turn on my heels and rush down the main hall, then right, down the narrow hallway that leads to Eve's office and bedroom. Will she even be awake? I imagine Eve sleeps lightly. I'm sure she'll be up. My heart is pounding so hard I hear it in my ears. I'd be lying if I said I wasn't a bit scared of Eve. She's so unpredictable I honestly don't know what to expect. She's turned into something, or someone, completely different over these last few years.

These last few days, however... Maybe she *is* back.

There's a bright yellow crack under her bedroom door, which means that's where she is. I walk up slowly, take a deep breath, and stare at the sign beside the room. It's a piece of metal, something that looks like a bracket, but it's empty. I bet the warden's name used to be here.

I stare at the door handle, but that's when I realize it didn't click closed all the way. The bright yellow line extends up the doorframe; only it's much thinner along the vertical crack than the bottom horizontal crack.

Did she leave her room and forget to close it? If so, where did she go?

But then I hear something.

"Get your shit together, Eve."

Footsteps pace back and forth behind the door. That was her voice. Why is she referring to herself in the third person?

She lets out a long, frustrated grunt, and although I can't see her, I'm guessing she's pulling at the short hair on her head. I move closer to the door and press my ear against the cold wooden surface. I feel like I'm back in our old apartment, spying on Mom when she thinks I'm sleeping.

She's talking again, but I'm not sure what she's saying. The door suddenly slips open a bit farther, probably under the weight of my face, and I pull back with my eyes nearly popping out of my skull. I'm ready to run back down the hall. The last thing I need is for Eve to catch me spying on her. That's not why I came here, but she'll see it that way. And I shouldn't be spying, but I don't want to knock and then have her think I was spying, either.

There's no winning right now.

It doesn't seem like she noticed the door move. Her feet are still shuffling around. I take another step, and this time, move my face toward the crack. It's big enough for me to see a bit into her room.

Where's Eve, though? All I see is a closet, and beside that, a full-length mirror.

My heart skips a bit when I see her appear in the mirror, staring at herself. She's huffing and puffing with all her teeth bared and it looks like she's about to lunge at the mirror and strangle herself. She looks nothing like herself, which freaks me out. What's wrong with her? Is this her other side? Is this what Nola was talking about? The whole Jekyll and Hyde thing? Was she right? Is Eve's mental health going south?

"Oh God, Eve," she says, and her face is once again smooth and young-looking. She combs all of her fingers through her hair, flattening it backward against her head. "Pull yourself together. This whole thing... It isn't real. She didn't mean what she said. I mean, how could she? I've been there most of her life." She starts pacing again, and now I can't see her. "She didn't mean it. She didn't mean it. Of course, she cares about you."

Oh my God. Is she talking about me? Does she know what I said to Nola? How would she know that? Nola wouldn't have come here, would she? No, not after everything that's happened. Nola's on my side. Isn't she?

Shit.

Eve suddenly reappears, her twisted face inches away from the mirror. I can see the back of her head now, her uncombed hair and the back of her white blazer. But it's that reflection... It's like there are two of her. Her nose is crinkled so much that it looks twice its size and her eyebrows look like one giant one. Her head is bowed forward, casting dark shadows under her bright eyes.

"It's Nola's fault... That fucking bitch," she spews, and saliva splatters the mirror. "She's turning Lucy against you." This time, she throws a crooked finger at herself in the mirror and half her body jerks.

She's lost her mind. Although I'm terrified now, I'm relieved to know that Nola isn't the one who told her about our chat. Eve must have overheard us, and it sent her flying over the edge.

Is this Eden's brave and confident leader? This crazed woman talking to herself? Because this isn't Eve. At least, not the Eve I thought I knew.

She's hunched forward with her fingers forming claws at her sides. Her rounded back moves up and down and she breathes hard through flared nostrils. But then, as if injected by some serum, she straightens her posture and raises her chin. Now, she looks like the Eve that I know.

She smiles at herself in the mirror, something I wasn't expecting.

"The women of Eden worship me," she says. "I can have, and will have, whatever I want."

I pull away from the door and plant my back against the wall, my eyes firing all over the place and my heart pounding against the solid surface behind me.

Worship?

Is that what she wants? To be worshipped? Is that the kind of woman leading Eden? I suddenly start seeing flashes of memories floating around in my mind, most of them surrounding my unhappiness here in Eden. The only thing that's been keeping me sane is that one day, I'll get to leave Eden.

I'll run away and leave this prison sentence.

But now... Now that I've seen who Eve is... I can't run. How can I? Hundreds of women are under her spell. They follow her like lost puppies, waiting to be told what to do. And the tea she's been giving them... She doesn't mean well. She's trying to control everyone. She's completely insane.

If we were in the old world with hospitals and medical care, she would be in a psychiatric facility somewhere getting treatment.

Not here. Not ruling Eden. She's going to destroy everything.

She needs to be stopped, and that's exactly what I'm going to do.

Visit **www.shadeowens.com** for more works by Shade Owens, including **Genesis**, the third book in the Garden of Evil series.

www.ingramcontent.com/pod-product-compliance
Ingram Content Group UK Ltd.
Pitfield, Milton Keynes, MK11 3LW, UK
UKHW041953190726
13854UKWH00005B/1947

9 781990 271076